I0870439

The WISHING STAR

The WISHING STAR

Elizabeth Andrews

ST. MARTIN'S PRESS NEW YORK

Copyright © 1981 by Elizabeth Andrews
For information, write: St. Martin's Press,
175 Fifth Avenue, New York, N.Y. 10010
Manufactured in the United States of America

Library of Congress Cataloging Publication Data

Andrews, Elizabeth
The wishing star.

I. Title.
PS3551.N4173W5 813'.54 81-8836
ISBN 0-312-88416-8 AACR2

Design by Manuela Paul

10 9 8 7 6 5 4 3 2 1

First Edition

To Jerry

Chapter One

"I'm going to find him," Jessica told her mother firmly. "It's the only reason I'm going to the United States; you know that, don't you?"

Lettie smiled reassuringly at her.

"Yes, dear," she said, placing the last of the white linen nightgowns in the open wooden chest.

The chest sat in the middle of the common room before the fireplace. Jessica had brought her clothing from her chamber upstairs to make the carting of the full container easier. As she came back and forth she looked lovingly about the paneled walls and beamed ceilings to fix them forevermore in her memory.

"I'm taking too much with me."

"We were told one trunk—that both the ship and the stagecoach on the other side would be better able to manage it."

"Yes, but will I?" Jessica laughed.

Together, the two women buckled the leather straps that closed the box securely.

"He is there, somewhere; he must be. He would not simply disappear."

"You will feel better for having gone," Lettie said. "Staying here and continuing to grieve will do you no good."

"He would never leave me of his own accord," Jessica said proudly.

"But there might have been some . . . misadventure," Lettie said cautiously. "You must be prepared for that."

"Some mishap, yes. But I know, deep within myself, that he is alive, Mother. And I'm going to find him."

It was their last evening together before the voyage. Both women were tired and sad that they must part. Earlier in the day they had traveled into the city of London, in the surrey that they still kept, to see Josiah Barrows, Jessica's uncle. Josiah had a small fleet of ships to keep his cotton goods business operating efficiently. He imported raw cotton from the United States–he sometimes still referred to the New World as "the colonies," even though it was now 1840; he had a healthy respect for Empire–and sold the raw stuff to the British textile mills. The hulls of his ships going over were filled with bolts of beautiful and varied cloth, for the men and women of the New World still liked the fashion of the Old. Jessica's husband Jason Coopersmith had been in the employ of her uncle, who was Lettie's older brother. It was Jason's job to visit the plantations and the cotton auctions, buy the best of the bales, and then travel from the South to the North to make sure the most important and best distributors stocked the cloth from the English factories Josiah represented. It was rumored that Josiah owned many of these factories himself, but he would not admit to it for fear of appearing too wealthy. He remembered Lettie's husband Matthew Steele scoring the foul conditions of the factories in London and in Manchester, and the poor state of the working people, including children, laboring long hours yet barely able to feed and clothe themselves. "Bad food . . . poor health . . . a pestilence and . . . poof! . . . off they go!" Matthew had fumed.

Jason had proved to be an excellent factor, and he carried on some of his uncle's other business as well, especially–when he was in England–in the design of machinery. Through the past ten years Josiah Barrows had put up the money for huge spinners and weaving looms and exported them to the northern states of the New World, where industry had been steadily growing. It would seem that he was creating competition for English and possibly his own cloth, but he was a wily entrepreneur who knew that when competition was brewing one must have a hand in it–whether to lessen its impact or to turn it away, only time would tell. He had been a child when the Revolutionary War was fought but he was really a Tory at heart. He would prefer the colonies to be importers rather than manufacturers. He had interested Jason in manufacturing techniques, as well as cotton buying, and hoped that one day Jason might develop this part of the business and succeed him as surrogate son.

"Even in the New World a man doesn't just drop out of sight never to be heard of again," Jessica said.

Her voice was certain, but she was not. She knew that the relatively young United States was not so well developed or organized as to make one man's movements in its great territories known to the authorities. Even in England, with its Scotland Yard, a person could vanish completely. She tried not to think of the hazards, but she knew them all and had catalogued them in her nightmares and in her moments of logic—swamplands, fluxes and agues, Indian raids, thugs and rascals, all sorts of outlaws. Yes, it was possible for a man to disappear . . . to die . . . and his relatives would never know for sure . . . but she would not accept it. Jason was too vital a man. He must have left a trace somewhere.

"Your Uncle Josiah had his agents make a thorough search," her mother said, as though divining her thoughts.

Josiah Barrows had gone over it again with them this very day, as he had six months ago when Jason had failed to return from America. The captain of the ship Jason sailed on in all his voyages had waited an extra few days for him, but when no note or message arrived, he could delay no longer. Josiah did not tell his sister or niece that the captain thought the young man might have dallied with some wench who had caught his fancy.

"I've written letters to all my factors in the States and to all the plantations Jason visited, and to the auction houses . . . nothing. To the factories . . . nothing. I've had notices posted, with promise of rewards, in the inns where he was known to stay . . . north and south . . . nothing. I've advertised in the newspapers of every state . . . nothing."

Josiah made a steeple of his fingers and then turned it inside out.

"I know you've done everything you could, Uncle Josiah," Jessica told him. "I appreciate your concern."

"Concern!" he said indignantly. "I loved the boy! If he were my own nephew, my son, I couldn't have cared more."

"I know. And I'm grateful that you have provided passage for me on the *Elizabeth.*"

"I'm sending you aboard the *Elizabeth* because the captain's wife travels with him and you'll be in safe hands."

"Thank you, Josiah."

"I knew you'd be pleased, Lettie," he nodded in his sister's direction. "It has more comforts than the *Gypsy* that Jason was wont to travel in. The captain and his lady have nice quarters on the *Elizabeth* and Jessica will fare very well, I assure you." He picked up a straw fan to stir the air about him and handed extra fans to his guests. "Clerk!" he shouted, "open the door!" In the outer cubicle a boy hastily made some movements, and the strong stench of the Thames, on which the building fronted, made them wince. Lettie held the fan before her nose.

"Warm day for early April," Josiah commented. "A good day tomorrow to begin a voyage, my dear," he said to Jessica. "And warm weather will prepare you for more of the same in Virginia, where I hear it grows insufferably hot in the summer."

"It's better than Georgia, or Mississippi, where Jason went many times to buy cotton."

"That's true, Jessica. No need for you to go there. Jason was not scheduled for those areas on his last trip."

"But he may have gone there nevertheless."

"Most unlikely. His itinerary was set for Virginia, Maryland, Delaware, New Jersey, Pennsylvania, and up through Rhode Island and Massachusetts."

"Jessica will not travel so far," Lettie said anxiously. "She will go to her cousin Eleanor and her husband and stay with them in Virginia."

"Yes." Josiah nodded. "It will be a fine change for you, Jessica, and the sea air will do you much good."

"That is not why I'm going," she said angrily.

"Of course not, but nonetheless. . . ."

"It will be a proper base to begin my inquiries. It's in the heart of cotton country—and tobacco, too."

"Yes," he said, "but you must not have false hopes, my dear."

"I am hopeful," she said, "and it is not false."

"Yes, yes," he said hastily. "Boy!" he shouted, above the din of the street noises—horses' hooves on the cobblestones, the call of the vendors, children at play, a drunken doxy, a procession of carts loaded with goods thumping over wooden wheels—"close the door. We've had enough air, such as it is . . . garbage," he grumbled. "They throw their slops right out the door and off the boats directly into the river. . . . Excuse me, ladies, but they do foul the air . . . Jessica, Captain and Mrs. Northrup will call for you in the morning and take you with them to the *Elizabeth*. It's a long journey to Yarmouth, where she's docked, Lettie, and it would be wise for you not to come. You must take your leave at home, where it is best, in any event," he said, looking sharply at his sister, "in private."

Lettie smiled at him.

"Yes, Jessica," she said gently. "That was my intention. Our farewells can indeed be made at home."

"I shall miss you, Mother."

"And I, you."

"You don't mind my going?"

Her mother shrugged.

"It would be dishonest to say that I don't mind . . . but it is honest to tell you that I think you should go."

Her long skirts swirling around the trunk, Jessica ran to Lettie and placed her arms around her.

"It won't be for long. We'll come back together—Jason and I."

"I hope so."

"We will . . ."

The two women sat down before the table where a tea service had been placed. Jessie felt the silver pot. "Still warm," she said. "That will calm us before we go to sleep."

"Yes."

"Will you be all right staying on here?" Jessica said softly, watching her mother's fingers tremble as she filled the china cups.

"Of course."

"Anna will be here?"

"Certainly. She's part of the family by now. Charlady, nurse, cook, friend. . . . Don't you worry."

Jessica felt uneasy nevertheless. Since Jessica's father died two years ago, her mother had seemed to grow increasingly frail. It had been a long, slow process; it had not shown right away. But her mother seemed to have shrunk physically, Jessica realized now with sorrow. She was going on this long journey, to be months at sea with no news from home; anything could happen. Perhaps she would never see her mother again. The thought made her fingers tremble, too, and before she could control it her eyes began to tear.

Her mother noticed.

"Now you're not to worry about me," she said firmly. "Josiah will look in, too. With all his bluster, he is a good man. . . . How many mothers, Jessie, have seen their sons and daughters off to far corners of the earth . . . and especially these past few centuries with the promise of explorations and then the colonies and the New World. . . . You are taking a long voyage, my dear, but it's not the first of its kind, and it is not the last, and it is in circumstances better than most. I know you are in the good hands of Captain and Mrs. Northrup and with dear good Eleanor and her husband in Virginia . . ."

"I wish you would come, too."

"Home is too precious to me, and you will be useful to Eleanor. . . . I would be just another guest . . ."

"I am glad she has asked me to tutor the children. . . . Or was it her husband who asked me?"

"Yes. It is better that way."

"And I'll enjoy it."

"Your father prepared you well."

Jessica thought of all the books her father had set out for her to read and the course of study he had demanded of her. He liked to talk to her of the philosophers and the history of the world, and he wanted her to be well versed in these subjects. He had been a great admirer of Napoleon and the revolution in France until the revolution had become too bloody and Napoleon's statesmanship became war and Empire. "Ah, the idealism of youth that turns as one grows older," her father would mutter sadly. "Pragmatism . . . pah! France was to have been the ideal society. . . . Ah, well, I still believe in the teachings of Rousseau . . . his views of equality are my own. . . . And the New World could have really been the Ideal Society, but for the scrambling for land and the scourge of slavery."

He would have long discussions with Jason about the conditions Jason had already witnessed and deplored in the southern states.

"It will take much bloodshed to resolve the problem," Matthew had said. "A slave society cannot last. Look at the spoiled glories of ancient Greece and Rome. What are those countries today? Pah! Napoleon should have given heed to Caesar! Did the Roman Empire last? Ah, well, Nelson taught Napoleon a sad lesson. . . . But Napoleon's French Civil Code—ah, that was another matter . . . liberty and equality there . . ."

While he revered the writings of Jefferson, Matthew denounced the statesman for keeping slaves. Jason, in defense of his livelihood, and looking self-conscious and sounding apologetic, had argued that the plantation system of the New World South depended upon slave labor, and Matthew had roared his loud lawyer's roar. "Then it should be changed, sir!" he fumed. "The system should be changed, I charge!"

As a young man Matthew had read law at The Inns of Court, in the Inner Temple, just before their importance began to wither away and the Inns became social clubs. He had gone on to teach law at University then and to practice his profession. Lettie still kept his powdered wig, under a glass dome, on top of a large cherrywood wardrobe in her room, and inside the cupboard the black robe hung limply upon the pegs. Once, when Jessica was a little girl, she had gone with her mother to see and hear him defend a client in the Old Bailey, and the barrister up front who had to shout to be heard above the unruly crowd of spectators seemed a stranger to her, though her mother whispered it was truly her father. He made an impassioned appeal for a man who, he claimed, had been falsely accused. The prisoner standing in the docket seemed so thin and obviously grieved that Jessica had felt a tremendous sympathy for him, and she was overjoyed when her mother had told her that the case had been won. There was such an expression of joy upon the face of the stranger-father that she said, "It is truly wonderful, isn't it, Mother?" And Lettie laughed, and said yes, "It is wonderful . . ." and added, "but it would be even more wonderful were he to collect a fee."

Jessica asked her about that but her mother would not explain. When she asked her father, now familiar in his everyday clothing and at ease in his study at home, he laughed and said, "That's pragmatism for you. Remember when I taught you the meaning of the word?"

"Pragmatism and idealism."

"Yes," he grinned and flashed a smile in her mother's direction. "Womanly pragmatism and masculine idealism."

That had stung Jessica. Mostly because she wanted to go to University with him and read law, too. He regretfully told her this was not possible for a girl or a woman—and she raged internally—but she could read every book in his extensive library at home if she so minded.

"You must learn the womanly arts at home with your mother."

Her mother looked keenly at her daughter.

"And they are many," she assured her. "You have the best of both, Jessica. You study with a true scholar . . ."

"And," her father finished gallantly, "with the best example of the social graces."

Her mother had given him a mocking curtsey, and they had all fallen, laughing, into each other's arms.

"I placed the gifts for the children in your carrying case," Lettie said. "And some of the lesson books to refresh your memory."

Jessica nodded.

She took her mother's hands and pressed them in her own.

There was a lovely bond between them, she thought. Always, as Jessica was growing up, each seemed to know what the other was thinking or feeling. If she fell and was bruised, her mother would appear at the right moment. If Lettie were troubled, Jessica would say the right words. If she had a bad dream, her mother appeared at her chamber door. When Jason Coopersmith had been brought to their house the first time by a former colleague of Matthew's at University, Lettie seemed already to know when Jessica said she was in love . . . and Lettie smiled her approval.

Jessica had departed from her mother's house before. She had gone happily in marriage to Jason. The visits back and forth had been pleasant ones, full of women's talk and warm sharing, and when Jason had not returned from his last journey it had seemed natural for Jessica to close up their little cottage and live once more in the Steele family home. They did not go into mourning, as the two of them had done when Matthew had suddenly died. Then, overcome by shock and grief, they had clung together. On Jessica's return, she came as a married woman on a visit, in a time of trouble but not in grief. Periodically Jessica hitched the old mare to the battered four-wheeled carriage and drove to her cottage to see about it. They were days of quiet communion for her; her mother tactfully refrained from offering to accompany her. She wandered through the still rooms with their quiet whitewashed walls and sheet-covered furnishings. She went to her little spinet and plucked off its covering. She played some of the music that she and Jason had enjoyed together. Somewhere in the world, she was certain, one of the chords would spark a vibration that would reach him.

Then she went into the bedroom and lay upon the huge bedstead, staring into the canopy above. She sniffed at the big bolster, for it still held the fragrance of their hair—often sweat-drenched hair that had twined together in passion—and she knew he had to be alive. Such a vibrant man could not be snuffed out without leaving a mark, a sign behind him.

She would come back to Lettie hours later, less restless, more at peace with herself, and resume her endless task of writing letters to every newspaper in the New World, not caring if she duplicated Josiah Barrows' efforts.

When Jessica mentioned the voyage overseas, Lettie merely nodded as if she wondered why it had not been planned before. Lettie talked to Eleanor's mother, who was delighted that her daughter would have company from home. Lettie spoke to her brother Josiah as well, and the details of the journey were quickly attended to.

And yet, Jessica thought, looking at her mother's weary face, Lettie would miss her when she was gone. It would be so lonely for her. This closeness had its drawbacks, too. Separation was all the harder, and yet—when one was very close to someone, separation could be borne because there was love. There was comfort in the knowledge of love, the feeling of oneness. One carried the essence of the other person in one's heart—or mind—wherever the seat of emotion was. It was the same between Jason and herself.

* * *

Jessica and the captain's lady stood before the railing outside their quarters, as they usually did on fine afternoons, to take pleasure in the fresh air. They both wore light capes against the spring ocean coolness. Half the voyage was past, and Jessica trusted that she was now over the seasickness she had suffered the first weeks out when there were rough seas. Many days she had been prone in her bed, except for the times she must raise her heavy head and clutch the basin that lay beside her, retching into it. Then Constance Northrup would come, unsteady as the ship pitched and tossed, with a wet cloth to place over her forehead—sometimes to hold Jessica's hand as the younger woman pleaded with Constance to throw her overboard. It will pass, Constance told her over and over, and finally it did. When the storms abated, she found she could tolerate the easy rolling of the ship and at times even found it soothing. There were days when they did not move at all, when the wind disappeared entirely and they were almost motionless in this huge body of water, with nothing in sight even at the horizon, and the terrible sense of isolation and infinite space began to oppress her after the first forty-eight hours. She could feel the current that moved sluggishly under the wooden timbers and the lethargy that seemed to fall over everyone, from their cabinboy to the seamen and almost to Captain Northrup himself. He would mutter into his beard, damning the doldrums, and pray for a squall or even a mighty gale. And then, after days of nothing, when the wind would spring up, there would be spirited shouting and movement, with rapid adjustment of the wheel and the ropes, and the sails filling and then billowing, and there was the tremendous sense of release and joy as the *Elizabeth* finally skimmed over the stirring water and they were once again upon their way.

Now there was a stiff breeze ruffling the ocean, and Jessica adjusted her fluted bonnet more firmly over her ears, tightening the strings into a bow. She looked over the ship with a growing sense of pleasure, an emotion she thought she would never feel toward it. She was slowly beginning to learn some of the nautical terms and the names of the sails, now so beautiful at their fullest, dazzling white and puffed out like pillows for the gods.

The *Elizabeth* was a clipper ship and, as Jessica was amazed to learn from Captain Northrup, built in America. She expressed her surprise, for she had thought that her Uncle Josiah had only British vessels in his fleet. Not so, the captain told her, his eyes twinkling mischievously. "Matthew . . . he's a clever old fox, that one, far-seeing, benefiting from seeming disasters." Captain Northrup told her there had been an economic debacle in the New World–it had set in during 1837–and these past few years had been difficult for both the manufacturers of the North and the growers of the South. A number of Josiah Barrows' investments in the factories had resulted in his foreclosing for debts unpaid, and some of Josiah's American ships had been turned over to him in default of payments.

She thought about that now and wondered whether she had not listened carefully enough to Jason when he talked of his trips both north and south in the United States. He had been anxious to invest, too, in the factories–it must have been to bring them back to effective production, she was certain. Whatever schemes Uncle Josiah had to control the textile market, she was sure Jason would have only a constructive motivation in his dealings. Perhaps, she mused, he had assumed a role to serve Josiah well in buying and selling but at the same time to prime the pump overseas wherever he could to help get the foundering commerce back to its former rate of growth—their own fortunes could grow with it, too; it was not an impossible dream.

She should have asked Jason more questions, she told herself; then she would have known more about his movements. When he came home all she could think about was the joy of his presence, and their lovemaking—the more urgent for Jason's long absence—and bringing Jason up to date on the happenings in London. Men and women did not talk fully about business, she thought resentfully. It was not deemed proper. There was almost a taboo in their class. If she had been impoverished and forced to provide for herself, she would have had to be more aware of what went on in the world outside her own narrow preserves. Her reading of the idealist John Locke and the skeptic David Hume and the practical Adam Smith should have opened her eyes, if she had applied their theories, to what was going on in the development of the new country.

She remembered once talking to Jason about John Locke. Vaguely he had discussed Locke's theories about the natural goodness of man, but he had seemed more excited about Locke's having written a model constitution for the colonies that now were North and South Carolina. He had deplored the fact that Locke's constitution was never adopted. Jessica's thinking about Adam Smith's advocacy of free trade led her on to recall Jason's sparse and acerbic comments about Henry Clay and the Whig Party and tariff protection for the northern industrialists. Jason seemed to be caught in the double bind of importer and exporter.

She thought now particularly about Adam Smith and his book, *Inquiry into the Nature and Causes of the Wealth of Nations*, published more than a half-century before. Adam Smith had vigorously attacked placing restrictions of trade with tariffs on imports. She remembered a line of his work that had impressed her, at the time of her reading: "It is not by the importation of gold and silver that the discovery of America has enriched Europe . . . [But] by opening a new and inexhaustible market to all the commodities of Europe. . . ." His program—it was called the *"laissez-faire"* program of the Enlightenment—provided for the economic liberty of the individual, with division of labor and increased wages, and free trade among nations.

A sudden and great sense of excitement rose as it occurred to Jessica that perhaps Jason's involvement in international trade had stirred up a hornet's nest for him and accounted in some way for his disappearance. She would look into the matter further, she assured herself, discuss it with Eleanor's husband and read the newspapers of the United States and find some thread she could follow that would lead to her husband.

To calm herself she looked ahead at the bow ploughing a path through the waves, the white spray hissing against the wind. The masts stood tall against a cloudless sky, and all the sails were unfurled, carrying the narrow ship on a straight path.

"She clips along, doesn't she?" Captain Northrup punned cheerfully, joining the ladies as he came down from the bridge for tea.

"She is fast," Jessica said.

"Indeed, faster than the square-rigged heavier vessels—and requiring less of a crew."

"And the *Gypsy,* that Jonathan sailed in, was that a clipper too?"

"No, a schooner, rigged fore and aft, and fast, as well, like the *Elizabeth*. Good for trade, too."

"Well," Jessica said graciously, "I like the sails all around us. Topgallants, royal, skysails, and moonrakers . . . lovely, poetic names," she said, remembering all the varieties of sail the captain very patiently had taught her the first days she had been able to hold her head upright. He must think me a very soft landlubber, she thought ruefully.

"It's a new ship, isn't it?" she asked hastily.

"Yes," he said, "and weathering well, made with amazing skill in Baltimore."

"Amazing," his wife said mockingly. "Oh, do give them *that,* Abner!" She laughed and turned to Jessica. "Captain Northrup thinks everything native to England is the best."

Captain Northrup bowed to them.

"Like the ladies of England."

They smiled their pleasure. "Well said," Constance murmured.

A cry came from the watch in the crow's nest, heralding a ship approaching portside, though a wide expanse of sea still separated them. All those aboard the *Elizabeth* who were able rushed to her left decks, and for a moment Jessica thought the ship would surely tilt. There was a sense of excitement, for they had not seen another vessel for many days.

"Well, she's flying a Union Jack," the captain said, peering through the spyglass that Billy, the cabinboy, had handed him.

"Good," Constance said. "Then we can approach and perhaps learn news of home."

"Well, not so fast," Captain Northrup muttered, somewhat puzzled. "They're trimming the sails and seem to want to get away from us."

"Then they are not pirates," his wife said, trying to hide her disappointment that there would be no contact.

"But they are flying the British flag!" Jessica protested.

"You can't count on that!" Captain Northrup said acidly. "A pirate ship doesn't necessarily run up a pirate flag!"

They watched the other ship rapidly put more distance between them and gradually disappear from sight. They could hear the grumbling and sardonic laughter of the men.

"Why would they do that, why were they so unfriendly?" Jessica asked.

"Could be an illegal slave ship."

She gasped.

"A slave ship! Now . . . still . . . ?"

"Still," Captain Northrup said. "While by law no English ship may presently be engaged in slave traffic, there are many ship owners who lend their vessels for this purpose. . . ."

"Why doesn't the British Navy hunt them down?"

"It's a big ocean to police, and as long as there is a market the slave trade will continue. You never see the poor souls," the captain said. "They keep them down below in the holds, in unspeakable conditions, and throw out the dead ones at night. If you're close enough you can hear the awful splash. And if you're close enough," he said gravely, "you can smell the awful stench. Some seamen say the only sure mark of the slave ship is the stink."

Both women shuddered.

"There will be slaves on Eleanor and Charles' plantation," Jessica said in a small voice.

"Yes," Constance said, "but I'm sure your relatives would be most kindly in their treatment."

"It will be difficult to adjust to it."

"But you will," Constance assured her. "In your eyes they will soon become the serving class that we have at home."

"No, it's different," Jessica said.

"It *is* different," the captain agreed. "And there is a strong abolition movement developing rapidly in the North—especially with the question of admitting new territory into the Union. Perhaps in your time—not in mine, I'm afraid—you will see the slave system abolished."

"The abolition movement," Jessica said slowly. "I had not given much thought to that. . . . I wonder . . ."

"What, my dear?"

"Whether . . ."

Billy, the cabinboy, whispered to Mrs. Northrup.

"Tea's growing cold," she announced to her husband and Jessica.

Could he have become involved in that, the abolition movement? Jason had never said. Impossible . . . but, no, perhaps. An English factor buying cotton from the plantations? Could his thoughts about the southern economy and the slave system have changed? He traveled from the South to the North and then back again. The abolition movement . . . a dangerous activity for anyone and especially for an outsider, a foreigner . . . and yet perhaps logical . . . perhaps this was still another thread. . . .

The captain's quarters, though not luxurious, were indeed comfortable, as Josiah Barrows had promised. There was a small drawing room in which they now took their refreshment—a portrait of young Queen Victoria unsmilingly presiding over all—a private, very narrow galley, and two small bed compartments. A very snug little house, really, Jessica thought, that must have been very attractive to Captain Northrup and sweetened the voyages for him because he could have Constance along. Jessica often wondered how the other men reacted to having a woman (and now two!) aboard, with all the rampant superstitions about their shipwreck propensities and general attraction of doom. Too, it seemed to her they must be reminders of the men's abstinence from women. On the other hand, she thought, they must rationalize it, the same way they understood that through seniority and rank a captain should have a bed and a deckhand only a hammock, and a captain eat from china dishes set upon a polished table and a seaman from a tinplate like as not set upon a hatch. Nevertheless she did heed Constance Northrup's quiet restriction at the very outset of the voyage that she stay close by her and not wander about the decks herself. And she was aware that Billy was not sent back to the sailors' quarters at night and was permitted to sleep in the galley, or, when the seas were heavy and the pots and pans and dishes threatened to be thrown from their rails, on a pallet in the common room.

Billy passed the little bread and marmalade sandwiches as Constance busied herself with the teapot and pitchers of hot water. Jessica smiled at him as she took one. Though he worked so hard, Billy was only a child, between thirteen and fourteen years old, she thought; she had never actually inquired. And she did not know his last name. Perhaps this was what Constance Northrup really meant when she mentioned adjusting to the serving classes in the same breath that she talked of slavery. Jessica's face flushed at the thought. But she had noticed that he had gained a little weight since the beginning of the voyage. It was not his first time out—and he so young!—but it was his first time on the *Elizabeth,* and Jessica was aware of the motherly, but certainly not indulgent, eye that Constance kept on him. She set him to constant tasks of scrubbing and emptying the chamberpots, and doing all the chores of the scullery, but she also made sure that he had ample food and that he got his exercise—albeit in the form of running from the cabins to the quarterdeck or to the captain on the bridge. His face was still a little wizened, like that of an old man. His blond hair was flaxen from the sun and he pushed it from his eyes with a nervous twitch.

Perhaps he would have a growth spurt when he was fifteen or sixteen, Jessica thought, but now he seemed very tiny although not fragile. There was a tough fiber to him, she sensed more than she saw.

Early out, she had come upon him in her cabin staring at the books spread upon the bed. The expression on his face made her say to him, "Billy, please fetch me John Barrow's *History of England.*" She saw the puzzlement spread and color his cheeks with embarrassment as he poked among the books, confirming the reason for her experiment.

"Would you like to learn how to read?" she asked him softly.

He could only nod mutely.

"Very well," she said. "I'll teach you."

He stared at her with surprise and some distrust.

"We'll keep it a secret," she promised him. "We'll have our lesson early in the morning before the others awake." And for the first time she saw him smile.

Every morning afterward, before the sun rose—for since Jason had not come home, she had been a very fitful sleeper—she came quietly into the common room, bringing with her the primer she had intended for Eleanor's children.

And still she did not know his surname or anything of his history. Well, she was not the best sort of teacher then. Not the teacher that Matthew Steele had been—not only to his daughter but to all who came under his tutorial wing—whose gift was to reach the whole person. The rest of the voyage she would get to know Billy, learn what he really was like, who he was and who he had been—and possibly what he could be.

She realized that she had been staring at Billy and he was growing uneasy, and she turned to Captain Northrup.

"I can't stop thinking about the ship that we saw and how she turned away from us."

"Well, don't you fret, my dear; before you know it we shall land at Philadelphia, and you will see many more ships and many more people."

"No, no, it wasn't quite that . . ." But she couldn't put in words just yet the tantalizing ideas that slavery and cotton fields and factories had stimulated in regard to Jason.

"Years ago, before 1807 and 1808, when first the British and then the American prohibitive laws against slave importation were passed," the captain said, "the sea lanes were crowded with slave ships." He sipped his tea and then continued. "Some came directly from the African coast, some indirectly, and some stopped at the West Indies. The old-timers used to tell of it, the 'Middle Passage,' when I first went to sea—how the ships came from the barracoons, the holding pens where the Arabs sold black people, after buying them sometimes from neighboring African tribesmen, in wholesale lots to the captains. Passing these ships was an eerie business—there was not only the stink, but the clanking of chains and the keening of women and children, and the men like as not; it was one terrible chant of sorrow. . . . It is better now, even if not entirely wiped out."

"And don't forget the indentured servants," Constance prompted him.

"Oh, there is no comparison. . . . But that was before my time, too," the captain said. "The colonies' revolution put an end, for the most part, to that."

"Imagine, my dear, mortgaging your life to someone you didn't know for as much as three to seven years (and sometimes even more) just for the price of passage!"

"My goodness," Jessica said, smiling ruefully, "how much I have to thank Uncle Josiah for!"

"Yes . . . all would be well but for a husband lost," Constance said.

"Misplaced but not lost," Jessica replied.

Something about Constance's last statement piqued Jessica even more. Perhaps it was the way her mind was running this day. The talk of recession in the New World, and Uncle Josiah's and Jason's investments, and slavery and the abolition movement, and Jason's travels through the North and South of the country she was about to see for the first time stirred up fears—and even hopes—that she had not dared to face before.

The balance of the voyage passed quickly. The days sped by, and since one was so like the other, Jessica lost all sense of what day in the week it was, or which month of the year, or for that matter what time it was. Lessons with Billy (Jenkins, she had learned, but not much else) continued each morning before sunup. It gave her pleasure to see how well he was progressing. He had a keen intelligence that never failed to amaze her. He began to hang on every word she spoke. When she praised him, his face flushed hotly. His look became adoring. Probably, she thought, no one had ever given him so much individual attention.

After the lesson she would quietly read her own book in her cabin for an interval while Billy slipped into the galley to fix the morning meal as the Northrups stirred in their compartment. Then Jessica would bind up her hair in a more fashionable chignon, not thinking it suitable to appear with it flowing to her waist, and join her cabinmates. Captain Northrup would be off to his duties and Constance and Jessica would write in their journals. Jessica, too, wrote a continuous letter to her mother, which Captain Northrup promised to post with the first ship they found on landing that would be returning home. After Philadelphia, Captain Northrup was sailing up the Atlantic Coast to Boston, and he and Constance and the *Elizabeth* would not be back in England for many more months. He and his crew had much cargo to take off and put on before the return voyage.

Constance would send Billy off to Cook with a list of stores for the private galley and then plan the midday meal and supper. The two women would cook special dishes, with Billy's assistance, using their ingenuity more and more as the fresh foods disappeared and they had to deal with dried fish and smoked meats and rice and beans and whatever could be made of flour and other grains. "Not bad," the captain would say, "my compliments to the cooks, not bad at all." Sometimes they invited the first mate to share the evening food, and those were pleasant times. It was nice to have an unattached male to talk to, Jessica had to confess to herself. Mr. Graham was a most presentable man, somewhere in his thirties or early forties, and he paid her a respectful but admiring attention. He usually brought his fiddle with him and he would play and she would sing Elizabethan folksongs, while the Northrups tapped their feet and smiled appreciatively, and Billy shyly peeked in from the galley.

Afterward, when Mr. Graham had left and it was bedtime,

Jessica would take her little mirror from her handcase and study her reflection. Strange, since Jason had not come back, how rarely she paid attention to the way she looked. She went through the motions of taking care of herself, dressing, bathing, arranging her hair, but it meant nothing. This woman in the mirror was different from the girl she had remembered. The apple cheeks were now modeled into finer planes, the dark eyes more expressive, perhaps a little sad. She took inventory. A good firm body, slender and lithe, a long slender neck. She was twenty-four now, she thought with a pang; the first bloom was gone. She did not know that the deeper delicacy and intensity of feeling had surfaced to give her features a radiance they had not had before. Again she looked searchingly at herself in the mirror because she had seen the admiration in Mr. Graham's eyes, and it both excited and troubled her. Oh, she longed for the security of marriage and a man society sanctioned for her own. Jason, I shall find you, I shall find you, she vowed, or . . . I shall *find* you, she vowed.

Sometimes Mr. Graham would join her as she stood before the railing outside the Northrups' quarters. She stayed there for long periods of time looking out to sea. The sound of the waves against the side of the ship seemed to mesmerize her, and she liked to stare down at the valleys and troughs of the water. The changing patterns that swirled below seemed like the whorls on her fingertips. She felt like a sea person, remembering the stories her father had told her when she was a child, that she was a naiad, a nymph from the springs that came up to the ocean. She had seen herself then as a full-formed woman swimming to shore, trailing bright sea anemones in her long black hair. And little *v*'s of fishes and other creatures—turtles and seals—made up her retinue to the very edge of the beach.

She laughed.

"What are you thinking, ma'am?" Mr. Graham asked her.

"Oh . . . myths and fables."

"Serious thinking for a young woman."

"My interpretation isn't."

"Will you stay long in America?" he asked suddenly.

"I don't know."

"It's a rough country in some ways, Mrs. Coopersmith."

"Yes, but I shall be staying with my cousin and her husband."

"You don't want to get mixed up with . . . foreign . . . problems. Tempers run high."

She turned to stare at him in surprise.

"I hadn't intended to do that."

"Well," he faltered, "sometimes when you unravel a rope you find unexpected knots in it."

"And sometimes it comes away clean."

"Yes." He paused for a moment, then swallowed and said, "You need to know whether you are a married woman or not."

"Sir!" she cried. "I certainly am married!"

His tanned face grew even darker.

"Forgive me," he murmured. "I asked Captain Northrup if I could speak with you."

"You did?"

"Yes, and he said that I could."

"He had no right."

"He is captain of this ship."

She looked more fully into Douglas Graham's bright blue eyes.

"You both . . . you all . . ." she said, feeling pain, "believe there is no point . . . that he's dead. . . . Tell me," she cried, "do you and the Northrups know anything about my husband that I do not?"

"No. No," he stammered, "except we think you're only going to hurt yourself even more, setting an impossible task."

"No, not impossible," she said obstinately, then suspiciously, "unless you know—"

He shook his head sadly. His broad shoulders, usually erect, slumped.

"There's no turning you back? Won't you return with the *Elizabeth* to England?"

"No! I will not!"

He held out his hand to her, then drew it back.

"Perhaps it is sinful for me to speak now . . . not knowing whether or not your legally bound husband is alive or no . . ."

She smiled; then they—he and the Northrups—were acknowledging their doubt. Douglas Graham interpreted her smiles as encouragement and continued:

"I have no wife or child of my own," he said, "and I am a steady man . . ." He would not let her speak and hurried on. "I have a little place in Sussex and intend to settle down one day and farm it. . . . We don't know each other well, but those times we sang together, ma'am, there was such harmony . . ."

Her eyes dropped. She had felt it, too. He *was* a good man, she thought, very stable and capable of much feeling. She liked the sense of his presence—a tall figure, spare and strong.

"I am not a man to wish another harm, certainly not to wish away a man's life. . . ."

She shuddered.

"But if within a reasonable time you accept and make legal the fact that he is . . . no longer here . . . then I beg . . . to make you my wife . . . and care for you. . . ."

She took his hand and found it calloused and firm.

"I'm very flattered, Mr. Graham. I know you are a sincere man and I appreciate your offer . . ."

"Then let the offer stand. I shall come to you the voyage after the return sailing and ask for your answer. . . . No, don't tell me now," he admonished as she began to speak. "You will have time then to think on it."

He looked up at the bridge, and her eyes followed. The captain was looking down at them.

"I must relieve him," Douglas Graham said softly. He kissed her fingertips, touching her ring with the Coopersmith crest on it with his lips, bowed and left.

Chapter Two

The stagecoach bounced intolerably and Jessica was glad for once of the multiple petticoats she wore that protected her against the hard seat. Captain Abner Northrup had discharged his duty when he placed her on the coach at Philadelphia and entrusted her into the care of the drivers. His only wish was that he were going south, he told her regretfully, instead of to Boston, and could take her by sail to Norfolk and put her on a coach to Roanoke—where her people, south and west of that community, could easily come to meet her. She had already written them before she left London, she reassured Captain Abner and Constance. Her cousins knew she would arrive by stagecoach and were prepared to pick her up at the Abingdon stop, past Roanoke. They would check the Philadelphia lists of ship arrivals. Anyway, she would be glad to see some of the country before she settled in. Constance had thrown her arms around her—a frequent occurrence—and had bidden her to take care of herself. The two women had grown very fond of one another, and Jessica was particularly sad to take leave of her. Captain Abner gruffly patted her shoulder and wished her good luck, and promised he would report to her mother of their good voyage together when he reached England again. The sadness of parting was soon swept away by the excitement of being in the United States, still for Jessica the New World.

She remembered how she had eagerly looked at the harbor of Philadelphia and all the barges and ships on the Delaware River. They—the Northrups and she—had ventured into the town, on foot, amidst the piles of ropes and barrels and cargo on the wharves. Housewives and black attendants were inspecting the fish that the smaller boats had brought in and mongers wove around them hawking their wares. They had to dodge the horses and wagons. She could smell the stables facing the wharves. She had stared at the black slaves. They were the first men and women of color she had ever seen, though she had looked at sketches of them in her father's books. But to see them in the flesh produced a sense of shock. So much of it was fear. Then she settled down. They were people, she told herself—no matter that the color of their skin was different, and their facial features not the same as hers, or their hair or their clothing. She had expected something even more exotic. They were people, and in the realization of that fact their extraordinariness began to fade. The same with the red brick buildings she saw across the cobblestone street at the waterfront. They looked like many of the buildings back home. She did not want them to look the same, she thought unreasonably; a New World, a new look. And yet, of course, the English and the Scotch-Irish and the German and Dutch builders had brought their home skills with them.

They passed a tavern, with its colorful wooden sign swinging in what little breeze the humid late June afternoon offered. The able-bodied seaman who followed them with her trunk in a wheelbarrow glanced wistfully through its door, while Constance, a teetotaler, looked firmly away. At Second Street they came upon a church which the captain said was Christ Church, an elegant building, Jessica thought, with a lovely white steeple. Captain Northrup was so moved by her delight that he took her purposely—even if it was a bit out of their way—to Third and Walnut Streets to see the elegant new building that had been built only six years before, in 1834, where merchants could assemble and do their trading. Jessica admired its cobblestone court and elegant, round, Greek-columned facade. Captain Northrup was particularly pleased; it was his favorite landmark, and he had transacted much business there.

They made a turn or two and approached a building identified for her as Library Hall, with graceful columns and a statue of Benjamin Franklin in its niche over the front door. She was delighted to see the likeness of Franklin; he was another one of her father's heroes, firmly implanted in her mind. Then just a little farther they walked past another structure she admired and the captain informed her this was the previous Assembly Room now transformed into Independence Hall.

Soon they reached the inn where the stagecoach waited for passengers. Jessica was surprised to see Douglas Graham there talking to the driver who was supervising the hitching up of four fresh horses. Douglas turned to her quickly and swept off his hat.

"Ma'am," he said, bowing, "I was passing and wanted to see the trappings of these things."

Captain Northrup and his lady seemed surprised to see the first mate, too. The captain said something humorous about Mr. Graham's speed, and Douglas Graham turned scarlet. He quickly asked all of them to be his guests at tea at the inn, but the bustle outward of the other passengers indicated there was not time. The driver was on his box above the horses, and the coachman was assisting the ladies inside the carriage. Douglas gave a hand with Jessica's trunk as it was swung onto the rack above. Then he waited while the Northrups took their second leave of Jessica. He helped Jessica into the conveyance, his huge hand covering hers, pressing her crested ring into her finger. He looked deep into her eyes as she perched upon the step and told her firmly, "I'll see you again!" as she entered and the coach door was firmly closed by the coachman.

She thought of that goodbye often during the next few days as she traveled southward. His blue eyes had been even deeper than she remembered against the background of the sea. In the afternoon of the city they had glowed with deep reserves of turquoise and lapis lazuli—a beautiful mixture, she thought; strange that she had not noticed their depth so much before.

But most of her concern these past few days had been with the problem of travel. Not only the bouncing and the lurching and the fretting of an older woman passenger and the bold staring of the middle-aged dandy who sat opposite her. A few tradesmen were aboard, too, and they had brought along their panacea for discomfort. The smell of whiskey permeated the already stale air of the coach. The days melded into each other, with the noise of the inns where they stayed nights, often bedded down with two or three other women travelers in a single bed while the men went into dormitories of their own. The sleeping arrangements had offended Jessica greatly, and despite the affront to her roommates she had taken her cape, which she carried but did not use because of the heat, folded it, and placed it on the floor where it served as a pallet for her tired body. The community slop jars outraged her even more and she slipped outside in the mornings looking for a privy. Once they stayed beside a stream, and she rose much before the others, walked away from the inn until she was out of sight, and had a refreshing swim. It was so good not only to bathe thoroughly but to stretch her cramped and jostled limbs.

She was fortunate to have an end seat in the coach, near the window, and seeing the country unfold through the window frame made her glad that, despite the discomforts, she had not transferred to another ship at Philadelphia and sailed the last distance of her trip to Virginia. Now she could see the new country and share in the joy of discovery that Jason must have experienced, too. He must have seen these beautiful green lands, the flat surfaces of Delaware and Maryland, the vast networks of waterways and the interesting contrasts as they entered Virginia. One of the merchants told her they were going through the Tidewater region, and she was dismayed to see an area that was not only flat but swampy. Her cousin, and Jason too, must have exaggerated, she thought with disappointment, when they called Virginia one of the most beautiful parts of the United States.

But later, vast forests surrounded the road they traveled, and through the dense foliage she could make out stands of pine and oak intermingled with dogwood and rhododendron bushes that must have flowered earlier in the springtime. Then the land began to roll and they passed the edges of huge farms. She could see horses grazing in the fields and there were herds of cows and flocks of chicken and geese. They passed some villages on their route, and discharged some passengers and took on new ones. Jessica could walk around in some of the towns and admire the shops near the coaching stop inn and look at the clothing the people wore. A new passenger had to remove his high silk hat as he came aboard. Then came the farms again, and she could see some grand houses set far back from the pike—lots of apple trees—and farther along row upon row of a plant with broad shiny green leaves she knew immediately must be tobacco. She looked for the long low sheds behind the fields. These would be the "burning" cabins or the places where the leaves were dried before they were sold. It was so green, almost blue-green, as far as she could see in the last part of her journey—and sometimes, unbidden, it reminded her of the lights in Douglas Graham's eyes, bouncing off the deep, deep blue of the iris.

She shrugged that off. It was Jason she was seeking.

She had to change coaches at Danville. Her next, and last, stop was in the town of Abingdon, in the southwestern part of the state, not too far from the borders of Tennessee and North Carolina, the coachman had told her. She was the only passenger to leave the carriage and the man who was waiting approached her immediately. It must be Charles, she thought, and glanced behind him to see whether Eleanor had come to meet her, too. But with him was another man, a middle-aged black male; there was no woman present.

"Cousin Jessica . . . ?" He bowed gravely. "It must be you, Miz Coopersmith?"

He smiled at her. He was tall and very good-looking. She remembered the first letters that Eleanor had written describing him—he had noble features, she had said, and a great shock of white hair, though he was so young. . . . The silvery white contrasted remarkably with the freshness of his olive-rose skin and the deep brown-blackness of his eyes. It was startling to see the whiteness of his hair above the lean, muscled body that seemed so vital and strong. Eleanor was right, she thought; earlier she had suspected that Eleanor had written from the first flush of romance.

"Yes," she said, curtseying, then offering her hand.

"Charles Sedgely," he said, kissing it.

The black man was already transferring her trunk to a two-horse surrey that stood next to the hitching post.

"I trust the drive won't be too much for you. We have still a way to go—we are farther west." She shook her head, preoccupied about her cousin. "You must be very tired and unaccustomed to the heat we have here."

"Eleanor?"

"She doesn't like the heat of the afternoons. She takes to her chamber this part of the day. Many of the ladies of Virginia do the same." He smiled at her. "She sends her apologies not to be here but will see you shortly after you arrive at the homestead."

"Of course," Jessica murmured. "And the children—they are well?" He nodded. "I am so eager to meet them."

"And I am grateful that you have come to see to their lessons," he said earnestly.

He took her elbow and began to guide her to the waiting surrey. She was glad to see the canopy above it; she had not realized, especially after months at sea, how hot the summer could be. The town was quiet; just a few people were abroad this afternoon, mainly blacks in coarse cotton clothing. One black woman balanced a laden basket upon her head. The dust of the street swirled occasionally as a gust of wind, as humid as the surrounding air, stirred it. As Charles was about to help her into the carriage, the whispered sound of her name made her turn about quickly.

"Billy!" she cried, disbelieving.

But it was he—dirty and smaller than ever, it seemed, his flaxen hair dusty and matted. He looked so woebegone she was about to take him into her arms when the seriousness of what he had done made her stiffen in outrage.

"Billy!" she cried. "Did you run away?"

He nodded, and his face crinkled up into a smaller knot than before.

"From good Captain and Mrs. Northrup!" she said hotly.

"I had to," he said in a tight voice, close to crying. "He can get another boy."

"What have we here!" Charles said sternly. "This ragamuffin followed you from Philadelphia?"

"It seems so. Whatever are we to do?"

"Send him back!" Charles said firmly.

Her anger began to leave her as she wondered how Billy had survived these past few days.

"Where did you hide?" she asked the boy.

"Under the carriage," he said faintly, "between the front and back wheels . . . there's a little ledge . . ."

"Oh my goodness," she exclaimed, "it's a mercy you didn't fall under the horses' hooves and get killed!"

"Might have been a good idea," Charles said coldly. "Deserting a good master."

"I would have walked," Billy said stubbornly, "if I hadn't found that shelf."

"What did you eat?" Jessica asked. "When?"

"Sometimes at night . . . when we stopped . . ."

"Not very much and not very often," she said.

"No."

"Are you hungry now, Billy?"

He nodded, and a tear oozed from the pinched face.

"I imagine . . . Cousin Charles, Captain Northrup has already left Philadelphia . . ."

"And you want me to keep the boy here?"

"How could we send him back? Not until the next voyage anyway."

Charles looked closely at the boy.

"Doesn't seem very strong to me."

"Oh, he's a good worker. He was very useful to Captain and Mrs. Northrup and me . . . excellent in the galley . . ."

"Oh yes, sir," the boy said anxiously, "I'll work very hard . . ."

"Indeed you *will* earn your keep!"

The boy stared at him eagerly.

"I will! I will, you'll see!"

"All right," Charles said gruffly. "Up there, quickly, beside William!"

With agility, though Jessica imagined it cost his thoroughly jostled bones some pain, Billy clambered onto the driver's box. William looked at him impassively.

"We'll give him to Julia . . . she's the cook. . . . She'll take him in hand." Charles saw the fear in Jessica's face. "And feed him . . . put some meat on his bones. She was my ole mammy," he explained. "Ole slave woman."

"Oh," she said, trying unsuccessfully to keep the disapproval from her voice, and Charles looked at her and smiled.

When they were seated and the horses had settled into a steady trot, Charles said, "The boy must be very attached to you."

"I think it was the reading," she said thoughtfully.

"Reading?"

"Yes, I was teaching him to read."

"A ship's hand? Really?"

"Yes."

"And was he an apt pupil?"

"Yes, very."

"Hmmm. You must be a good teacher. I'm eager to have my children begin their lessons in earnest. They are ready." He looked out the side of the carriage for a moment. "I expect you will be a good influence on them. God knows they need it."

They turned off the road down a lane that was planted with poplar trees on both sides. At the end of it Jessica saw a large house looming through a shield of shrubbery before it. As the lane opened into the circular drive, a large veranda constructed around tall stone pillars supporting a slate-shingled roof became apparent. A portico opened from the middle windows of the second story. The building seemed massive to Jessica. Its structure was so elegant that she was surprised to see that the cluster of additional buildings to the side of it were mean in appearance. Two rows of log cabins trailed from one of the mansion's sides into the backlands.

William reined in the horses and a bevy of little black children gathered quickly to see who had arrived. They were barefooted, the girls in short dresses of a blue-checked material and the boys in nothing but nankeen pants. They chanted and called to the master, and then, just as quickly, at the sound of some granny's sharp voice, they disappeared completely.

"We'll take you through the land some day soon," Charles promised her as he helped her down to the ground.

She could see very far back the beginning of the fields stretching into the distance. At the very edge of her vision were tiny black figures dotted through green plants.

"We have more than five thousand acres," Charles told her. "Land rich and money poor."

As she stepped into the house she could not think poor but only rich. A large center hall extended from front to back and there were many rooms branching from it. In the wide hallway she saw numerous gleaming mahogany tables and a massive grandfather clock and an abundance of chairs, damask-covered and plain wood with graceful Windsor bows, supported by delicate spindles. Off to one side, with its door open, was a great drawing room, with a full piano and a harp at one of its ends and a spinet at the other—with lounges and wingchairs and Persian rugs upon the random-width plank floor, portraits of ancestors, no doubt, gracing the walls. A quick look across the hall took in the dining room, its double doors also drawn aside, showing a huge banquet table in its middle, with rows of chairs along its sides and also against the wainscoting. The size of the gleaming buffet indicated it could support a great quantity of food. This was a house meant for entertaining.

A black houseman, dressed in a black coat exactly like the one worn by Charles Sedgely, came gravely to greet them. Jessica wondered whether he had been chosen for size so that he could easily slip into hand-downs; he was as tall and slender as his master. A young houseboy appeared to relieve William of Jessica's trunk.

"We must see to Miz Coopersmith's comfort, Cicero," Charles told the elder man gravely.

"Yassuh," Cicero said quietly. "We's got Miz Coopersmith's room, by the chillun, ready. Would Miz Coopersmith lak to rest befoh dinner?"

"I should think so after such a long trip," Charles said, not giving her time to make her preference known. "Why don't you get Sally to see to her needs?"

Jessica was soon settled in her room atop the long winding stairway. Sally had unpacked her clothing, put it in the clothespress, filled the water jugs, and brought her a tall cool glass of lemonade. She chattered away incessantly as she went about her tasks, but it took some time for Jessica to become accustomed to her speech—it was thick and slow and very melodious but sometimes unintelligible to her ears. Cicero's had been relatively clear; she supposed it had something to do with where each had been raised and how much he or she had been exposed to the speech of white people. She was glad when the girl went away, though she appreciated the things she had done for her.

She needed to sort out her thoughts and impressions. Charles, her cousin by marriage. He was an attractive man who might be difficult really to know, and yet perhaps not. Eleanor. Why had she not at least come from her room to greet her? When they were young girls, she bubbled over with energy and pounced gleefully upon Jessica—no matter that Eleanor was older—whenever they had come together. Of course it was nine years since Jessica had last seen Eleanor, but the long separation should have made her cousin all the more impatient to be reunited.

And the matter of Billy. She was appalled by his disloyalty to Captain and Mrs. Northrup, and worried about what might become of him. She must trust to Charles' good instincts, that he would see to it that Billy was fairly treated on the plantation. Perhaps it was because Eleanor had not yet appeared, and because she was feeling a bit forlorn and lonely and far away from home, that the thought of Billy close by began to become more of a comfort than an annoyance.

She made her toilette quickly, slipping from the heavy, stiff black bombazine of her traveling costume. The cool water poured from the pitcher into its matching china basin felt soothing to her warm skin. She wished for a huge wash tub or whatever they used for a full-body bath, but at least she was able to sponge herself completely. She chose a cool white muslin dress, cut in the simple shepherdess style her father had so loved and that had been made fashionable for a while years before by Marie Antoinette. One petticoat was all she could bear. She cared more for comfort now than for fashion. She tied the pink ribbon sash loosely, and pulling her long black hair to the top of her head, Jessica caught it there with another pink ribbon.

She looked for the presents she had brought the family—the China teas, some China silk for Eleanor, a fine old French desk clock for Charles, books for the children. Laying them upon the table by the window, ready for presentation, she saw the fan that had been left there by Sally. Gratefully she began to use it, sitting in the rocking chair beside the table.

There was a tap on the door. Perhaps it was Eleanor, she thought excitedly, and rose to open the door, at the same time calling to the person knocking to enter. She was still in the middle of the room when two small heads peered through the door frame. Sally hovered behind them.

"Nurse done say they kin come," Sally murmured and then disappeared.

"Come in," Jessica said softly to the little boy and girl, and they curtsied and bowed and came and sat upon her bed. The little girl, who was younger, clung tightly to the boy's hand.

"Now let me see," Jessica said gravely, "I imagine you are Jennifer," pointing to the girl, "and you must be Charles Junior," turning to the brother.

"My father is Charles," he said firmly, "and I am Char*lie* for Charles *Lee.*"

"Oh yes," Jessica said. "And Jennifer is Jenny."

The little girl's face brightened.

"Howja know that?"

"Your mother wrote me so in her letters."

"Mama is sleeping," Charlie said.

"She gets headaches," Jenny offered.

"And we must not trouble her," Charlie said.

"Indeed not," Jessica agreed, surprised.

It was not long before Jessica gave them the books she had brought and then she was on the bed, too, reading to them. Jenny curled happily against her side and Charlie peered over Jessica's shoulder. They were beautiful children, Jessica thought, reading automatically for a few moments as she looked at them appreciatively. The little girl was a miniature of her father, except for the blondness of her hair, and the black velvet of her eyes contrasting with it was striking. Charlie had a fine-boned look about him and his delicate features were like Eleanor's.

She subtly tested Charlie with a few words here and there in the book's text and found that he read badly. Upon questioning, later, she learned that there had been a tutor for a little while.

Charlie did not like him, and anyway Papa had had a quarrel with him and had sent him away. Jessica could see that she had considerable work to do, and the prospect made her spirits rise. The relief she felt made her realize how disheartened she had been by Eleanor's nonappearance.

The children liked being read to; Jessica was not sure whether it was her attention or the story that appealed to them so much. And when Sally came to return them to the nurse for supper in the children's dining room, they were reluctant to go. Jessica promised to see them later in the evening, and Charlie informed her that he and Jenny always came into the family dining room, after the adults finished their dinner, to say goodnight. Jessica walked them to the hallway, pleased that Jenny permitted her to kiss her cheek and Charlie responded to her hug.

She thought of the children long after they had gone and of the last time she had seen Eleanor. Then her cousin had been preparing for her voyage overseas. She was to be the guest of other relatives, not kin to Jessica, who were to entertain her in Connecticut. Eleanor had been so excited during the evening she and Jessica spent together, showing her the elaborate ball gowns she was taking with her and talking of all her suitors in London who were brokenhearted at her impending absence from the social scene. Laughing a great deal, she danced Jessica around the room. Eleanor glowed with anticipation and said that she wished Jessica were old enough to come with her. Eleanor's parents were accompanying her, so she would not be too lonely, though she would pine away for her favorite cousin, she assured Jessica, during the six-month stay abroad.

First came word that Eleanor's hosts had introduced her to a fine dashing young man who was finishing his education at Yale. Then, the news of the wedding already preceding them to London, Eleanor's parents had returned without her. It was an exciting romance, according to Eleanor's letters and the story told by her parents as they paid their family calls upon coming home. Jessica hung upon their words—the handsome suitor, the wedding at the huge plantation in Virginia where he lived, the beautiful uncrowded land, how happy Eleanor was, how desolate they were at the distance between them but what a good and suitable match it was for their daughter. Charles Sedgely was part of the landed aristocracy of Virginia. Matthew Steele had shrugged but, in response to a meaningful glance from his wife, held his tongue. Later, after they had gone, he talked scathingly of the aristocracy in Virginia. Slavers, he said angrily. Thomas Jefferson should have insisted that the paragraph he had originally drafted into the Declaration of Independence condemning human bondage be retained. Should have stood firm against the members of the southern delegation, Matthew said sadly. That document, with justice and freedom for all, was a mockery. Like the French Revolution, of which he had been so fond, Lettie had reminded him gently but with point.

Jessica sat again at the table, fanning herself, waiting for the summons to dinner. Sally had informed her there would be a dinner bell and that she would come to escort her to the dining room.

Jessica thought again of the children, how beautiful they were and responsive to affection. True of all children, gently reared; Jason had written of them in his letter to her from Virginia. He had scribbled glowingly of them and, with longing and no circumspection, expressed the hope that one day they would be blessed with children, too, as lovely as they.

Jason loomed vividly in her mind. She could see the beseeching eyes, the glow that came into them when he was ready for lovemaking, the warm feel of his arms, the joy of two bodies responding to one another. She shivered.

She was closer to him now that she was in Virginia. This was the reason for her voyage, why she was here. Not just to tutor Eleanor's children and see Eleanor again and get to know her husband—though she wanted to accomplish all these, too—but to establish a home base from which she could make inquiries, to enlist Eleanor and Charles' help.

On his last business trip to the States, Jason had visited the Sedgely plantation for a few days, when he had written the letter. Perhaps Charles and Eleanor—no, Eleanor had not been there; Jason had written that she was away, in Maryland—perhaps Charles would know of some stopover he had made somewhere that had not officially been listed in his itinerary. Charles might have a lead for her to follow, someone to see, some place to go where Jason may have left a clue. She must talk with Charles about a plan of action, perhaps tomorrow, if not tonight—no, not tonight when she had just come. But she would not forget for a minute why she had journeyed to the United States. She had a mission to accomplish and accomplish it she would.

She thought again idly of Eleanor, pushing down the hurt that her cousin had not made a special effort to greet her. And that she had not cut short her visit elsewhere when Jason had come to stay at her home. Then Jessica fretted that there was no breeze to stir the curtain at the window; she must adjust to the heat. She could hear the vibration of the cicadas outside, and the droning of cicadas and bees and the fragrance of the rosebeds and the shrubbery beneath her room made her drowsy. She could feel her head nodding, sometimes almost descending into her lap, then quickly almost unconsciously jerking back to lifted level again. She was dreaming, and once she thought she saw Eleanor standing above her, Eleanor in a soiled wrapper—but it couldn't be, so unlike her—and her hair wild and uncombed about her shoulders—it couldn't be, not Eleanor, so fastidious and caring about herself. Jessica drifted in and out of sleep and when she reached the upper levels of almost-consciousness, she saw Eleanor again, near the door this time, blowing a kiss to her as she floated through it, and vanishing. Jessica could hear herself sighing as she came out of her nap.

Sally stood there. Perhaps it was Sally she had seen, or dreamed of, but no—the thought of Eleanor persisted.

"Goin ta dinnah now," Sally said softly. Jessica was adjusting to the slurring of her speech. "Bell done rung."

Sally took her not to the dining room but to the drawing room, where Charles stood before the dark fireplace and an elderly lady sat in an easy chair. He came forward to take Jessica's hand and bring her before the *grande dame.*

"My grandmother, Miranda Donahue—my late mother's mother," he explained.

Jessica curtsied. Miranda took her hand, searching her face.

"Good bones," she said.

Jessica almost laughed aloud.

"Grandmother is here, visiting for a fortnight. She lives in Maryland," Charles explained.

The houseman she had seen earlier brought sherry and bits of cheese.

"Good, good," Miranda said, "these late dinners make me famished. Now in Maryland we aren't as formal as these Virginians," she smiled at her grandson as she said the word scathingly, "and eat at decent hours."

"Is there that much difference?" Jessica asked. "Between the customs of Maryland and Virginia?"

"Yes," the grandmother said promptly. "Marylanders are much more red-blooded. Virginians are effete."

Charles laughed.

"Grandmother doesn't really believe that."

"Oh, yes," Miranda said. "I do. My daughter married a blue-blooded gentleman and look at the son they produced. In a black swallowtail coat, the tails trailing against equally black leggings—trousers, I should say, to keep up with the times. When I was a young girl in Maryland, many years ago," she said proudly, "men knew how to dress. They were like the birds of the field, as nature meant it to be, in brilliant plumage. Damasks—crimson and gold and white, with silver buttons on their waistcoats—and kneebreeches and silken hose to show a manly leg. Powdered hair and wigs and silken bows to catch them back, ruffled stocks and silver buckles on their shoes. And now—just look at him—somber as a crow, pooh!"

"Nothing can compare with Grandmother's girlhood," Charles said solemnly.

"In the big houses, of course," continued Miranda. "In the outlying districts the men were in their buckskins and raccoon hats—meaner but manly still. These crows today, it's against nature! And ah, the Maryland feasts. Sides of ham, suckling pigs with apples, legs of mutton and joints of beef, and the pie—fruit and meat, and all the gallons of cider . . ." She went off into a fond reverie.

"It's all right, Grandmother," Charles said soothingly. "Cicero will call us to dinner soon."

"About time."

"Will Eleanor join us?" Jessica asked anxiously.

"She sends her regrets," Charles said. "She is still in the throes of her sick headache. Tomorrow . . ."

"Perhaps," Miranda said tartly.

"Tomorrow, she said, she would see you surely."

"Could I look in on her after dinner?"

"It would be better not to," Charles said. "Even the candle-light bothers her when she is this way. She prefers to be in darkness."

"Yes, she does," Miranda said.

"Wait until tomorrow. She will see you then. You've seen the children?"

Then the conversation turned to Charlie and Jenny, and Charles and even Miranda beamed as she praised their beauty and their manners. Charles told fatherly stories about them and Miranda vied with him as she told tales of Charles' own youth.

"He was a hellion," she said proudly. "He had no truck with his father's polished ways. Took after his ole Grandma. Though some of the Virginia velvet could not entirely be sloughed away." She seemed thoughtful. "Alexander Sedgely," she nodded her head, "I must give him credit, and not dishonor the dead. He was a fine man and he loved my daughter, his wife, and I was pleased at that." She sighed.

Jessica remembered Eleanor's mother's information that Charles had lost both his parents when he was not yet twenty and that the estate had come undivided to him as an only child. Some kind of pox or flux had decimated the area, she had heard, and whether Charles had been away at college or was strong enough to resist it, she did not really know.

"She knew how to keep a better table," Miranda said tartly. "You'll have to keep an eye on Charles; he'll starve you to a rail. Just look at him—no flesh. No wonder he keeps his legs covered, probably has no calves."

Jessica flushed as Charles roared with laughter.

"I'm not responsible for the fashion. Or for the kitchen for that matter."

"Eleanor?"

They brushed her word aside.

"Mammy is completely in control."

"Oh, that Julia," Miranda said, "she'll fill you so full of gumbos, the okra will come out of your ears."

"Now, Grandma, you know she's the best cook this side of the Tidewater."

"Well, in some things," she conceded. "But," she turned to Jessica, "I hope you'll influence her in the way of Yorkshire puddings and treacles and steak and kidney pies—oh, I'm absolutely ravenous, Charles . . ."

Fortunately just then Cicero summoned them.

Julia was a good cook, Jessica found, and Miranda had no cause to complain. They sat at one end of the huge table, attended by Cicero and a young black boy. Cicero, his hands covered by immaculate white gloves, served the food in highly polished silver bowls and tureens and platters, and during the evening the boy, who was nameless, cleared away. Cicero poured the wine, the coffee. There was some murmuring in the outer room and the sound of a door opening and closing. Miranda saw Jessica's questioning glance and explained to her: it was the pantry door opening as the little "nigra," whose job it was, ran back and forth to the cookhouse to get the hot food from Julia.

"I'm going to have an ell built, a covered areaway, to join it eventually to the house," Charles said absently.

"Not a good idea at all!" Miranda snorted. "Julia will burn down the house, with fires going all the time."

"There is a way," Charles said, "to make it more efficient."

"With all the hands you have," Miranda said tartly, "you needn't worry about extra labor. Idle hands and still legs only lead to mischief."

"No, no, we can then release more hands to the fields."

"How is the crop this year?"

"Very good, Grandmother, but the price has been low. We have been in a depressed market situation."

"What? Still? You should have stayed with tobacco."

"No, I know I'm right. Cotton is king and the market will

change. Now that we have steamboats and a locomotive, too—though not near this community yet—the economy will boom again."

"Jason wrote me that the factories in New England are putting in new improved looms, and, of course, he has been active in it . . ."

"Good," Charles said, surprised. "He did not tell me of his involvement, or maybe he brushed over it so lightly . . . good. The more industry in this country the better. Maybe we'll gallop out of the depression, rather than creep from it."

"Wouldn't it interfere with his sale of English cloth?" Miranda asked him.

"No. There's a big market for both. I think he believed that competition can only stimulate commerce."

Jessica was glad to hear that. Jason had said the same thing when she asked him about the conflict of interest in selling English cloth and setting up American competitors. Jason explained that there would always be women and men who preferred English goods—while there were those who needed the economy of American materials without tariffs and shipping costs. More business—and extra income—in national trade could spark more business internationally. There would be prosperity for all. Tooling America was just as important—and as profitable—as selling finished goods. And of course England needed American cotton for her own weavers and other markets. It was a two-way street, or ocean, it seemed.

The talk then naturally turned to Jason. Charles spoke kindly of him and told Jessica how much he had enjoyed his visit. He had gotten to know Jason and admired him immensely, but not all his sentiments. "He was too much the reformer for me. I am a more conservative man. And a Southerner," he smiled at Jessica.

Jessica was alarmed by his use of the word *was.*

"He is distressed by slavery," she said quickly. "It didn't trouble him so much at first, but as he was exposed to it more, his feeling grew . . ."

Miranda reared at this. She said that slavery was not as bad as the Northerners made it out to be. Of course there were some miserable overseers and owners, but by and large the "nigras" were well treated. And labor of course had to be valued for what it was. To work hard was a respectable enterprise. After all, she had come to America as one of the last indentured servants. Jessica was completely surprised. Miranda's elegant appearance seemed bred in the bone. Her face was still lovely despite the wrinkles and liver-colored spots on her cheeks, which she tried to camouflage with rouge. Her hair was carefully coiffured, and she was handsomely dressed in billowing folds of silk, a handmade lace fichu over her shoulders and across her ample breast. Her hands, amazingly smooth, though one or two fingers were bent with arthritis, were covered with rings, fine gems as Jessica could see. At Miranda's throat was a diamond and amethyst brooch on a velvet and pearl collar, and in her earlobes were gold-framed diamonds.

She looked at Jessica, aware of her amazement, and laughed.

"You didn't know?" She laughed again. "So many of the ladies of Maryland—and of Virginia, too—a few generations ago came to the new land and found their fortune and, of course, their husbands in this way."

She continued to talk, unaware of or not caring about Cicero and the serving boy standing at attention against the walls of the room. They were not seen, therefore they were not there. Even if they listened now, no doubt they had heard it before. Miranda told how she had bound herself to seven years' servitude to a Maryland tobacco planter through a man in London who solicited young women and men to join the ranks of emigrés. A good way to leave the poverty, and the hopelessness, of England at the time, she said drily. A chance at a new life. And it was. Hard work, too, she said. She had not worked long in the fields, however. More and more the "nigras" had taken over that labor. The family she was indentured to brought her into the house as a parlormaid. And when the lady of the house passed on to her "just deserts," she said coldly, Miranda married the man to whom she was legally bound.

"Made a decent woman of you," her grandson teased.

"Your mother wouldn't have permitted you to speak this way!" she snapped. "His mother was very much a lady," she said to Jessica. "Her father and I saw to *that.* And she married into such a fine family." She glared fondly at her grandson. "Who knew she would bring forth such a scalawag!"

Charles laughed.

Then Miranda began to describe the early days of the indentured servants, and Charles explained how the system had been abolished. There was no need for it with the influx of the "nigras," his grandmother interjected. She continued that she had been a mere slip of a girl when she had come to Maryland, barely fifteen.

"Oh, I came voluntarily, but so many were crimped."

"Crimped?"

"Taken without their consent. Strange stories were told of men and women sold into seven years' bondage against their will, people from all sorts of backgrounds. And convicts were summarily indentured. They were a sorry lot—pooh!" she said contemptuously, "—gave the rest of us a bad name."

"It must have been a difficult servitude," Jessica said.

"Not for everyone. Most redemptioners were treated well," Charles explained. "And when their indenture time was over they were released by their masters and given full suits of clothing and some implements and most went on to till their own land. Some upstanding families grew from these beginnings."

"Upstarts mostly," Miranda said. "Not like my husband."

"That's Maryland for you," Charles grinned, knowing his grandmother would explode. "Rough unmannerly country."

And Miranda did.

"I should box your ears, Charles!" she exclaimed. "My husband, his *grandfather,*" she turned to Jessica, "ran a gracious home. Oh, the balls, and the rich gowns the women wore . . ."

"And the silks and velvets of the men," Charles said sardonically.

"Yes. My husband, with a sword at his side. And the sedan chairs for the ladies . . ."

Sedan chairs, pulled by men, like oxen in the yoke. How her father would have glowered with rage, Jessica thought.

"Sounds heathen," she said boldly.

"Yes," Charles agreed with her mischievously, "and the

vagrant preachers drunk in their pulpits. Or cavorting with the women."

"Like Tartuffe," Jessica said, remembering how she had read the rhymed play in French with her father.

"Not all of them," his grandmother said acidly. "Oh, there was roughness, but we had a good life. Not as grim and serious as you are here, Charles. Oh, the balls," she said again. "And the way my hair was dressed. I had a 'nigra' trained by the French in Santo Domingo. Ah, my husband, the lovely things he did for me . . ." she went off into a brief reverie. "Danced a fine minuet. . . . Now *he* had a fine leg—wonderful calves, and velvet knee breeches and silken hose to show them off. . . . Ah, those were the days. . . . And made a fortune with tobacco. Tobacco was money. You could buy anything with tobacco. I always said, Charles, you should have stuck with tobacco, instead of all that cotton." From her repetition of this comment, Jessica gathered it was a sore point between grandmother and grandson.

"Tobacco has worn out the soil here," Charles told Jessica, "all those years the Sedgely family grew it, with no crop rotation."

"Pah," Miranda said. "Tobacco is gold."

"Cotton is solid. And now that I have that fine new gin . . ."

"Oh, those little boxes that scholar made?"

"You're behind the times, Grandmother. Those little Whitney boxes have been developed into large machines that have an excellent record for combing out the seeds."

"Tobacco," his grandmother said fretfully, "that's the currency of the South . . ."

"Cotton is Jason's business, too," Jessica interjected. "He was a factor for you, too, was he not, Charles?"

"We were just in the negotiating stage," he said kindly, "and I had hoped he would represent me. He was a good figure of commerce despite all his reforming impulses."

"He talked to you frankly . . . because you are Eleanor's husband and part of family . . ."

"I hope he talked only to me in that fashion." Charles shook his head as if in astonishment.

"He would be more circumspect elsewhere," she said, as if to reassure herself. "I will find him. I know he is somewhere here in this country and will continue his commerce."

Miranda and Charles looked at her blankly.

"But my dear," Charles murmured, "nothing has been heard from him for such a long period . . ."

"No body has been found," Jessica said, finding it difficult even to say the word *body,* "and that means that he is still alive."

"Alas, child, you do not know this country," Miranda said compassionately, "swamps, great forests . . ."

"He could not just disappear."

Miranda shook her head.

"It is sad for young people. . . . Ah," she sighed, "how cruel and unjust it seems for old ladies like me, well over eighty, closer to ninety to be honest, to be here when Charles' own father and mother . . . my poor dear daughter . . . are taken so young."

"I am determined to make inquiries. Charles, you will help me," Jessica asked urgently.

"I'll do whatever you wish," he said, "though when you first wrote, I did go to the neighboring planters and speak with them." He paused. "Without result."

"That was very kind of you, and I thank you. But, Charles, perhaps at another time, not at dinner, we can consider other territories—perhaps farther south or even north of Pennsylvania—that Jason could have gone to?"

"Yes," he said, "we can do that." But his look of sympathy and hopelessness sent a chill through her.

"You must have a ball," Miranda said, to change the subject. "Positively before I leave, Charles. I should like to see the reel even though I no longer dance it."

"It's a busy time. We must make all the cotton we can . . . and Eleanor . . ."

"Pooh!" she said. "It would do her good. It might be the very thing."

"I am anxious to see Eleanor," Jessica said. "I've missed her."

"You will, tomorrow," Charles said. "She told me to tell you so. And the next day, if you wish, I shall take you riding around the plantation so that you get a good sense of it. You do ride, don't you?"

"Yes, I learned as a child."

"Good. Though we could take a surrey."

"No need. Father insisted that I ride well."

"Excellent."

She began to ask questions about the plantation and Charles answered them patiently. The Sedgelys had come to Virginia in the early seventeenth century, a plot of ground granted to them by the graciousness of the Crown. The land had gone from father to eldest son through the years. Many of the sons had gone to Princeton College, the favorite of most Southerners, and to Yale, too, but they had always returned to the land, even as he had. Sometimes the wars interrupted, the battles with the Indians and the French and the Spanish and the War of Independence and the infamous War of 1812. It had been difficult for Virginia's people, especially, to resist becoming Tories, because of their close ties to England. The question of self-rule and fair taxation had been of more importance, however, and one of Charles' relatives as a matter of fact had sat in the first Continental Congress. Virginia, Charles said proudly, provided many men for the new country's leadership. Jefferson, Jessica interrupted; he had been another of her father's heroes. Yes, Charles said gravely, and George Washington and Patrick Henry and James Madison and many more. And his father, Charles continued, had been livid about the attack on American ships by the British and their burning of the cities was intolerable. He smiled at her apologetically, remembering his manners as host.

"And now we are all good friends," he said, "and business is growing between us all the time. We weathered it all, through the bad times, and enjoying the good," he ended, still smiling at her. The New World was so beautiful in its freshness and its bounty, she must see as much of it as she could manage. She nodded, thinking she would go its length and breadth if necessary to find Jason.

All the time they were talking the courses of the meal were faultlessly served. There was fish and then fowl and a vast assortment of vegetables, some she knew and some unfamiliar to her, and a salad of many greens. A new kind of pudding was presented at the end of the meal, with good English tea, by way of India. Hot tea reminded her of home and the times that she and her mother had shared a pot, and what a comfort that had been, and a wave of homesickness overcame her. The young serving boy must have seen how her hand quivered as she reached for the sugar and cream and he set it carefully close to her cup so she would not spill it. She had a fleeting sense of sympathy with him and then forgot about the incident in the conclusion of the meal. Charles gallantly pulled back Miranda's chair, and then her own, and they went into the drawing room.

Bowls of fruits and nuts had been placed on the tables. Miranda sat in a large wing chair and took a brandy from the footman. Jessica refused. Charles went to the piano and played one of the new Chopin preludes. It was a sensitive rendition, Jessica thought, listening carefully. His touch was light and sure and the sound of the instrument had much more richness than that of her little spinet at home. She stared at Charles' face as he swayed with the music. The light from the wrought-iron candelabras around the room and the single silver stick above the keyboard brought out the sharp, interesting planes of his face, the high cheekbones, the cast of his features. His hair gleamed brightly as he moved his body in time with his hands.

She turned to Miranda, who sat listening with her eyes closed. In repose, she seemed older, and Jessica saw that she kept flexing her hands, whether in emotional fullness or to relieve the pain of their joints Jessica was not sure. But it was apparent that she took much pleasure from the music her grandson played, and her eyes flew open when he finished. She blew a kiss to him and produced a series of hoarse huzzas.

"Lovely," Jessica murmured.

He rose.

"Do you play?" he asked.

"Oh, just a little. Nothing compared to you."

"I imagine you are modest."

"No, it's the truth."

"Well, then, will you play a duet with me the next time?"

"I'd like that," she said, smiling, thinking how kind he was, making her two promises—to take her about the plantation and to play the piano together.

The children came in at this moment, leaving Sally at the door. They had probably been waiting in the shadows, knowing they should not interrupt. Jenny went immediately to her father and curtsied before him. Her long skirts spread out around her grandly as she bent her knee. She was dressed in the fashion of a miniature adult. Charles kissed the top of her head, saying they were late; they could have come for pudding in the dining room. Tomorrow, he promised Jenny, at her look of disappointment. Then Jenny turned and curtsied to her great-grandmother and to Jessica. Charlie followed her sedately and offered his hand to everyone and bowed. Miranda interested them in the nut bowls and even more in the tin of sugar-drops she found in her silk reticule.

"Well, now," Charles said, "are you ready for your lessons tomorrow? Or," he added, turning to Jessica, "forgive me, is tomorrow too soon to begin?"

The children looked at her in suspense and she said she would like to start classes without delay. To her surprise and delight, Charlie seemed relieved. His smile widened and Jenny clapped her hands.

"Who will take Cousin Jessica to the schoolroom tomorrow after breakfast?" their father asked, to test the extent of their enthusiasm.

"I will! I will!" they both cried simultaneously.

"Then you both shall," he said, laughing.

Their first sedateness had completely left them and they danced about the room, going from one to the other of the adults and exacting the ready attention of each. Jenny particularly liked the feather in her great-grandmother's headdress, and Miranda generously plucked it from her hair and tucked it in the little girl's curls. "There!" she said, "now you are the great lady!" And Charles quickly found something for the boy. He took an arrowhead from his waistcoat pocket and showed it to Charles. "I found it in the fields today," he told his son; "I thought you'd like it."

"Indians," the children said, in frightened voices, their eyes growing round. "Will you tell us an Indian story, sir?" Charlie asked, carefully pocketing the arrowhead trophy.

The grandfather clock struck the half-hour.

"Tomorrow," their father promised. "It's time for Sally to take you to bed."

Sally, listening, came as if on signal. The children bestowed and accepted kisses all around and made their departure noisily.

"They're lovely," Jessica said.

"They have good bones," Miranda murmured.

"They are good children," Charles said. "But if you have any trouble with them, just let me know."

"Trouble? There won't be any."

They talked for a little while longer until Charles seemed to grow restless. He kept springing from his seat and walking around the room. Miranda looked at him shrewdly and suggested they play a game of cards. It seemed to Jessica that he was reluctant as he fetched them from an ivory-inlaid cabinet. They moved to a game table set in an alcove in the room. Charles played badly; he did not seem to care.

"If we had four players we could play whist," he grumbled.

"Oh," his grandmother said. "Who would you suggest?"

They played halfheartedly for a half-hour and then the old lady threw down her hand in disgust.

"When I play, I play seriously. Oh, you Charles! I'm off to bed!"

Charles peremptorily summoned Joseph—now when Charles called him Jessica knew his name—and instructed him to get Fanny. Jessica was thus made aware of another house slave when the young girl who obviously was assigned to Miranda came to assist her out of her chair and up to her room. Fanny was younger than Sally, Jessica observed, but looked enough like her to be her sister. They were both cocoa-colored with pleasant faces. Fanny was dressed in the same loose-fitting homespun gown that Sally wore, only at her neck there was a lace collar loosely sewn on. It looked of the same handiwork as the fichu about Miranda, and Jessica guessed that Miranda had given it to Fanny. Miranda seemed to have grown tired and leaned heavily on the girl. Once on her feet, she pulled herself together and turned haughtily to Charles.

"When you can keep your mind on the game," she scolded, "then I'll take some pride in beating you."

"Watch out for her," Charles said laughingly to Jessica when Miranda had gone. "She can be rough at times. I often think she ran my mother's life, even from as far away as Maryland, until the day the dear soul died."

"Family ties are difficult to loosen."

He looked down at her, suddenly distant.

"Shall I summon Sally to fetch you to your room?"

She felt a great sense of disappointment she could not understand. It seemed to her he was dismissing her summarily. The disappointment turned to anger.

"No, thank you!" she snapped. "I can find my own way."

"I know you must be tired," he said, more kindly, "after your long and arduous trip. I won't see you at breakfast, but at the noon meal. I'm off at sunup with the field hands, and in the late afternoons I work in my office—in the next room off the hall. The schoolroom is set up in the library upstairs. The children will show you. Don't set too-long hours for yourself and for them. It's summertime—and if the children weren't so badly in need of instruction, Charlie especially—we wouldn't have school at all until the fall. I would suggest just a couple of hours each day after breakfast. Everyone in the house takes a nap after lunch. The manor grows cooler toward evening."

"Then I shall say goodnight. I hope Eleanor feels better—please tell her."

"Thank you. Goodnight."

He bowed gravely to her, and just as gravely she curtsied to him. She was about to offer him her hand, as she usually did with her friends, but thought better of it. She left in a state of confusion. Was she to breakfast alone? At what time would Eleanor leave her room? Perhaps she would appear at lunch. Would she not have a chance to see Eleanor beforehand, alone? And she would need to find out about Billy, too. Perhaps a good night's sleep would clear up the muddle in her head. She went quickly to the foot of the great winding stairway in the center hall. A soft giggle distracted her. She paused, looking behind the stairwell. A little girl, about ten years old—Jessica wondered later in amazement why she should even think of the child's age with the shock of it all—darted out of a room at the back of the house. The small graceful frame was convulsed in merriment; the child had evidently played some trick or balked some authority, and she began to laugh aloud.

"Aletha, come back here!" someone whispered sharply.

A tall and slender beautiful mulatta came into the hall, snatched the child's arm, and drew her back into the shadows. Jessica had a vision of the woman's café-au-lait skin, smooth and shining, and long auburn hair and wide-set large soft brown eyes—the blend of colors was riveting. But it was the look at the child, not the adult, that truly astounded her.

Aletha, but for the color of her skin and the blackness of her hair, was the image of Jenny.

Chapter Three

Jessica did not see Eleanor until noon.

The morning was a busy one. After she breakfasted alone in the dining room, served by Cicero and feeling miniaturized at the vast table, with its huge spread of mahogany on either side of her, she determined hereafter to have a morning tray sent to her room. She asked Cicero whether she might visit the kitchen. He hesitated for a moment and then he bowed slightly and said he would take her when she was ready; she realized he would never say no outright to a white person. She wondered wryly whether he thought she wanted to examine the kitchen facilities, whatever they were. She was interested in cookery but not that much; her real intention was to find how Billy had managed. She had confidence in the wiry strength of his young body and his ability to cope. His long journey on the ledge under the carriage had signified that very well. Nevertheless, she was determined that he was not to be mistreated in any way.

Though Charles had spoken the night before of constructing a passageway to connect the kitchen to the main building, Jessica was still surprised that it was necessary to go outdoors to reach the cook house. She followed Cicero, only now seeing closely the great breadth of his back and the fine cut of Charles' castoff coat. They had to walk about fifteen feet over a well-worn path surrounded by black-eyed susans and buttercups. There were poles for beans surrounding the bleak wooden structure, and it made her aware of a tiny vegetable garden at one side. She wondered idly how hot dishes could be kept hot during the wintertime as they were run to the dining room—she imagined that speed was the answer and thought what an inconvenience that must be. The poor runner could catch the lung disease running from the heat of the house to cold then to heat again. She thought of the town houses back home in London where kitchens operated by cooks and maids were in the basement—there was no compulsory running out and in, only up and down the stairs. Both systems were very inefficient, she decided, and Charles was right in his intention to join the kitchen to the main structure of the manor.

The interior of the cabin was more interesting than the outside indicated. Perhaps it was the people, Jessica thought quickly, as her eyes tried to register everything at once and therefore missed details that would come later. The thing that loomed up large and was second in interest was the huge cookstove. It practically danced, big as it was, from the force of the fire burning in its interior. It was covered with outsize copper pots, and there was an exotic aroma of gumbo and okras in the air. But it was the cook, called Julia, who dominated everything, people as well as objects. She was a large woman, carrying a lot of firm flesh; she could not be thought obese. A white blouse covered her huge bosom and most of her skirt was hidden by the floured table before which she stood, punching down the dough of the breads she would bake. A red bandana covered her massive head and shining hoops hung from her ears. She had fine brown eyes that looked unwaveringly at Jessica—no subservience here!—and the flaring, aquiline nose of an Indian. Julia turned questioningly to Cicero then back to the table again. Cicero, though much older, was her man or her husband, Jessica could immediately sense; there was understanding between them that went further than ordinary rapport. Jessica looked away for a moment and saw the young serving boy Joseph who had helped at dinner. He was seated at a smaller table and was polishing silver. He did not look at her. He appeared to be no older than eighteen; she thought he could even be less. Then she was distracted by the huge fireplace that took up the entire breadth of one wall. It had a brick oven built into one side of it, and while the fireplace hearth was an empty and dead cave in the midst of the summer, she could see smoke curling from the door below its bake oven, separately fired, and she realized that the slowly increasing fragrance of baking loaves was beginning to overwhelm the redolent fumes from the stewpots.

Julia brushed the flour from her hands.

"Howdy, miz," she said heartily, bobbing clumsily in lieu of a curtsey. "Kin I hep yall?"

Jessica introduced herself. She complimented Julia on her cooking and told her how much she had enjoyed the dinner the night before and the breakfast this morning. All the time she was searching the room for Billy. A small child darted out from the back room and Julia turned sharply to shush her back again. It was Aletha, whose mother had called to her the night before. Poor child, Jessica thought sympathetically, her maternal instinct aroused, was she never allowed to show herself?

Julia looked directly into Jessica's eyes again.

"I keeps her fo her mammy," she said evenly.

"Her mother?"

"Chloe, my godchile," she said abruptly. "Bes seamst'ess en de county, ax ennyone en dey'll say dat's de troof."

"Does the child live with you?" Jessica asked, looking beyond Julia and seeing the little head poking out from the inner doorway.

"No'm," Julia said shortly. "Jes when her mammy am busy."

"You like children, I know," Jessica said. "Mr. Sedgely told me you had been his nurse."

Julia's manner softened.

"Ah yassum," she said, "foh I 'came cook. Mos lovey chile I evah done see, 'cep Joseph, mah younges," she nodded at the silver polisher, "en mah po fus chile dat died when he wuz birthed." She sighed. "But he gimme de milk to nuss Massah Chahles. De Lawd has His ways." She began to punch at her dough again. "Mos lovey chile." She looked up at Jessica again. "En yall, miz, am de new teachah?"

Joseph's head momentarily rose from his work and Jessica could see him looking at her from the corners of his eyes.

"Yes," she said. "I must go soon to begin my lessons with Charlie and Jenny."

The heat of the room began to overwhelm her and she could sense Cicero becoming restive; wearing a coat in this room must be smothering, she thought. She must release him by leaving; she knew he would never take it off in her presence. But she was determined to see Billy. Charles Sedgely had told her he had entrusted him to Julia's care.

She asked for a snack of milk and cookies to be sent to the classroom in midmorning. Then the matter resolved itself, for the outer door opened and Billy entered, his arms full of kindling wood and at his heels a group of small giggling slave children loaded with branch cuttings. When he saw her, Billy almost dropped his burden, then caught himself, nodding his head at her and grinning from ear to ear. Seeing him smile set her doubts at rest. He looked better than he had the day before. Oh, the disturbing memory of that bedraggled, gaunt, tired boy; it had shocked her so, and made her feel responsible for his arduous journey.

"Good morning, Billy; I see you are well."

"Yes'm," he said, still smiling. "Julia gave me a good supper and a soft pallet on the floor at night and . . ."

"Yall done bettah see 'bout dat woodbox," Julia said gruffly, "en nevah mine all dat nonsense. Massah Chahles say yo mus wuk foh yo keep."

"Oh, I will, I will!" he assured her, filling up the box with his armload and the wood he took from the restless children.

"I'm glad to see you, Billy," Jessica said clearly, "and I will check on you from time to time."

He turned to smile shyly at her, and her breath caught in her throat. He was such a young, vulnerable child.

"And I shall come here to the kitchen," she said impulsively, "a few hours a week to continue our lessons."

It was as if she had shot off a musket ball. Julia and Cicero became extremely agitated, Joseph looked up eagerly, the little children stopped prancing about the room, Aletha advanced further from her door post.

"Lessons!"

Jessica was not sure who said that.

"Not heah," Cicero protested in a muffled voice. "It ez not puhmitted."

The silver clattered angrily from Joseph's hands.

"Not permitted!"

"No'm. No miz. Gainst the law . . . no readin lessons wid niggahs present."

"How ridiculous!" Jessica exclaimed angrily.

She heard Joseph bang down a spoon.

His mother evidently heard it, too. "Mebbe," she said slowly, "mebbe, Miz Jess'ca . . ."

"Julia!" Cicero warned sternly.

An uncomfortable silence fell about them.

"Well," Jessica said decisively, breaking it, "I'll be back tomorrow to see you, Billy."

He looked at her lovingly.

"Whatever you say, Miz Jessica . . ."

It was a pleasant room, the library, that had been set aside as the classroom for Charlie and Jenny. It was on the second floor, not far from the bedrooms. The walls were lined from floor to ceiling with shelves of books. Old maps and charts had been pinned to stands. A ship captain's desk dominated the front of the room; she was intended to preside there, Jessica imagined. There were smaller desks for the children and on them ground glass jars of ink and feather quills to write with. An artist's easel took up one corner with ample supplies of pigments and brushes of all sizes and pieces of charcoal and an assortment of paper.

From the open windows came the fragrance of newly cut grass and the roses and myriad flowers that bordered the mansion. For a moment Jessica found herself listening to the birdsong, but it did not distract her or the children for long. Charlie and Jenny came with serious faces, little hornbooks in their hands, Jenny with a pinafore over her pretty cotton dress and Charlie in a jacket, which Jessica immediately had him remove. First they looked at the pictures in some of the books she had brought, then at the paper that had been provided on another easel of sorts set alongside the teacher's desk. Jessica carefully drew the letters of the alphabet on the paper and she had them memorize their shapes and what their names were and what they stood for. Later she would show how they could be arranged together to spell a word and then re-arranged to spell another.

They counted numbers, and she started with the fingers of their hands, writing figures down on the paper at the easel for them to see and remember. They counted and counted, using their fingers and then venturing beyond them to their toes and to objects in the room and to the bag of beads that Jessica had brought with her. Jenny was completely enthralled. She moved the wooden beads around the table, putting them in the piles that Jessica told her to—first the twos pile, then the fours pile, then the fives pile; Jessica was about to go on to the tens pile, but she realized she was going too fast, expecting too much.

She had Charlie draw what he thought flying was and he drew a picture of birds; she wrote the word *flying* under the wings. She drew stick figures in a row with the slash of their feet lifted behind them and asked Charlie what he thought it meant. He immediately said *running*, and she let him write the letters of the word under the figures. She was excited. Charlie would surely make up for lost time and for the poor tutor he had so disliked. She looked at his careful printing with great exhilaration and told him to look carefully at the word and the figures of the make-believe people running and to remember both of them together. She drew pictures of fruit and gave them names; pictures of nicely padded women and men and labeled them *mother* and *father;* little stick figures of boys and girls, with skirts or breeches, and labeled them *boy* and *girl* and *brother* and *sister.*

They were exhausted when it was time to stop. The children wanted to continue nevertheless, but Jessica this time stayed firm. "Tomorrow," she promised." "Look at your books," she told them, "try to figure the stories out from the drawings you copied. Try to find the words we covered today. Tomorrow, show me the words you see that you know. Tomorrow we will continue."

They hugged her, coaxing her to go on. "Tomorrow," she said. "How long is tomorrow?" they asked. And despite herself she continued the class long enough to contemplate the abstraction of time. She drew illustrations of the sun and the moon for them, the sun rising and setting, the moon rising as the sun set and the blackness of night and the light of day. She drew a sundial. "Not today, but some other time," she said firmly, "we shall learn the meaning of time; the difference in the sunlight at different times of the day and what it means in the relative terms of time."

"What is revelant terms of time?" Charlie asked, stumbling on the word.

"You are learning," she said. "You ask the right questions."

Sally led them reluctantly away to their lunch in the nursery.

She drew upon her courage and knocked on the door Sally had said was Eleanor's.

"Eleanor?" she called softly.

For a moment there was silence, then a husky voice, "Jessica?"

"Yes."

"It's open. Come."

Almost timidly, Jessica pushed open the door. It took her a moment to adjust to the half-light. A magnificent room shimmered in the darkness. A huge canopied four-poster cherrywood bed dominated most of the space, surrounded by polished floors and rugs that had evidently come from the homes of Indian or Persian princes, and soft chairs and a Grecian sofa, high off the floor, with tight little pillows at its ends. Little black children came bearing powders and paints; a young black woman was dressing Eleanor's hair. Eleanor sat at a table, facing a mirror.

Jessica could not believe it was Eleanor. Her cousin had been a rosy-cheeked, almost plump, bubbling young woman. Before her sat a haggard person, cheekbones sharply defined, the tremulous recessive jaw now apparent, the hands—obviously trembling—drawn to the high translucent bony forehead. In the mirror they saw one another, and the at-first expectant expressions of their faces altered to sorrow, for Jessica, and more despair, for Eleanor. Eleanor turned. "Jessica!" she cried. She pressed her palms firmly on the table to raise herself, but the weight seemed too much. She half-tumbled back to her seat. Jessica ran to her and gently raised her up and put her arms about her.

The two women clung to one another, the slave women and children gaping at them.

"Leave us!" Eleanor said sharply, and her attendants disappeared.

"Dear Eleanor," Jessica said softly, "at last! I've been wanting so much to see you!"

"I wanted . . . to come to you . . . I did . . . I really did. . . . Oh, it's so good that you are here, Jessie. I can scarcely believe it. I'm so glad you are here."

Jessica gently disentangled herself from the other woman's embrace.

"What is it, Eleanor? Are you ill?" Anxiously Jessica searched her face, but the fumes of alcohol answered her question.

"Sick . . . sick . . ." Eleanor said, almost incoherently.

Jessica guided her cousin to the couch and, as she lay back, found an afghan to cover her. Jessica sat silently beside her, pressing Eleanor's pale hand in her own. After a while Eleanor seemed to rouse herself; the translucent eyelids fluttered open.

"Look at me, cousin," she said bitterly. "What do you see?"

"My dear Eleanor."

"No, really, not the dear old Eleanor."

"My kinswoman, my friend."

Eleanor closed her eyes, then bestirred herself and tried to inquire of news at home, but her words began to trail away. For a while they stayed in silent suspension.

"A burnt-out woman," Eleanor burst out finally, hysterically. "Given to sherry and rum—a state constant and sustained—a state of being in which I care nothing of the world outside me, what my husband thinks and what he does . . ."

"Oh Eleanor, you must stop!"

"Easily said."

"Eleanor . . ."

"I want to sleep away my life, past caring."

"Oh, Eleanor," Jessica wailed, wanting not to, but unable to hold back.

"Sorry, Jessie. You have your own troubles. . . . I'm sorry . . . I was truly sorry about Jason. . . . I'm still not past caring, I guess, but I keep trying, I'm on the way . . ."

"No . . . no . . . your parents . . . aunts and uncles . . . they all send their greetings and their love . . ."

"I miss them sorely . . . or I did. . . . But you won't tell them . . . will you, Jessie, about the . . . when I'm up to it, I write long letters . . . all lies . . ."

"Why does he give it to you!" Jessica said angrily, looking around for bottles. "Why doesn't he take it all away!"

"Oh, Charles," Eleanor laughed hoarsely, "he tried . . . oh, he tried." A crafty smile hovered about her lips. "But I outfox him. . . . There are ways . . . sources of supply . . . always, if you want it badly enough . . . and I do." She laughed again, cruelly, mocking her husband or herself, all the people in complicity. "An uprooted woman, Jessie," she said pointing crookedly at herself. "But the roots didn't take in foreign soil."

Jessica felt sudden anger.

"You have so much, Eleanor! The beautiful children—a husband—your obligation to them. How can you forget that?"

"I *want* to forget," she said savagely. "The children don't need me. There are so many hands here to look after them. And Charles . . . Charles doesn't need me." She seemed overcome by a fresh wave of despair. "Unneeded . . . unloved . . . why don't I just *die!*"

Unthinkingly, Jessica shook her.

"Don't talk that way! How dare you talk that way!"

"How dare I? Oh, I dare . . . Jessie."

"Life is so precious, Eleanor."

"Precious to some."

"You have to fight for what you want, Eleanor!"

"Did you see him—her, his mistress? Did you see the child, Jessica?"

Jessica nodded. "But . . ."

"Fight? What chance have I, really? You saw her. This is a

cruel land, Jessica. Go home soon, after we visit and much as I want you here. . . . Go home. . . . You don't know how cruel this land is! It is not for white women!"

"You are giving up too easily," Jessica said, trying to sound sure of herself. "No matter what happens, or what has happened, you are still the mistress here. He is *your* husband and this is *your* house."

Eleanor shook her head, and the motion seemed to sicken her. After a moment, she said, "You don't understand the way it is here . . ."

Then she seemed not able to contain it any longer; she had to pour it all out, to tell Jessica everything. At last here was a friendly ear to hear her.

Charles and Chloe had grown up together on the plantation. When they were children no one had cared that they played together. And no one had cared—not Charles' father then—that as young adolescents they had become lovers. It was the expected thing with young masters and slaves; it served to keep the southern belles chaste. There were plenty of black wenches, and no one need worry about getting a respectable girl of good family in trouble. And later, they could always whisk the slave out of sight. When the child was born, Aletha was turned over to Julia, and Charles did not come home for vacations from Yale. Chloe was quietly given to a good fieldhand in a neighboring plantation—jumped the broom, Eleanor said sarcastically. Then Charles and Eleanor had met. And they were married.

"That should have ended it!" Jessica cried out.

"But it didn't!" Eleanor said dolefully.

The first years were good, she told her cousin. Oh, it was so good, for a short while. The passion, the fire, the tenderness. It had been so wonderful. . . . "You understand, Jessie . . . you are a woman, married too; you know how it can be . . ."

Jessica felt the pain, for Eleanor, for herself.

Eleanor continued. All the bottled-up grief, the resentment, the hatred, welled up and over them both. If Jessica had tried, she could not have stopped the torrent. She realized that all that was needed was a sympathetic person from home, a familiar face from the time when Eleanor was happy and the world was before her promising everything lovely and true.

After Charlie was born—when an heir had been produced, Eleanor said ironically—a fever seemed to overtake Charles. At first she could not understand it. She thought childbirth had made her body different, repugnant to him in some way, or that he had come down with some strange illness. He avoided her, or when he needed her physically it wasn't the same. Jenny had not been conceived out of love. Then Eleanor had learned cruelly one day when she saw the mother with the child Aletha—the child looked so much like her father, didn't she?—that Chloe had been brought back. Chloe's husband had been sold; Charles had had a part in that, she knew. Anyway, Chloe was back. And in his bed—in Chloe's bed.

Jessica pressed the hand that now was shaking again.

"I can't bear it!" Eleanor cried wildly. "You've seen the child, born before my own, but still a bond that can't be broken. I can't stand the sight of her! It's not her fault, but I hate her. I hate her mother! I hate her!" Jessica tried to soothe her, but she pushed her away. "There's no fighting it, Jessica, the terrible life here. Everyone accepts it as a matter of fact, a way of life. No one speaks about it. The white mistresses all pretend that it doesn't exist!"

Eleanor's pale face became mottled with red spots of angry emotion. She looked at the dressing table, as if for reassurance, where in the disarray was a glass containing her whiskey. Slowly she drew her eyes back again to Jessica.

"I hate her! And yet I love her, too. My sister," Eleanor said savagely. "That negress!" she spat. "That mulatta whore, born of white masters and colored slaves. I hate her! . . . No, I love . . . her . . ." she sobbed. "I *hate* her."

"Why don't you come home?" Jessica whispered, reversing her earlier position in the face of such pain. "Surely, it's not good for you here. Come home, Eleanor. . . . I'll go about my mission; I'll find Jason, then come back for you and take you home."

"Your mission!" Eleanor cried, overwrought. "As unrealistic as my going home!" Jessica cringed. "Oh, I love him!" Eleanor sobbed. "How could I leave him?"

Jessica was silent.

"Oh," Eleanor said. "You see me coming from under a bout with rum. I am low and ugly today but sometimes . . . Jessica, I am almost beautiful again . . . or at least I think I am . . . and . . . almost . . . fit. Sometimes he looks at me . . . and comes to me, Jessica . . . and that's why I am here. For those times . . ."

Jessica felt shame for her cousin, then anger at herself for passing judgment, then compassion.

"I love him," Eleanor said, more softly. "That's why I stay."

"This rum . . . this is not the way to get him back."

"It lessens the hurt . . ."

"For the moment."

"I'm only happy when I can't think."

"You must pull yourself together."

"Sometimes," Eleanor muttered, "I hate her so much, I could kill her, and him. I could beat her to death. I could arrange for her sale."

"But then . . ."

"I would lose him forever. I would lose the little bit I have." Her voice dwindled away to a whisper. "And that little bit means so much to me . . ."

"Eleanor, you must come away before it destroys you."

"Or *she* must be sent away! But that will never happen," she said sadly. "He would not permit it—never again. I must adjust," she said bitterly, "like all the other women of the plantations . . . Miranda says it is so, and that I must conduct myself like the other wives."

"Oh, Eleanor, perhaps now that I am here, you will pull yourself together. We shall do many things."

"What things?" she said disconsolately. "What is there to do in this backwater place?"

"We shall! You'll see."

Eleanor seemed to remember something. She fumbled for a small vial hidden beneath the sofa. Jessica watched helplessly as she drained it. Eleanor smiled a cat's smile at her.

"It's very good, really. You always were a do-gooder, Jessie, even as a child! A holier-than-thou! A martyr, a saint. I'm not cut from the same cloth." She hiccupped. "Are you not human and just crave the touch of a man, the man you love?"

"Oh, Eleanor!"

"I forgot . . . I'm sorry, Jessica, I'm sorry. I really didn't mean to be so cruel. I have changed, as you can see. . . . Each day I promise myself I'll stop . . . I'll stop drinking . . ."

"And then?"

"Then he stays away, and I know he is with her—and I begin again."

They were silent for a while. Tears began to spill from Eleanor's eyes and she closed them.

"It will soon be mealtime," Jessica said softly. "You do want to come, don't you?"

"Will he be there?"

"He said he would. If you cry, your eyes will be swollen. You do want to look your best. You do want to come to table?"

Eleanor dabbed at her cheeks.

"Yes, I do. I want to be there, I do want to see him. And I only wish I looked well."

"Just rest there for a few minutes. Mother sent you a pair of her jade earrings. I have them here with me for you. Do put them on, Eleanor."

"Oh, how nice!" her cousin said, as Jessica opened the small silk pouch for her. "Her very own earrings, dear Aunt Lettie. You won't write her how I am, will you?"

"They look lovely on you—so good for your green eyes and your red hair. . . . No, perhaps there will be better things to write about."

Eleanor sat up and let Jessica hang the jade drops at her earlobes. Jessica brought a silver-backed hand mirror for Eleanor to see.

"They are beautiful," Eleanor said. "How could Aunt Lettie part with them?"

"Because they were for you. You are her favorite niece, Eleanor."

"And how is she?" Eleanor said softly. "Tell me about her—and about you. I'm so wrapped up in my own misery I forget about the world sometimes . . . and all the people I have held so dear. . . ."

The were on less-charged ground now and Jessica talked softly about her mother and London and news of the Court.

"How can a person be so torn by hatred and love at the same time?" Eleanor interrupted, and Jessica wondered whether she had heard what she was saying.

"Because you feel so strongly. . . . Try to think of something else . . . if you can," she added apologetically, knowing the difficult period of adjustment she herself had made.

"If I didn't care. . . ."

"That's not the way we are."

"Dear Jessica, I am truly sorry . . . But there's nothing I can do about it."

"You can be busy."

"Busy? At what? Looking after the 'nigras?' "

"Why not? Don't many of the planters' wives?"

"Oh yes," Eleanor said wearily, "at first—before—I did some nursing, sat with sick children, attended births . . . but it's all so dirty and squalid . . . and now they *know!* Oh, Jessica, when I leave them or they leave me there is whispering and, if they dared, they would sneer in my face! I can't bear it." For a moment she covered her eyes with her shaking fingers.

"No," Jessica said firmly, "you only imagine it."

That angered her cousin.

"Do you think," she said furiously, "that I don't know it! The high and mighty mistress brought low by a slave, her husband's concubine!"

"Then maybe," Jessica whispered, "you shouldn't be so high and mighty. You should hold your head up high, yes," she said, her mother's voice appearing in her own, "but there are many good works that you can do proudly and with dignity. *Then* they will respect you, Eleanor."

Eleanor snorted.

"Do you think I care about them?"

"And so will Charles."

Eleanor's quick anger had subsided.

"Do you really think so?"

"Yes, I do, and I know you will feel better."

"Poor Jessica," Eleanor sighed, "with troubles of her own, set down into a hornet's nest. . . . I should not have burdened you, the first time I've seen you after so many years . . . but then you could see for yourself. . . . I have changed, haven't I, Jess, getting old before my time . . . and ugly."

"Nonsense!" Jessica said brusquely. "You're much too thin is all. Do you eat?" Her cousin didn't answer. "You probably don't. And some fresh air and exercise will help bring back your color . . ."

Eleanor laughed caustically.

"Color. He'd like that."

"And if you exert yourself, you'll sleep better," Jessica persisted, "and the circles will disappear from under your eyes. They are lovely eyes, Eleanor. It's up to you to use them. Look beyond yourself. And there are the children. . . ."

"Oh, they are whisked away by all their nursemaids and mammies. There's no use for me. . . ."

"You're their mother."

"Will he really be at table today?"

"Charlie or Charles?"

"Charles. Will he really be at table?"

"He said he'd see me there."

Eleanor stiffly swung one leg over the edge of the sofa and rose unsteadily. Jessica helped her back to the dressing table. The curls piled high had lost their pins and were straggling down untidily.

"I'll call . . ."

"No, let me," Jessica said. "You always had such beautiful hair, Eleanor, I'd like to brush it out for old times' sake. Remember when you let me do it when I was a small child?" Swiftly Jessica removed the remaining bone pins. The red hair flowed down below her cousin's waist. Jessica found the brush in the welter of things on the table and set to work gently. The brushing should bring back the sheen. She noted the softening effect the hair had about her cousin's pinched face and she begged her to wear it this way, tied back by a velvet ribbon Jessica had found. Eleanor protested at first, said she would look too much the country dolt, but Jessica was persuasive. She brought her cousin to her feet, fluffed out the crushed watered-silk voluminous skirts, removed the kerchief from Eleanor's chest and pinned the cameo that had held the prim cloth together just where the cleft of her bosom appeared. Then she took a yellow rose from the vase almost hidden by the clutter and fastened it in the cameo's pin.

"There," she said, "now you are beginning to look like the Eleanor I knew."

The peal of the midday bell sounded through the halls. Jessica almost had to lift Eleanor from her chair and guide her to the door. Disconcertedly she realized how unsteady her cousin was, and when Eleanor moaned that she could not make it, she almost had to agree. But she was determined. She chided Eleanor for not trying, fastened her arm more securely about the other's waist, and slowly walked her out the door, down the winding stairway one step at a time, past Cicero who tried desperately to maintain the impassivity of his face. Charles, who had heard them coming, met them at the foot of the stairs. Jessica could see the pleased surprise in his eyes.

"My dear!" he said heartily to his wife. "I am so glad you are joining us." He nodded pleasantly to Jessica. "I know how much Eleanor has wanted to see you."

"And I, her," Jessica said softly. "Could we not go right into the dining room?" She disengaged herself from Eleanor and directed her cousin's arm onto Charles'.

"Indeed," Charles said, firmly taking his wife in charge. He directed Cicero to fetch Miz Miranda from the drawing room; they would forgo their aperitif today. Eleanor was seated and managing well when Charles' grandmother came to table. Charles rose as Cicero attended to Miranda's chair, and only a raised charcoaled eyebrow showed the old lady's amused amazement. The meal progressed with little difficulty. Charles complimented his wife's hairstyle—"In the fashion it was when I met you," he said gallantly, and Eleanor's cheeks flushed brightly.

"And the jade earrings!" Miranda boomed heartily, "wherever did you get them?" Eleanor haltingly told her and the lady wisely directed her conversation to Jessica, who began to talk about her mother again. It could not be accomplished so easily, Jessica realized, even as she made small conversation. There would be many trials, and perhaps errors, but this was a beginning. Charles and Miranda had evidently not expected Eleanor to come downstairs even though they had told her Eleanor would see her today. Jessica understood this was quite a milestone. She surreptitiously watched the trembling of her cousin's hands as she tried to use the soup spoon. It was impossible; there was too much wavering, and in fear of spilling, Eleanor set the utensil down on her saucer. The chicken was a little easier for her to manage, but she took only a few small pieces. Jessica was determined to take a tray later that day to Eleanor's room and coax her, even feed her if necessary. If she could only strengthen Eleanor physically, then the emotional strength might follow . . . *would* follow, she thought doggedly.

Miranda talked gaily of the jewels her husband had given her, and of the gems she received from the other men who had sought her favor when he was gone. She talked more of the parties. "You must give a *party,* Charles, a *ball!"* she exhorted her grandson. "That's what this beautiful house needs!" She talked on, but not thoughtlessly, Jessica thought; Miranda knew what she was doing. She saw Charles reach out and pat Eleanor's shaking hand, and she saw the hunger in Eleanor's eyes and the gratitude for the small favor, and she grew angry when she saw the tear on her cousin's cheek. *You will not cry, Eleanor!* she willed fiercely, *you will not cry.* And miraculously there were no more tears.

Jessica talked, when Miranda would let her, about the children and the classroom and what they had done and what she intended to do. Charles promised her any equipment she needed and hung on every word. She told them she had promised to read to the children later in the afternoon.

"Then I must give you the grand tour tomorrow," Charles said.

"Oh yes," Jessica said. "I do want to go through the grounds and see everything."

"And so you shall," Charles promised. "Tomorrow afternoon."

Between them they walked Eleanor back to her room.

"Everyone naps," Charles said, "in the heat of the day . . . a southern comfort." They paused before Eleanor's door. "But I have work to do, matters that need attention."

Jessica could sense Eleanor's disappointment.

"You go too, Jess!" Eleanor snapped.

Charles left abruptly, and Jessica walked into Eleanor's room with her and saw her to bed. Eleanor quickly fell asleep.

* * *

Jessica awaited Charles in his office. She looked forward eagerly to the tour. She had been here for two full days now and had not ventured farther than the kitchen cabin.

It had been a very full two days. She thought of what she had already accomplished this morning. After breakfast she had gone to see Billy again and had promised to set the time soon for his daily lesson. Then back to class with the children. She smiled as she thought of them. How seriously they regarded their work. How quickly they were learning, how they responded to stimulation.

Eleanor had not come to dinner again last night. As she had not done for a long, long period, Jessica gathered from Charles' and Miranda's remarks to each other. Jessica had peeked in Eleanor's room when she heard the tray come up. Evidently, it was sent automatically every evening and automatically it came down again–sometimes empty if the little serving children were hungry, certainly not through Eleanor's doing. Jessica sat with her, tempting her with a morsel of this or a bite of that, and sometimes Eleanor tried, mainly to please her. Eleanor talked of the midday meal and promised that she would make the effort once more the next day. Jessica saw that she had been drinking again.

But she appeared at the noon meal the second day in a row. Again, Jessica brushed her hair down and saw that she wore the jade earrings. She had Eleanor take off the dress she had worn the day before and put on a fresh, bright one. Eleanor had managed a little better at table this day, Jessica thought, pleased. A little step at a time. Maybe she would backslide; she surely must, but eventually she would find her way back to sobriety and purpose, Jessica had no doubt. At least she was determined to help Eleanor find the way. Perhaps the best way was through Charlie and Jenny, and Charles' pride in them. She had promised to bring the children to her later in the week, and Eleanor vowed faithfully to be in condition to receive them.

Jessica looked about Charles' office. His desk was covered with ledgers and bills and other documents and letters. She wondered that he did not have a steward to tend to these matters and for a moment thought idly of Douglas Graham, the first mate who doubled as ship's steward, and how he managed so well for Captain Northrup. It had been good of him to see her off at the stagecoach stop. He was a good, dependable man, so different from Charles with all his grace and excitement. She shrugged. Charles Sedgely. Where was he? Probably with *her,* Chloe. Though his afternoons and nights were his own to spend as he wished. Eleanor said he came to her but seldom, and his chambers were removed from his wife's. What a sorry pass their marriage had come to. But she must not sit in judgment, she caught herself up sharply. She must guard against that.

When he came, they quickly went outdoors where the stableboys had brought the horses. Jessica rode sidesaddle—she was pleased to see an English saddle had been provided her—and she smoothed her black riding skirt against the horse's flank once she had mounted the mare. She noted how well Charles sat his sorrel stallion, and he led the way at a slow trot. Once they had cleared the kitchen building, he waited for her to come abreast, and they rode side by side so that he could talk with her about the plantation.

She saw first—now at close range—the slaves' quarters, which extended a couple of hundred yards behind the big house. There were two parallel rows of small log cabins set close together directly off the dirt lane they shared. As her horse slowed near one of them, Jessica had a quick glimpse inside. She had a fleeting impression of a dirt floor and an uneven or lumpy mattress set upon it; she saw a table, some boxes, a peg on a wall with a pair of trousers hanging from it. A few chickens scattered as they passed.

"We let them keep chickens," Charles called to her. "It varies their diet."

"Is that unusual?"

He laughed.

"Yes," he said.

Outside one cabin she saw an old black woman, her head tied with a rag, who smiled toothlessly at them and nodded respectfully to Charles, calling the ragamuffin children to her side out of the way of horses' hooves.

"A good afternoon to you, Auntie!" Charles greeted her. "Auntie Blossom, a good woman," he said to Jessica. "A wonderful fieldhand in her time, could pick, and chop, cotton as quickly as a man. . . . Now she's too old, her bones pain her, so she stays behind and cares for her grandchildren . . . helps with the cook crew sometimes, too."

"Cook crew?"

"There's the hands' cook house over there." He pointed to a larger cabin with a huge chimney coming through its roof.

"Doesn't every family cook its own meals?"

"No. Not here. That would not be as efficient as a central kitchen."

"Oh?"

He explained to her how the rations were all doled out together–each slave was entitled every week to three or three and a half pounds of fatback, or pork, or sometimes it was better bacon, and a helping of sweet potatoes and corn and greens. "We run a special farm beside the individual garden patches to provide these."

"Doesn't every plantation?"

"No," he said shortly. "And we permit fishing and trapping–they find coons and possums and rabbits to supplement their diet. And we also provide the hominy grits."

"Milk for the children?"

"Only if the mother cannot nurse or another woman won't take the baby while she feeds her own. Or if the child is sick. . . .

They do very well. . . . Notice their teeth—of the young ones—sometime, so white and strong."

"Their African heritage?"

"Perhaps. . . . And, oh yes, we import peanuts, or pinders or goobers as they call them, from Africa for them. It's expensive to feed hands. Corn pone and mush—it all adds up in the end."

Jessica thought of what her father would have said about owning a body and soul, and bit her tongue.

"Do they all eat together?" she asked instead.

"Sometimes. Or they take their meals back to their individual cabins and eat separately with their families."

"Oh."

"We never split families apart," he told her gently. "And we never go to extremes in maintaining discipline. Our slaves are reasonably happy here."

"It's all so different from home."

"I know. It takes getting used to."

She was glad that England had abolished African slavery. She remembered how it had happened about ten years ago and how her little family had rejoiced. Great Britain had abandoned the West Indian slave trade as well and the press gangs and the transportation of felons. She was proud of the advance and felt homesick for her mother and her country.

"If ever you can become used to it," she murmured so softly he could not hear.

"Beyond are the vegetable gardens for the hands' food that I told you about." He gestured ahead and she saw corn in the fields and greens. "And over there we still keep a patch of tobacco." She looked where he pointed. "Use it as currency some places, but it's mostly for home consumption here. We have prizes of tobacco for hands who exceed the quotas."

"Oh, you are advanced in your thinking."

"Is that irony I detect?"

Before she could answer, the cotton fields spread before them and Charles reined in his stallion. The mare halted. As far as Jessica could see were rows of green leaves and brown husks and the tufted white fuzz of still-tight cotton balls, mixed with the pink and white and red blossoms that had not yet fallen from other plants further behind in their development. Charles told her that each field bore several yields and ripening of the bolls was uneven. The bushes, which looked quite strong, were about three and a half feet high and were quite fruitful, he went on. The seams of some of the bolls in any one field would burst one month, some the month afterward. Later, he promised, he would take her to the sunniest tract, where picking had just begun. The picking started at full peak in August and continued through November.

There was always much work to be done besides the picking–continued sowing, weeding and hoeing, thinning out choking plants–the chopping, Charles explained. That's what the hands were doing now in the field before them. Jessica looked at the black women and men and children chopping the plants. There were water boys and girls walking between the rows with buckets of water and gourds for the slaves to drink from. In different sections there seemed to be one large black man who led the others. "Drivers," Charles replied when she asked, "they set the pace. We need a hundred hands to a thousand acres of cotton," he sighed. "You see, there's not much we can do about it if we raise cotton."

She wondered whether she had been frowning.

"Then there's the clearing and sowing again that go on nine months of the year; the other three we finish up with the ginning and the baling, which we do all year long as well but don't have time to complete. There's no respite on a plantation–always so much to do on the land and to keep buildings and equipment in repair."

The black men saluted as they drew near them. And the women and children bobbed, the females' skirts not far below their knees and billowing out like sails in the occasional puffs of hot wind. Many of the younger women had their babies with them, strapped to their backs with a cloth sling. Sometimes a black child about ten years old would come and take the baby from its mother and remove it to the end of a row, where other babies slept under plants still flowering and under the vigilance of yet another child, and where a third might be waving a frond over their heads to keep away the flies. Or a mother, before transferring the child to the little attendant, would take out her engorged breast and let the child suckle as she supported it with one hand and still worked with the other.

"The women are considered half-hands," Charles said with amusement, as if, she thought angrily, he knew it would provoke her. "And the children quarter. Of course, the bucks are full hands."

She looked at the sturdy figures in their dusty, really dirty, jackets and pants and then looked away. The driver, evidently chosen for his size and aggressiveness, was shouting at them.

"It's for my benefit," Charles said slyly. "Come. We'll go see the new field they are preparing."

He signaled to his horse and they moved on, picking their way carefully between the plants that crowded the lane. At another sector of the land they saw men working with light wooden plows with wrought-iron shares. "They are not much use," Charles said with exasperation as one snapped in the hands of a worker. "We bring them down from Connecticut but they can't penetrate the soil more than two or three inches." The driver shook his fist at the slave whose plow had broken, and Jessica glared at him. "They all know the tools are no good, but the hands do abuse them and the driver must show his authority." Jessica had hoped Charles would intervene. He did not. The driver brought another wooden plow to the man he had chastised. "You might take note our drivers carry no whips; on other plantations they do."

Jessica turned to watch the plowing and the furrows that appeared in the black soil. They then proceeded to the sections where seeds were being sowed, the workers dipping into hemp bags tied to their waists, and to others where plants were sprouting—and on to still others where they were springing up into relatively tall, green-leaved stalks.

"We collect all the cultivators at night and count them," Charles said matter-of-factly. "Some of the hands have sticky fingers."

"Perhaps they think they have earned them."

"Then they are wrong. . . . I see you have been badly influenced by your father and Jason."

"Influenced," she said tartly. "I don't know how badly."

"Well, it got Jason into a lot of trouble, it seems. You must be careful," he said, and she thought she heard concern in his voice, "that you don't speak out of turn to the wrong people."

She halted her mount.

"Do you think that's what happened to him?"

Charles shrugged.

"I don't really know. . . . Come. . . ."

He led her then to the cotton field that was being picked. She admired the full-blown balls of cotton, large as the viburnum blossoms she loved back home. The sun glinted off the threads as the pickers pulled bolls from branches, and she could not believe the quickness of their fingers. It was stoop work, just like the chopping, and her back ached in sympathy.

"We must go on if we're to cover everything," Charles said, rousing her. "There's the gin-house ahead. If you are to know about cotton and planting, you must visit there."

They dismounted at the entrance of a huge barnlike structure. Men and women, carrying baskets of cotton on their heads, were going through its door. They made way for their master and his guest. Inside she saw another mass of black men and women. The men were taking the baskets of cotton from their bearers and sending the contents down a high chute to a receptacle that to Jessica looked like a large trough. When Charles brought her closer she observed a huge cylinder with teeth within it revolving against a grate. She could see the bolls thickly peppered with black seeds go through the grate and come out clean without the seeds. Charles then had her look out the window. A black man was leading a horse around and around in a wide circle. The horse was supplying the power to turn the gin and keep the cylinder in motion. Charles proudly pointed out to her the connection of the leather thong snaking out of the barn to the horse's collar. Jessica watched the women at the trough guiding the cotton down the chute into the gin's teeth. They did not look directly at her as she passed, keeping their red-bandana-covered heads down to their work, but she could see the corners of their eyes sliding around to catch a little glimpse.

Their legs were bare and covered with white cotton fuzz. It must be in the air, too, Jessica thought; she could feel it in her throat.

Then they continued into another section of the barn. Men were baling the cotton. The size of the bales and the speed with which they were bound astonished her. The bales were then taken to a storeroom where they would be held for shipment. The storeroom was packed with the white bundles. She had not imagined there would be so many, especially since it came from only one section where the picking had begun. But, she realized, Charles' plantation was huge, and one part of his land was equal in itself to a large farm.

"Do the factors come here to bid on the bales?" Jessica asked, trying to see the cotton industry through Jason's eyes.

"Yes. And sometimes we haul the bales to auction elsewhere."

"And where do they go then?"

"Some overseas, and some to the factories in the North."

"You don't manufacture here?"

"No," he said shortly. "Some say once we industrialize in the South we are lost."

"Why?"

"Let's go," he said. "There is still so much to see."

They rode far beyond the storehouse and soon came upon a meadow with a stream running through it. He told her there were many fish in it, particularly the sunnies and catfish that Southerners liked so much. The banks of the river seemed lit with sunshine; the field glowed with dandelions. His horse led hers onward as they rode away from the narrow river and to a field where other horses grazed. They were beautiful beasts, Jessica saw, and she imagined they were carefully bred. "I only keep a few and the rest we sell," Charles told her. "There are a few foals—there—" he pointed, "—that I am raising for the children. They must learn to ride and soon I shall teach them; I am already late with Charlie." They rode on and came to another field where the cows were. "Just a small herd," Charles explained, "for our own domestic needs—milk and beef. The 'nigras' are not very good with animals. They often mistreat them."

"Perhaps taking out their own anger upon lesser creatures."

"Why, Cousin!" he said, "I think you are hostile to me."

She blushed.

"I cannot help but show my feelings about slavery. After all, you know Jason's stand, and now my own only grows stronger seeing your system at work. . . . I must apologize, however, to you, Charles. After all, you are my host and it was good of you to accept me into your household knowing that Jason and I are opposed to slavery."

"It is wise that you are saying this here where there are not dangerous ears to hear you," he said gravely.

"I realize the difficulties."

"But I like talking with you," he said, smiling at her, "hearing your point of view. It shows me what the opposition is, outside. We tend to live in our own private worlds and not listen to other voices."

"That attitude is commendable."

"No, *really*. I need the stimulation of talk fresh from London. From cities. We sometimes grow backwater here. I often miss what I had at Yale," he said pensively. "Yes, we grow provincial, all of us, in time."

"You don't seem provincial."

"Do you know business?"

"A little. Jason and I would discuss it, but not enough."

"I would like to talk business with you sometime. I want to tell you what it is like to run a plantation and make it work, make it pay."

"And I would like to hear about it."

"Then it's a promise."

"Good. Just tell me one thing more now, Charles, and we'll keep the rest for later. What did you mean when you said that once you industrialize here you are lost?"

Charles thoughtfully patted his horse's shoulder.

"It has been said that once you make a slave a mechanic he is halfway free . . . does that answer your question?"

"Partly."

"More about that later," he said and smiled.

They circled back around the land. She saw the woodlands, the beautiful oak trees and pines, and liked the dark somnolence of the place. He told her they cut enough wood every year to heat the big house and the cabins in midwinter and had a small sawmill where they planed some boards for building needs. They were going to make cupboards for the slave cabins come December, and maybe some other improvements.

"Do you mind if I walk for a while?" she asked suddenly.

"Not at all."

He swung agilely from his horse and then helped her dismount.

"The woods are lovely," she said, stopping to examine some ferns. "It reminds me of home."

"Oh, are you sad to be gone so far from it?" he asked sympathetically.

"But I am glad to be here."

"And I am glad you are here, too. Already, there has been an improvement in Eleanor, and the children are delighted with their teacher."

He smiled at her gratefully and she smiled back at him.

"Perhaps I can get Eleanor to walk outside with me."

"Yes," he said, "that would be excellent, indeed."

They heard voices and soon came out upon the cotton fields, which they saw now from another vantage point.

"I think we should ride again," Charles told her and helped her onto the mare's back. He cupped his hands for her to boost herself upward. She swayed against him and felt the hardness of his arms. He turned quickly away once she was seated and mounted his own horse.

The slaves in this section of the fields were singing as they worked. The songs were not spirituals. They were work songs, in the rhythm of their body motions.

"Do they sing all night?" she asked, thinking of stories she had heard.

"Sometimes," he smiled, "when the moon is right, they sing and dance the patting juber."

"What's that?"

"A dance they brought with them from Africa."

"And the drums?"

"No drums; they are not permitted in the South."

"Why not?"

"They are traditional signals," he said gravely. "They could talk to each other in drums. We do not permit that."

"You mean, plan insurrection?"

He blanched.

"We never, *never* say that word, and especially not in the fields."

"Another gaffe," she said apologetically.

"They often play the bones with their singing," he said. "That's harmless, and very pleasant really. Beef ribs from the plantation house kitchen, saved by Julia, cleaned thoroughly, then polished and knocked together. Clunking sound but rhythmic if the player is musical."

"And when there is no full moon?"

"Then usually to bed after the evening meal. Darkness and the pleasures of the night."

She blushed and then felt foolish. After all, she was an experienced and married woman.

"When the families increase, it is good for all of us. The plantation thrives. A good strong man brings seven hundred fifty dollars, sometimes more, sometimes a thousand or twelve hundred fifty."

"That's a lot of money," she said.

"Yes. And a beautiful woman, not meant for the fields, can bring as much as twenty-five hundred dollars."

She looked at him sharply. She thought he was trying to get at her, to punish her dislike of the system.

They rode in silence.

The afternoon was waning. It would be light for some time but now the sun was in its descent and its beams diffused more softly. The earth and its crops seemed tinged with a dull copper glow, and there was a stillness in the air as if the day creatures were pausing before the night creatures emerged. The breeze had quieted but there was a cooling moistness all about them that portended a storm. The horses' hooves stirred up the crickets and praying mantises and small toads that hovered in the grasses. Jessica stifled her low cry as a garter snake slithered across the path.

Charles whipped off his hat, and his thick white hair gleamed even in the half-light. It contrasted vividly with his suntanned skin. He had a handsome head, Jessica noted once again—large, almost massive, set upon a long, strongly muscled neck. His features were sharp and finely drawn. His dark eyes were fine, too, attenuated into a long almond shape, thickly fringed with black lashes that brushed high cheekbones. As he blinked, she thought of hummingbirds quivering in the air. The hand that rested lightly on the saddle was long and slender, the fingers lean but blunt at the tips. They had the look of strength about them, those fingers, she thought, a fineness and strength.

She wanted to hate him, she suddenly realized. He was opposed to everything she believed in. And yet everything was not merely good or bad. There were so many gradations. She could not dislike him. As he helped her down again with the assistance of the stable boy before the veranda of the big house, she realized she had leaned on his arm a little too long. She had enjoyed his company, perhaps a little too much.

"It was a pleasant afternoon," Charles told her solemnly. "I must thank you for coming and taking such an interest."

"It was truly fascinating. And of course I'm interested. I want to go further into the economics—or the business—you promised to discuss with me. You will, won't you?"

"Of course," he said. "I value your point of view."

"Thank you. Thank you for taking me. I want to know more. Perhaps it will help me understand about Jason."

"You don't give up, do you?"

"Of course not!" she said spiritedly.

He towered above her and she could see the compassion in his eyes.

"Sometimes we follow courses not best for us," he said and sighed, "and yet we are helpless in our pursuit of them."

"We are not helpless."

"I wonder. Anyway, my dear," he said, and he seemed very intense, "don't take to task those who flow with the tide."

She thought of that statement that evening, after they had played cards with Miranda and been badly trounced by her. Miranda had retired and she soon followed her up the stairs, and in the back hallway she heard the whispering of Chloe—she would never forget the timbre of her voice—and the low response of Charles. She thought of it a few afternoons later, after Eleanor had made successive and successful appearances at the midday meal, when Charles had walked her back to her bedroom for her afternoon nap and had gone inside with her and not returned for a long while.

Jessica had sheltered her hot face in her hands as she dwelled on both incidents.

Chapter Four

They were going to have a ball after all. Miranda had gotten her way. It would be held the following week, just before the *grande dame* returned to her home in Maryland. Jessica helped Charles write the invitations. They worked side by side at the huge dining-room table, copying from lists Charles said were really not up to date. They had been idle for a number of years, he explained, since Eleanor had done nothing about parties, and he crossed off entries and added some, too. She noticed he had a fine script, a little too many curlicues for her taste, but graceful and flowing nevertheless. He showed her how he liked the invitations to be folded, heated the wax, and gave her a sample of his seal. On the first one he pressed down on her hand, to make the seal come up better, and she was annoyed with herself that her fingers began to tremble and that she became all thumbs so that for a while he had to repeat the pressure until she had it just right.

"So many people," she murmured.

"Well, it's *de rigueur,*" he explained, "when you have a ball, you invite everyone from all the plantations within miles of your own."

"Everybody?"

"All the plantation families."

She wrinkled her nose.

"Why don't you invite only those you really care for!"

"Do that again!" he commanded.

"What?"

"Make that face again. It's delightful!"

"We'll never finish here," she said.

"We're in no hurry."

"I have classes tomorrow . . ."

He grinned at her.

"So you do."

She was furious that he teased her.

Cicero delivered the invitations by hand, making the route in the small cart he handled so well. It took him two days to travel the course. He went around half the circle one day and completed its arc the next. He seemed excited by the chore. Jessica had not seen him look so pleased since she arrived. The tempo of the household sped up. Charles had charged Jessica with the job of conferring whenever necessary with Cicero and Julia about the make-ready tasks to be completed. Julia presented a supper menu that Jessica thought overabundant in rich foods; Charles studied it and approved it and even added a few more hams and said he would see that proper supplies would be sent to the kitchen. Extra bedrooms were to be opened for those who cared to stay on for a day or two. And the ballroom on the second floor was to be aired and dusted and the gilt chairs arranged around the walls for those who did not want to dance, or who had danced too much and had to rest. Cicero would need to see about getting trestle tables set up and Julia to supervise the laundress on the linen cloths and napkins. Charles himself would see about the local musicians. Joseph would bring in the flowers and would she, Jessica, kindly see to the arrangements? Perhaps, Charles said slowly, that was a task in which she could involve Eleanor. Eleanor had a lovely way with flowers. It would be good for her to be occupied in making a contribution to the success of the ball; it would cause her to take an interest in the coming festivities. Miranda looked so elated about all the bustle, Jessica wondered whether she could have used the stimulating effect upon Eleanor as one of her final arguments in favor of the affair.

The kitchen house was in a bustle as Jessica continued the sunrise lessons she had begun there. She had returned a few more times after the first visit to see about Billy. She had decided not to begin the lessons immediately or set any place or time, until she received more signals from Julia and Joseph. Of what Joseph was saying to her with the clatter of his spoons and the urgency in his eyes before they darted away from her, she had been certain. She wanted to make sure of Julia.

Jessica asked Julia to teach her to make the beaten biscuits whose fame, she had been told, had spread through the length and breadth of the state and beyond. As they worked she talked of her home back in England and how she had often helped her mother bake long loaves of bread. Then she spoke of her father and the lessons he had set before her and how he had seen to her education. She talked about reading and what it had meant to her, how it had opened up the world and made it possible for her to know about all sorts of people and how they felt about many things. She could feel the presence of Joseph, sitting at his task in a far corner—the excitement of his unspoken response was thick in the air.

By the time they took the trays of golden biscuits from the bake-oven, Jessica knew that Julia was her friend. The next day Jessica came again, in her free time, to learn about pies. Sometimes in her work her floured hand would touch Julia's floured hand. This went on for a week before she spoke of the lessons she would begin for Billy. It would be best to give them here in the kitchen, she said, so it would not upset the rest of the house. Julia listened, her face impassive.

"Spoze so," she said.

The earlier the better for her, Jessica continued, and for Billy, too—this way it would not interfere with either one's chores.

"Spoze so," Julia said.

They could just sit at a side table, where they would not get in the way, and she could recite the lessons to Billy. And she could read stories to him and tell the meanings of the words.

Jessica stopped, nervously. She did not fully understand what the laws and the restrictions were in the South about reading and just who could read and who could not, but if she were circumspect enough perhaps she could get around all the rules. She was her father's daughter, indeed, and believed there were means to put into practice all the principles she believed in.

"Spoze so," Julia said.

"Billy, I'll be here before sunup, before breakfast," she said loudly. "Be ready, please."

"Yes'm," he said, grinning. He already knew the game.

In the morning Joseph sat at another table, not far from the teacher, cutting up fruit for jam. When Jessica, after reading aloud, asked Billy a question about the book and Billy answered, Joseph would nod his head or shake it; and Jessica replied to Billy. Julia would see about the breakfast, but her eyes grew round. Her lips moved silently as Jessica spelled out some words for Billy.

And so it had gone on from there. This morning, before the party, Joseph continued with his silver polishing chores as Jessica read a new chapter from *The Life and Strange Surprising Adventures of Robinson Crusoe of York, Mariner.* Billy sat goggle-eyed, and Julia, as she mixed up a new batch of bread, kept shaking her head in wonder. Cicero usually kept out of the kitchen; he did not want to know of it, the learning that was going on there.

Joseph and Billy cried out in despair as Jessica closed the book. They wanted to know what happened next. Next lesson, she said firmly. Then Jessica reached for the Johnson's dictionary. She wrote out some of the words they had heard in the story. She instructed Billy to see what they looked like. Then she talked about their meaning and had Billy use the words in sentences of his own. The next minute she began to talk directly to Joseph. No one seemed to notice the difference. Joseph responded. They proceeded as before, but openly including him now. Both boys were shy about expressing themselves, afraid to make mistakes. Jessica patiently drew them out. Later, she promised them, she would turn to *The Swiss Family Robinson, or Adventures in a Desert Island.* If they liked Robinson Crusoe, they surely would be fascinated by the next book. First they must learn some of the words, she said, for she was going to let them try the new book, a page at a time, on their own. She had a list of words most often used and she made them say them after her and then repeat the letters in the words and the order in which they must be arranged to be recognized. She had first considered using a primer for Joseph so that he would catch up with Billy, but he was quick and she discarded the idea; he would just have to work harder, she decided.

After *The Swiss Family Robinson,* they would go on to Swift's *Gulliver's Travels,* which Jessica's father had regarded so highly because of its appeal to reason. But she would finish the lesson today with a reading of some of the poetry of Tennyson, not for their erudition but for her own sentimental pleasure of the lines. She was glad that Sedgely Manor had an adequate library. She had already found there, and set aside for her own reading pleasure, a copy—quite new—of Nathaniel Hawthorne's *Twice-Told Tales* and Henry Wadsworth Longfellow's *Voices of the Night.*

As she read the Tennyson poems, she heard a humming sound come from Joseph's lips. They moved slightly and she realized he not only was repeating the words after her but was putting them—unconsciously, she believed—to music. The rhythm had elicited a musical response. One time she had surprised him, playing on the taut, thin, strung-out leather strips of a wooden box he had hollowed out and fashioned into a crude fiddle. He had quickly put it behind a pile of potatoes he was supposed to be peeling. Now that she had worked with him on the books, perhaps he would get it out and play for her.

One of her lessons had been spelling out their names. Billy had proudly shown her he had not forgotten her instruction on the ship and he wrote his name largely on the scraps of paper she had brought with her. Cicero unexpectedly came into the kitchen and began to tremble. He snatched Joseph's paper from his hand and tore it up.

"Dat only means trubbel!" he said in anguish. "Don larn it, Joseph, don do it!"

"Naw, Cero, don stoppim," Julia said quietly. "He's gotta larn, jes gotta."

"Yall see im kilt!" Cicero cried. "Yer own son!"

"Naw, Ahll see im *live,* thas whut—yer own son, Cero. Reely live."

Joseph stubbornly took a new sheet of paper and traced out

again the letters that Jessica had shown him, that spelled his name. Doggedly he finished it, as Cicero angrily left the room, and he handed it to Jessica.

"Dat–*Th*at says me, who I is–"

"Am," Jessica corrected.

"Tha . . . tha*t* says who I *am,* don't it?"

"Yes," Jessica said. "It *does,* Joseph."

"It shows a pitchah ob me?"

"A picture of Joseph."

"Jes dis Joseph?"

"No," she said slowly, "not just this Joseph. Any Joseph."

"How come jes–jus*t* not me, Miz Jess'ca?"

"It could be Joseph anybody," she said slowly. "Anybody given the name Joseph. It needs another name beside it. A second name, the name of his father or his house? Sedgely?"

"Naw!" he said angrily. "Ain mah–my–ole man, ain my house."

"Shush!" Julia said sharply. "Yall gotta larn but no hatefulness, Joseph!"

"Joseph Cicero," Jessica suggested.

"Pa won't lak it. Git im in bad trubbel," he said dubiously.

"All right. I know, make it two times. Joseph Joseph. Then there will be no mistaking who you are."

"Joseph Joseph," he said proudly. "Den–" remembering, "*then* that really means me, dis–this–slave boy, me."

"Yes. People will quickly learn who that is–you learn it, but save it for another time, when it will be safer, Joseph Joseph and more useful to you."

He nodded. Laboriously he wrote Joseph Joseph over and over again until Jessica finished her writing lesson with Billy, which turned into a letter to his mother back in England.

"But she won't be able to read it," Billy said, crestfallen, when they had finished the simple message.

"Someone will," Jessica told him. "She will find someone to read it to her."

"Will it say the same thing to that person that it does to us?" he asked anxiously.

"The very same thing," Jessica reassured him, "if he knows how to read then he'll understand the words and tell them to her."

"Good, he said, smiling brightly, "maybe she'll take it to the preacher. He reads the Bible, so he should know the words."

"Yes," Jessica said. "And your mother will know where you are, that you are safe." Billy's young face, that was filling out and looking more boyish all the time, radiated joy.

"Tell her," he said excitedly, "I'll come back to see her . . . and . . . and I'll bring her . . . a new dress!" Jessica restrained herself from patting his golden head.

"Yes, I'll write that," she said. "Now watch how I make each letter and words: I . . . s . . . h . . . a . . . l . . . l . . . c . . . o . . . m . . . e . . . h . . . o . . . m . . . e . . .

The Tennyson poems finished the session this time, and they reluctantly watched her go. After breakfast, she switched to her younger pupils.

Charlie and Jenny were patiently doing their sums—on the two age levels she had set before them—and she looked at their heads bent seriously over their work. Jenny was frowning—almost imperiously like her father. Her golden curls cascaded down her back. She looked up once to study her hand and count on her fingers; she was so intent she did not seem to see Jessica. It troubled Jessica that Eleanor had so neglected the little girl. The child was well taken care of physically; the house slaves had seen to that, and Charles conscientiously spent those precious minutes with both Jenny and Charlie before bedtime every night. But they needed more. Jessica remembered the closeness of her own relationship with her mother—and her father—when she was Jenny's age and she knew well what the child missed. She went over to Jenny and impulsively kissed the top of her head. Jenny lifted her dark eyes and smiled delightedly at Jessica, then went back to her work, the smile still lingering on her lips. Jessica was amazed at the child's diligence. When she peered over Charlie's shoulder she saw he was drawing horses instead of doing the times tables she had specified. They were good drawings. She had seen some of them before and they were consistently fine. He had a strong clean line and an imaginative eye. She must talk with Charles about his son's talents. Charlie could develop into a remarkable artist, with training. Perhaps there was a local artist Charlie could begin studying with and then, later, go on to Philadelphia, or even to London, to work with some of the masters. She must certainly speak with Charles about this. In the meanwhile, she complimented the boy on his drawing and set him a problem of multiplication. If two mares had a foal apiece every year, how many additions would there be to the stable in six years? Charlie was to draw that many foals on the fresh sheets of paper to show the right number. He seemed to like that and enthusiastically worked on the problem.

While they were occupied, Jessica leafed through an old botany book she had found in the library. She would take the children on a field trip. She would ask Charlie to sketch the different plants and the insects they found. Jenny could pick flowers to press into a book they would keep for that purpose.

Then Jessica looked up sharply at the familiar sound of rustling in the hallway. Usually she was aware of it when she was reading aloud to the children. This she did at the end of every morning class. They were now into the story of Robyn Hoode. She had brought a copy of the book with her from home; it had been her own when she was growing up and she still enjoyed looking at the woodcuts of Robyn Hoode with his bow and arrow and Lytel John, with his mighty staff.

Jessica, careful not to turn abruptly, saw the tip of a small bare foot extending into the open doorway. She carefully closed the botany book and picked up *Robyn Hoode.* Quietly she told Charlie and Jenny that if they were not yet finished with their problems, they could complete them later that afternoon and turn them in for her inspection at the next day's class. She would like to begin reading. Charlie reluctantly put down his pen, torn between the pleasure of his craft and hearing a favorite story. The story won; he was a reasonable boy; he knew he could always pick up his drawing at any time. And Jenny was enchanted by Maid Marian.

Jessica read in a loud voice. Charlie, as she had begun reading louder and louder each day, had asked her whether a reading voice should be different from a speaking voice. She had considered that carefully and replied well, one must be sure that everyone could hear; yes, a reading voice should be different.

"Well," said Jenny, who was more outspoken, "we're not exactly deaf. You need not shout. Mama says it's not good manners to shout."

Jessica did not exactly shout now, but she pronounced each word especially clearly and let it bounce about the walls. Occasionally she peered up from the page. She saw the little foot in its entirety now. This was as far as it had come on all the previous occasions. Maybe if it continued, the entire leg would follow.

Sometimes her alerted ears would hear a sudden gasp quickly stifled, or a giggle swallowed before it developed. Jessica decided to try an experiment. When she came to an especially exciting part that had Charlie and Jenny leaning forward from where they sat, rapt, at her feet, she lowered her voice dramatically, so that even her two pupils strained. They looked at her anxiously, wondering what was wrong. Jessica looked from the corner of her eye again, and sure enough, there was a coarse blue cotton bit of skirt and flash of creamy-beige calf showing in the doorway. Now Jessica began to whisper, and Charlie looked at her patronizingly—silly woman playing games.

"Lose your voice?" he said disgustedly, knowing well she had not.

She shook her head, placing a finger over her lips. Now both children knew she was up to something.

She read in a very loud voice again, then abruptly lowered it. In another surreptitious glance at the doorway, she saw Aletha standing there, fully exposed. Still without looking directly at the child, she said in the tone of voice in which she was reading, "Aletha, please come in."

Charlie and Jenny turned sharply and Aletha stood transfixed and trembling before their eyes. She seemed about to turn and take flight.

"Aletha, come here, please!" Jessica said loudly, in the most authoritative voice she could muster. She felt vaguely excited.

The child slowly advanced, reluctantly but inexorably, as if she could not disobey the call of any mistress. Her lovely little face was puckered with fright, and the eyes brimmed with tears. The long black hair quivered with the rest of her and she tossed it as if to make a screen that she could hide behind. She could not possibly see where she was going, but her bare feet propelled her before Jessica.

"I sorry," she said unhappily.

Jessica looked at the fine tucking in the child's dress, such beautiful handwork on inferior cloth. Chloe was a very gifted seamstress—Jessica had seen it in the shapes of Charlie's and Jenny's clothes and in the cutwork of the tablecloths and napkins and the drawnwork of the pillowslips and coverlets. She knew Chloe was nearby. The linen room, where Chloe worked, was in a little ell at the end of the back stairway. It occurred to Jessica that perhaps Aletha had been encouraged to listen, perhaps not to show herself—or the child would not seem so frightened now upon discovery—but to listen and to learn along with the other children.

"Aletha . . ."

The child shook the hair out of her eyes and looked shyly at Jessica. She seemed pleased to hear her name spoken; she probably thought, Jessica told herself, that I did not know her name.

"Yassum?"

"Aletha, wouldn't you like to come in and sit down and hear the rest of the story?"

Jessica was stunned by the illumination of the child's smile.

"Kin I, miz?"

"You may, Aletha. What a pretty name. Come, child . . ."

"Oh, but Mama wouldn't like that!" Jenny cried, shocked.

"I don't know . . ." Jessica said slowly.

"Mama won't let us play with Aletha," Charlie explained gravely. "She's told us many times not to."

Jessica looked at him compassionately, wondering whether an eight-year-old looked at a female replica of his father and understood the meaning of it. Perhaps he was still too young. And perhaps not. One could not live on a farm and not see the ways of nature. One's ears, no matter how callow, could not fail to pick up the innuendoes and whispers.

"Well," Jessica said, looking again at Aletha, her heart constricting as she saw the misery there and the tears beginning to fall down the smooth honey-beige cheeks. "This is not really playing, children." And she assumed her authoritative voice again. "This is working. We are working to learn things and to make us grow into more useful and good human beings. Like you learn in church."

"We don't go to church," Jenny said primly.

Jessica remembered Charles Sedgely's allusion to Tartuffe-like preachers.

"It's too far away," Charlie said.

"We're wasting time. Soon the afternoon meal will be ready. Don't you want to hear the end of this adventure?"

"Oh, yes, yes!" they cried as Aletha fidgeted.

"Well, then . . . Aletha, sit here," Jessica ordered and pointed to the open space of the circle, Teacher at bottom, Charlie and Jenny on either side and Aletha now closing the gap. Aletha seemed stunned and almost fell into her place. The air seemed tense to Jessica. Perhaps it was her vision of Chloe at the back end of the hall, who strained, listening for her child.

"Now," Jessica said, picking up *Robyn Hoode* again, "remember, we are working and not playing." She felt a pang of conscience but firmly put it down as misguided; she must follow the path that her father and, she was sure now, her husband had set upon before her. "There is no need to trouble your mother. We are not really hurting her. And Aletha may come each morning and work with us."

Jessica did not look at Aletha, but anxiously at Charlie and Jenny.

"It's all right. Father likes her," Charlie said gravely.

"And your mother would, too, if she came to know her." She added quickly, "But she's too ill now to try—and we must spare her."

" 'Sall right," Jenny said, content to mimic her brother. "Let's go on with the story."

Jessica began to read again, in her normal tone. She thought she saw Charlie grin at her.

People, carefully dressed and coiffed, had been arriving all day. The sound of horses' hooves had been music to Miranda's ears as she stood, flanked by Charles and Jessica (Eleanor promised to appear later that evening), in the center hall to greet the guests. A pre-ball feast was spread upon tables on the veranda for those who came early, and Cicero and Joseph and Sally and many other househands—adults and children—passed around juleps and punch and plates of salads and fried chicken and ham.

After the siesta hour, with the rooms of the house crowded with visitors, fanned against the heat with tied bundles of chicken and rooster feathers by the little handservants they had brought with them, still more men and women arrived. A supper—called light but which nevertheless had the boards creaking under its weight—was spread on the dining-room table.

Now the ball really began. The ballroom doors were swung open, the musicians took their places, and the iron-work candelabras were set ablaze against the deepening dusk. Charles and Miranda and Eleanor—and Jessica, too, the others had insisted—formed a receiving line inside the ballroom entrance while Cicero, white-gloved and proper as he had been taught by Charles' parents before him, stiffly announced in the best English tradition the names of the guests as they ceremoniously entered with measured tread.

Miranda wore all the jewels she had brought with her and she shone and twinkled merrily, her white satin ballgown also alight with seed pearls sewn in concentric waves about her skirt and enlarging into full-sized pearls at her bosom. Jessica had stared in open admiration at Charles, before she caught herself, in his formal dress. He wore a well-cut fawn coat with a velvet collar, despite the heat, and narrow, close-to-the-leg beige-colored trousers that seemed to flash in motion beneath the flounce of the cutaway jacket as he turned and bowed over the outstretched hands of smiling ladies. His white cravat was ruffled and finely stitched with handmade lace. His hair was recently cut—by his valet or by Cicero? she wondered—so that it barely came to his shoulders, and the whiteness of it shone diamondlike in the glow of the candles. She was glad that he was cleanshaven—like Jason, she sighed. Quickly she turned to look at Eleanor. Charles' arm was draped lightly about her waist, perhaps to support her. Eleanor looked beautiful tonight,

Jessica realized with pleasure mixed with a modicum of other feeling she would not really acknowledge. Eleanor's face and figure gradually filled out as she had continued to take a few more forkfuls of food at each meal—until one night, to the amazement of everyone at table, she had progressed to a full dinner. Sally had carefully dressed her hair in a bouffant and elaborate upsweep with puffs and curls held by ornate tortoise combs and circled by a velvet band. Now Eleanor, like Charles' grandmother, wore a satin gown, but hers was cut low at the bosom, showing a shadow that Charles occasionally looked at with appreciation. The dress fell from under the bosom in a small bellshape around her form, with intricate trapunto work at the hem, which just allowed her satin shoes to peep out, and there was more trapunto decoration at the tiny cap sleeves. She wore golden bracelets on her arms and a diamond necklace at the throat; Jessica vaguely remembered hearing from her aunt about such a necklace given to Eleanor as a wedding present by her husband. She herself was more plainly dressed, though it did not really matter to her, Jessica thought. Her dress was scoop-necked, too, but not so deep as Eleanor's, and had a demure ribbon sash about her waist. The material was a thin blue china silk her mother had added to her trousseau and which she had fashioned with the help of her mother into the simple shepherdess style that, shaped by her father's taste, she had grown to like so much. Her string of pale coral beads matched the color of her sash.

When the guests were all properly acknowledged, the receiving line dissolved. Charles opened the dancing as he led Eleanor away in a waltz. Jessica could see the craning little heads of Charlie and Jenny at the doorway, with Sally standing anxiously behind them ready to pounce if they should dash in. Jessica was happy that the children should be witness to the unaccustomed sight of their mother in their father's arms, in happy pose, as they lightly pirouetted about the ballroom. Jessica had not seen an expression so ecstatic on Eleanor's glowing face since they were girls in London.

She turned away and was quickly claimed by a neighboring planter. He was a good dance partner and Jessica was swept up into the excitement of the evening, liking the sudden popularity she experienced and the gallantry of the men. In between dances a knot of them gathered about her clamoring for attention. She realized she was the new woman in a fairly closed society and her presence created something of a ripple. The Virginians were quite a handsome lot, she thought happily, as she gazed upward at one good-looking face after another. She was somewhat out of breath, spun around so vigorously, and finally she had to beg for time out.

Her last partner danced her to the sidelines where Miranda sat regally in a gilt armchair. One of her little child slaves was fanning her with a large-plumed gaily dyed ostrich fan. Occasionally Miranda placed a heavily perfumed handkerchief to her nose as if for revival—a pose, Jessica quickly divined. Miranda's eyes twinkled wickedly; there was no question she delighted in the scene before her and the obeisances made to her by men and women both. Her highly dressed hair quivered as she acknowledged the curtsies and the bows and the kissing of her hand. Her nodding did not prevent her from observing everything before her, the trysts going on behind palms in the dark corners, the anxious mothers and wives and husbands, the amount of whiskey being consumed, the pale faces growing redder from the spirits and dancing and stirred-up emotion, and the black house slaves standing in the background, whom she periodically snapped to attention with a smart clapping of her hands in their direction. She motioned Jessica to a small chair at her side.

"Good party," she said, with satisfaction. "Just what this plantation has needed." She nodded gravely to an elderly gentleman on his way to the liquid refreshments. "Look at that old sot," she said maliciously, "he's outlived five wives and is looking for another. . . . You must come to me, Jessica dear, when this household can spare you. I'll give you a series of balls you will never forget and have all the eligible men of the state of Maryland at your feet."

"I'm not looking for eligible men."

"Nonsense, my dear!" Miranda scoffed. "Every woman without a man keeps looking until she's dead. And even those with husbands, too, unless they're blind. . . . Look at that hussy over there," she waved at a beautiful lady who smiled sardonically in their direction, "she's had every man in a five-mile radius who's still able. . . . Oh, my dear!" she cried, looking at Jessica's shocked face, "you're not a child!"

Jessica laughed, despite herself.

"It's good for Charles to get back into society," Miranda said sagely. "Charles is obsessed with the land . . . and other things. . . ."

"Eleanor looks so well tonight."

"Yes, due to your loving ministrations."

"No, of her own doing."

"Nevertheless . . ."

A dowager came to sit on the other side of Miranda and quickly drew her attention.

Jessica thought of her breathless conversations with her dance partners. Yes, the countryside was very beautiful . . . the weather was hot . . . the price of tobacco . . . they were watching Charles Sedgely and his insistence on cotton growing . . . no, they had not heard of Jason Coopersmith, who was he? . . . her husband? . . . each seemed disappointed . . . feeling better when she said he had been missing for some time . . . wild country hereabout, they commiserated . . . he was a cotton factor, did she say? . . . well, there was a young factor who had come a couple of years ago to make an offer on his crop, but he himself scarcely remembered what happened after the sale, and the factor had never returned . . . yes, perhaps his name was Coopersmith . . . was it not morbid, one young man said lustily, to live in the past when the present was so alluring; you are an alluring lady . . . Jessica smiled. This was fertile ground for any woman looking for a husband . . . the males outnumbered the females in eligible families . . . the land was still relatively new . . .

"May I?" Charles was before her, bowing slightly.

She looked at him in surprise and then searched for Eleanor. Eleanor was already claimed for the next dance. Jessica rose delightedly, and Charles took her hand to lead her out onto the floor.

"Are you having a good time?" he asked, as they stood poised waiting for the music to begin.

"Oh yes," she said happily.

"A happy shock for our neighbors."

"Really?"

"We haven't had a ball for years, or gone to any either . . . refused all invitations . . ."

"This one is very pleasant," she said, somewhat breathlessly, as he nearly swung her off her feet.

And growing pleasanter all the time, she must admit to herself. That recent afternoon Charles had helped her from her horse and she had known how enjoyable his touch was to her. She liked the pressure of his arm now at her waist. With her other partners she had paid no attention to arms and their contact. But there was a vibrancy to Charles' arm; it almost pulsated against her. And the hand that held hers was warm and strong. Charles led her through the motions of the waltz, the dance that had originated in Germany and gained popularity in Europe and later in the United States. Once the pressure of other dancers pushed them suddenly closer together and she felt the length of his body against her. It made her gasp and she could feel her cheeks redden. "Sorry," he murmured, unperturbed, "those clumsy louts."

Before the dance was finished, someone called for a Virginia reel and the fiddlers swung into the merry tune. Men began to form a line on one side of the room and women on the other. They extended the length of the hall; everyone seemed eager to participate.

"Do you know this?" Charles asked her, as the couple at the head of the lines moved toward one another.

"Oh yes! Back home we call it the Sir Roger de Coverley. How delightful!"

Eleanor was the head lady and she twirled each man happily as she came down the line. It was evident how blissful she was when it was time to engage her husband. For a moment Jessica could only stare at her with a tug at her own heart before she was claimed, too, by Eleanor's partner. She was glad when Eleanor must go on to the next man. She and Charles smiled across the space between them.

Soon it was their turn to be the head partners, and when she and Charles came together at the proper turns it was as exciting as before. When he took her hand, he pressed it ever so slightly, and she was annoyed that he should feel her fingers flutter. It was with dismay and relief that she greeted Eleanor, who came at the end of the set to claim Charles. An earlier partner came to beseech Jessica, and Charles and Eleanor went off to the tables where the candles were now being lit and the buffet supper was ready to be served.

Cicero and Joseph and other male slave attendants presided over the food and sliced and served. Other slaves, some Jessica had never seen before or had failed to recognize, set little tables in front of the gilt chairs, and bundles of white monogrammed linen napkins, exquisitely laundered and pressed, were distributed among the guests. Charles was the gracious host, helping the ladies to seats and joining the men at the punch bowl, finding places for those without a group of their own. The fiddlers disappeared at the first clatter of the china, and during the intermission and when the noise of serving had settled into the lower hum of eating and light supper conversation, Eleanor slipped to the spinet, so much smaller than the piano in the drawing room, and began to play a Beethoven sonata. Jessica stood entranced, listening to her. She had forgotten what an accomplished musician Eleanor had been from early childhood onward; it was legendary in the family. It made her think of Charles' musical ability, too, and how well he had played the evening she arrived and the other evenings that followed. He and Eleanor had so much in common, she thought sadly; how tragic that their lives had taken such unfortunate twists.

Jessica could see that Charles, never out of her view, was deeply affected by Eleanor's music. He had been hovering over an elderly guest, seeing to her comfort, and had straightened up and stiffened at the first few notes. He stood rooted at his place, eyes on his wife and her gently swaying figure over the keys. He led the applause and, when it had finished, went to her and asked her to play again. She did, and he pulled up a chair and sat by her side. As if there had been a score before her, he looked ready to turn the pages; indeed he bent over her at intervals and whispered small bravos, not to distract her but to urge her on. Eleanor went on to Chopin, Charles' favorite pieces, and he began to nod time for her which she did not need—she knew them so well. They must have played them together, Jessica guessed; she knew that for a fact when Eleanor's eyes lifted from the keyboard and fastened on her husband's remembering face.

The assemblage was hushed until Eleanor was finished. This time Miranda led the applause, pounding the floor with her elegant walking stick, which she did not use as such but held as a staff at important occasions. One of the planters proposed a toast to the beautiful and accomplished mistress of the house, going through the elaborate gesture of sweeping an imaginary hat from his head and touching it to his heart and then laying it at his feet. There were more huzzas, and Charles lifted Eleanor to a standing position, placing an arm about her and kissing lightly the top of her head. She rested against him, looking flushed and happy.

"Now," Miranda whispered *sotto voce* to Jessica, "if she doesn't get to the punch bowl all will be well."

"She doesn't need to," Jessica said thoughtfully. "She's back in her own element."

"Good for the reputation of the house, Eleanor showing her face at last."

"And doing it so well. Good for Eleanor," Jessica said, as she turned to the planter from the close-by estate. He was importuning her to walk with him in the gardens, where they could get a breath of air. It was growing unbearably hot in the ballroom. She offered instead to sit with him near an open window. Looking at her with exaggerated disappointment, he accepted the alternative arrangement and occupied her time for most of the remainder of the party.

Then, after the fiddlers had returned and there were more country dances and the waltz again, it was time for the host and hostesses to gather once more, this time for the farewells, and Jessica—who had not seen Charles since the piano recital—stood beside him and Eleanor and Miranda. Eleanor, she could see, had held up exceptionally well despite the long hours of the ball. Jessica wanted to concentrate on the good feeling of standing beside Charles, but she was distracted by well-wishers who welcomed her into the community and begged her to come to tea or come for a weekend or stay for a fortnight for that matter, and those who told her they would like to call on her in the future. Miranda left for her room, accompanied by an entourage, her body servant, and a gaggle of little black children. Houseguests asked to be excused and wandered to their quarters, or to chambers other than their own. It seemed that Jessica and Eleanor and Charles would be alone against a background of scurrying lackeys gathering up the leftover food and soiled plates. But soon her cousins said a hasty goodnight to Jessica and left the ballroom. Jessica felt a great sense of loneliness, and the old despair she had not felt for some months overcame her. Perhaps it was the letdown of a good party come to an end, she tried to console herself. But when she went outside and passed a dark hallway she thought she caught a glimpse of the beautiful Chloe, who disappeared almost as soon as she was seen. Chloe had been hovering there, Jessica realized, as disconsolate-looking as she imagined herself to be.

The house seemed in a turmoil the next few days, tending to the needs of the guests who stayed on and returning the ballroom to its former order and closing it firmly until the next celebration. After the last plantation master and his lady had departed, Miranda made ready to leave. Trunks of her clothing were brought down the stairs and stacked on the overhead rack of her elaborate carriage. Her coachman and groom were recalled from the stables where they had been put to work during their mistress's visit. Early in the morning the entire family assembled outside to see her off. Jessica stood with Jenny and Charlie, Eleanor with Charles, and in the background Julia and Cicero. The carriage was filled to bursting with Miranda's entourage—the little black children she had brought, some she was taking from her grandson's household, and two grown maidservants. Charles lifted his grandmother off her feet, kissed her soundly, and deposited her inside the coach. The children had quickly scrambled from her place and now sat anxiously around her pointed slippers.

Miranda looked out the window.

"Come here, Jessica," she called imperiously.

Surprised, Jessica approached the coach.

The old woman spoke quietly.

"You have been a good presence here, child."

"Thank you, ma'am."

"No. It is not for you to thank. As a token of appreciation, I'll give you one bit of advice–follow your own destiny."

Jessica was puzzled.

"To search for my husband?"

Miranda sighed.

"To do what you must," she snapped.

She pressed a ring of rubies and pearls into Jessica's hand and impatiently waved away her protests. She waved again to the assemblage, advised Jessica to stand clear of the horses, and gave her driver the order to begin their journey.

* * *

Jessica began a new campaign of writing to various newspapers in the United States, imploring them to carry stories about Jason and how he had disappeared. In her free time in the afternoons, and more frequently before she prepared for bed, she worked at her table penning descriptions of her husband. She addressed them to the newspapers of the South, published in Virginia and the Carolinas and Tennessee, she had seen in Charles' library. In London a friend had suggested she contact William Cullen Bryant, editor of *The New York Evening Post,* an influential publication in the North, and Jessica wrote Mr. Bryant a long letter. She had the names of editors of periodicals in Philadelphia and Washington and Boston, and she worked up appeals to them, too. It would take time, she knew, for replies, but it made her feel better to be doing something positive about Jason.

Charles raised a quizzical eyebrow at the many envelopes she gave him for the mail coach, but he promised to see to their posting. He looked at her ink-stained fingers one afternoon, as she handed the correspondence to him, and sent Cicero to fetch her a small bowl of milk–to soak the ink out, Charles told her gravely.

Charles seemed very preoccupied with the cotton yield. Many evenings after dinner he would disappear into his small office to go over his records, he said, and Eleanor would retire to her room and Jessica to hers. Sometimes Eleanor begged off coming to meals and Jessica and Charles dined alone, with Cicero and Joseph in attendance. Charles talked mostly of the crop, and Jessica learned more about cotton and its importance to the economy of the South. He seemed to want to educate her in the needs of the Southerners.

"You only learned about cotton from the factor," he said, not paying attention to the fact that she winced. "Only after the planting and the harvesting and the cleaning and the baling . . ."

Most of his neighbors, he told her, planted tobacco as the main crop. His father had, too. And for some years he also planted tobacco, as she already knew. But it was exhausting the soil. This was a serious problem. Some growers in the Tidewater were trying wheat. And he had decided, but for the few acres of tobacco she had seen for home use and exchange needs, to try his luck with cotton. Demand for cotton had replaced the demand for flax, he said, to a large extent throughout the world, and with the building of all the mills . . . he seemed to become excited thinking of the mechanization in the North and the huge supplies of cotton the mills would need. Jessica thought again of Jason and his desire to see more cotton goods manufactured in the States. But she turned back to Charles and his problems with the land.

"Won't you exhaust the soil with cotton, too?" she asked.

"We use guano," he said, "four hundred fifty pounds per acre, very expensive. But . . ."

"But then you don't have labor costs," she said tartly.

He took her up on that and lectured her on slavery. Slaves were not free—they represented considerable capital investment. He was a good slavemaster, he declared, well, better than most. He had done away with the overseer and the overseer's general abuses and saw to the management of the plantation himself. "And don't forget," he said severely, "I went to college in the North; I *saw* the conditions of the workingman there. They don't have the *security* of the slaves I keep here."

"Security!" she said incredulously.

"Yes. I take good care of mine. It's the natural order of things—there must be masters and slaves."

"The curse of Ham? I don't believe that."

"Every thousand acres of plantation must have a hundred hands."

"A hundred hands of slaves?"

"Slaves. But I told you that when we rode around the fields."

She wanted to argue with him about the immorality of the slave system but thought better of it. She ventured to speak on the inefficiency of it—a competent English servant could do the work of many house slaves combined; that had been seen with her own eyes back home. She was sure the incentive of a wage would increase productivity.

He countered that a master kept his slaves during hard times while white workingmen in the North—everywhere through the world—lost employment and must fend for themselves. Sometimes, he conceded, he could lease slaves out to other farmers who needed more help than they had themselves, but this only happened in good times when everything was at its peak and he, too, needed every hand on his own plantation. There were recurrent times of depressed economy in this New World, he sighed, most recently the panic of 1837. They were still recovering from that difficult period. Martin Van Buren—the president, he explained to her—was no help at all. "We were better off with Jackson, before him. Perhaps the advent of the steamboat and the railroad—that Tom Thumb steam locomotive!—will eventually help keep the South solvent. The German settlers in the Piedmont area built the iron furnaces. A railroad system is bound to come to Virginia. But development is slow, and the planters still have to resort to the rivers and wagontrails for movement of supplies and crops. We *need* to take care of our slaves," he said earnestly. "A prime buck hand brings a sizable sum in the market. That's part of our capital," he informed her.

"Very good," she said sarcastically.

"And women! Why, sometimes a man will pay as much as twenty-five hundred dollars for a beautiful quadroon."

That upset her. He had told her that before, but she minded it even more the second time.

"Disgraceful!" she cried, rushing out of the room, but not before she saw that he had divined her thinking and that his cheeks had flushed.

Another night they continued the discussion. He seemed eager to tell her how much difficulty the owners had with slaves. "Can't trust them with good tools, they break them," he said. She had seen that herself. "And if you're not careful, they will abuse the animals. Why, some plantations," he went on, "won't keep horses, only mules, because horses can't stand the mistreatment that mules will take."

He noted her horrified expression.

"My horses are treated well here," he said. "We tolerate no cruelty to beasts. And the slaves are treated well, too. They have a cabin as church and one of the hands is a minister, when he's not in the fields. Maybe one Sunday you would like to attend. You will be fascinated. They speak in tongues you will not understand and they twist and jerk and flop around. Sometimes," he went on, "we give a few of them at a time passes to attend a church in town. They can sit in the rear and hear the ordained white preacher. We like them to go because of our favorite sermon, 'Servants, obey your masters.' " He smiled sardonically at Jessica. "Or at a black church. We're sure they'll come back. At four o'clock in the afternoon a bell is rung to warn them to be out of town in ten minutes. And they know full well they had better heed the signal. . . . And at Christmas they come to the veranda of the big house and we give them presents. With dignity. We don't have them scramble for pennies, as some do. We permit them to have dances sometimes in the barn and there is whiskey for refreshment. You think we like to get them drunk, don't you? Yes, we do! Good for reproduction . . . and increasing our stock. . . . Oh, you're so righteous!" he flung at her.

She said nothing this time.

"Some of them even make some money," he went on relentlessly. "On Sundays slaves are allowed to fish and they keep their catch, and what they don't eat they may sell to us or to other folk. And we even allow them to keep a communal garden patch. No cotton permitted, of course; we don't want competition on our own doorstep," he said grimly. "Squash, peanuts—besides what we import—okra, melons, any kind of vegetables they want. Same privilege. Eat it themselves or trade or sell it to other 'nigras'—or poor whites, too, for that matter. . . . See, it isn't so bad. Your husband should have taken better note . . ."

"My husband?" she said with alarm.

"You can't talk antislavery in these parts," he said, even grimmer than before. "You only invite trouble—"

"Did he . . . ?"

"You cannot—with impunity—destroy a system that has worked well for a long, long time."

"Did the other planters know about his . . . his feelings?"

He refused to answer this directly but lectured her with increasing seriousness.

"The agricultural system here dictates our emotions. Some excitable individuals are incited to lawless activities."

She was silent, not knowing whether she was interpreting him correctly.

"We've tried to help ourselves in keeping the land fertile," he continued. "My father was active in the Albemarle Agricultural Society. In 1820 he and his colleagues demanded that an agricultural professorship be established at the University of Virginia and that steps be taken to assist the planters and farmers."

"And?"

He shrugged.

"Not much happened. In 1827, when I was a boy, a Virginia argricultural convention petitioned our state legislature for grants-in-aid and an appropriation of a thousand dollars for an advisory board of agriculture. We won. The board would be established to gather information and give instruction in the fields. But—" he said, silencing Jessica's approval—"it really didn't mean anything. A few years after the board finally was established, the legislature refused to appropriate funds other than the three-dollar traveling fee for each board member. Naturally the board fell apart. No one felt he could afford the time away from home and the expense. We have a few agricultural societies. We have a simple solution to soil exhaustion when we don't have the money for soil enrichments. We're slave wealthy. We just abandon the fields and have the slaves dig new ones."

He said this so savagely that Jessica could only stare at him.

They stayed at the dining-room table many nights, when Eleanor was not with them, long after Cicero and Joseph had cleared and gone off to the kitchen cabin. Charles seemed to like to talk to Jessica, if only to disturb her.

"Sometimes," he said, "Southern men have warmer feelings for their mammies than for their mothers. Do you know what that can do to a man? Why it often makes a woman of color so much more attractive to him than a white one?"

Jessica covered her face with her hands. She had been listening each night, against her will, for his footsteps—if they came, signifying his sleeping with Eleanor, and if they did not, his going to Chloe. Against her will she trembled. If he came to Eleanor, it was little comfort, despite her guilt. If he went to Chloe, waves of jealousy were so overwhelming they could not be checked. She felt she was approaching an abyss, attended by terrifying beckoning adversaries. Her instinct was to fling herself into it.

"When he grows up he plays with pickaninnies and it is all fine and good. And suddenly it is forbidden. His parents don't even have to tell him. It's in the air. He absorbs it in his bones. As the bones grow so do the prohibitions. All except one—and every white male knows it."

Her hands pressed more tightly against her cheeks. She wanted to tell him Eleanor had already enlightened her. But she couldn't.

"You really don't understand how it is here, Miz Priss. Outsiders come and they do not really know what they see. They only condemn. . . . or are jealous. . . ."

"Don't," she begged.

"You're like your husband—both reformers."

"Please."

"It will take a miracle," he sighed. "Or a bloodbath."

She took her hands away from her face now and tried to distract him.

"You've had some uprisings?"

"You'll be glad to hear that we have actually had rebellions." He smiled, thin-lipped, at her. "The Nat Turner insurrection, not long ago in '31. We had an uprising in Virginia as early as the seventeenth century, 1691 in fact, my neighbors have impressed that date forever in my mind. It was suppressed, of course, like all the others, brutally you would say, but for self-survival we would say. Those who weren't hanged or flogged to death were sold into the deep, deep South—the turpentine plantations or other godforsaken lands where they were worked and half-starved until they died. . . . Don't shudder, dear Jessica; these are the facts of life. Then there were the Island revolts—the carnage in San Domingo and other Caribbean territories. The French Jacobins helped the slaves of San Domingo. Your father would have loved that! And the slaughter that followed."

"He would not have liked the slaughter!" she said hotly.

"Rebellion and slaughter go together. . . . Your husband should have known that."

"No, no, no!" She rose from the table. "He is not slaughtered! He is still alive!"

"Perhaps. And perhaps not," he said cynically.

"Do you know for a fact . . . ?" she asked fearfully.

"No," he said slowly, "not for a fact."

"Well, then . . ."

"Shall I go on? Shall I tell you of other uprisings and repressions? I can go on. . . ."

"No, it's not necessary. I know what you're trying to tell me of retaliation."

"For your own good."

"Spare me that," she said sarcastically.

"You don't know," he said, reverting to his earlier theme, "what it means to suckle at a substitute colored mother's breast, even if it leaves only an unconscious memory—perhaps a dream. And the later days in her arms, or balanced on her hip carried around, or dusky hands bathing you soft on your body, soothing your bruises, singing to you. . . . You don't know. . . ."

Usually a full day of teaching, both in the classroom and in the kitchen house, taking walks with Eleanor to stimulate her appetite for food and keep her from her bottle—which did not seem so important to Eleanor now—and the other routines of the day made Jessica sleep soundly at night. After the last discussion with Charles she tossed and turned in her bed. Sometimes she slept fitfully, but vivid pictures of dark women and white men entwined in circles rolled like hoops behind her eyelids. Sometimes the circle opened and a mammy clasped a beautiful baby to her breast; then the mammy changed to a white woman, frighteningly familiar, then formed a circle again. There in the circle appeared Jason. Another figure in the circle, a woman; what was her name, was it herself? She was everywhere. She broke the chain and extended arms out of it to reach for Jason, but he eluded them and the circle formed whole again. And there was Charles; he was everywhere, and a white woman suckled a sepia baby at her breast, and then the baby changed color and the woman did too, and Jessica saw herself clearly this time, crying because she was out of the circle now and could not get back in.

Her crying woke her up.

The full moon lit her room brightly and she sat in the chair by the open window hoping the air would clear her mind. But the air was flower-perfumed and heavy, and she slipped from chair to rocker thinking the rocking would lull her. Distress remained like a heavy load upon her chest. She walked to the pitcher and poured water into the basin and laved her wrists and touched water to her cheeks and lips. She thought she might light a candle and walk down the stairs to the dining room where she imagined she had left her fan. A beautiful fan, originally from the Orient but brought to her from France, she thought irrelevantly, that snapped pleated paper open into a typically lovely garden scene with footbridge over a little brook. But if she lit the candle and went downstairs, the undercurrent of fear gnawed at her, she might not only find her fan and Charles, too; she no doubt would come upon Chloe as well. How could *she*, that base woman, Chloe, do that to Eleanor!

Visions of Chloe and Charles as teenagers walking hand in hand over wooded pathways, sinking down together on lichen-covered slopes. . . . Chloe standing stricken when Charles went off to Yale. . . . Chloe and her child. Chloe banished before Charles returned with Eleanor. . . . Poor Chloe.

Poor everybody, Jessica thought, abandoning the idea of retrieving the fan, or going below. She sat rocking beside the open window, watching the black of the sky change to navy blue and then to the paler shades, fading away the stars. She listened to the birdsong and marveled at the cheer of the world when she was so sad. Slowly she dressed for breakfast, trying to hide the circles under her eyes with some rice powder she had brought from home.

She had come especially early from the illegal morning class, cutting it short, to the boys' dismay. Julia had told Jessica that heavy food supplies were due to be delivered from the fields and it was better that a houseguest not be in the kitchen.

As it was still too early for her breakfast tray, Jessica wanted to be outside; she liked the grounds when the sun had just risen. She breathed the fresh air deeply, trying to distinguish its blend of special scents. The dew wet her slippers, but she did not care—she just wriggled her toes against the damp. Light seemed to dispel the despair of the nighttime hours.

With delight, she felt the quickening beat of the new day. Birds were particularly active now. Someone—she wondered who—had created bird stations throughout the gardens, and she watched as cardinals and mockingbirds and finches and bluejays fed on the seeds. There—she even saw a pair of parakeets—the bright yellow-orange of their feathers flashing against the green of the shrubbery. She saw the fighting for place and a turn at the trays, how the smallest birds waited on the ground for the kernels to drop, when they would seize them. The bluejays were given a wide berth even by the cardinals. Then her eyes were diverted by a brilliant flash of red as scarlet tanagers swept overhead in flight. She saw more the color than the form.

As she walked to the rose garden she could hear far off the rumble of the water wagons coming from the well. The water-wagon attendants would bring huge kegs to Julia in the kitchen house and then deposit even more in the pantry off the dining hall. In her mind's eye she could see the way the full barrels were substituted for the empty ones, how the depleted drums were tossed into the wagon for refilling for the next day. She had learned slowly but surely the operation of this huge plantation.

A formal rose garden stretched behind the back veranda. It was a place she especially enjoyed, enchanted by the beauty and serenity she found there. The red rose predominated but in great variety, in every color ranging from a blushing white through gradations of pink through scarlet and an almost purplish black. The bushes were planted in uniform rows and stone benches had been placed where the paths were the broadest. Sometimes she liked to rest on the benches and feel she was in a room with walls of blossoms. A house of flowers. Just for her. She smiled at herself. The fragrance was almost overwhelming. It seemed to whirl about her nostrils, into her mouth. She could almost taste it.

She was so at peace, finally, sitting there, that she did not know what she was thinking about when she was roused by a movement two aisles away. Squirrels and rabbits were abundant about the place—and she knew the oppossums and raccoons and muskrats came out at night—but this shaking of rose plants was too energetic to be caused by a small creature. She stood to see what it was, peering over a bush in front of her, carefully avoiding the thorns. The head of the other person—for person it was—lifted at the same time and she found herself looking beyond the separation into the surprised and pleased eyes of Charles.

"Well," he called, "good morning! You are an early riser!"

"Yes," she said happily, glad that he was here.

She walked around the rows to join him. He was so unexpected a sight, with his full cotton shirtsleeves rolled up, shears in hand, and straw basket at his feet, another Charles she had not met before.

"A gardener?"

"Of sorts . . . at times . . . very few times . . . not enough. . . . A cutter is all, really."

She saw the flowers in the basket.

"For the house," he explained. "For Eleanor to arrange later, if she will . . . if she does not forget."

"Oh, I could help . . ." And then she stopped, blushing.

"I'll leave them in the keeping room for Cicero."

"Yes. Then either Eleanor or I . . ."

"They would benefit from your touch."

"Oh, well. . . ."

"Your touch," he said softly. "Your hand in mine when we danced. . . ."

She shivered.

"You are cold?" he asked. "Perhaps you should have a shawl against the morning air."

"No . . ."

"Would you help me?" he said carefully. "It would save time–and effort–it you would hold the basket. As I cut I can place the roses–"

"Of course."

He talked casually about the types of roses grown in the garden. Some cuttings his grandmother had brought from Maryland, some plants he had sent for from England.

"Beautiful," she kept murmuring. Then, "I thought you left early for the fields."

"Usually," he said. "Today I am waiting for a buyer; he should be in my office in about an hour."

"I see."

He went on cutting and seemed to be concentrating on the job at hand.

"Not many things can keep me here in the morning," he said after a long period of silence.

"There is so much work to do."

"Yes. I don't permit myself many distractions from the fields—except perhaps one. . . ."

"Business?" A distraction. Her instinct was to say *me? Do you mean me?*

"Oh, business!" he scoffed.

She knew what he meant. She could feel it crackling in the space that surrounded them. They were strongly attracted to one another, there was no denying that. She did not know whether she would deny it if she could. But, she thought grimly, it must stay only attraction.

"Jessica . . . would you come to me?" he said quietly, examining the petals of a rose he held.

Her cheeks blazed.

"How would you find the time!" she lashed out, her sarcasm confounding her.

"That is unkind. Not like you, Jessica."

"I'm sorry," she murmured.

"I long for you, Jessica. . . ."

"I mean nothing to you."

This time he was really wounded. He put down the shears, reached for her shoulders, and then shook her.

"Please!" she gasped, flowers flying from the tossed basket, her head against his shoulder when he stopped.

He gathered her closely to him.

"Jessica . . . You are very special to me . . ."

"No." When she wanted to say *yes.* "I could not . . . she is my cousin!"

"Jessica . . ."

His arms around her were warming and good, but she shook them off.

"No!"

"Would you give me any hope?"

"No."

"Our talks together. Your caring for my children. Our meals together. Your closeness—don't you see?"

"No."

"Can you not imagine what it is doing to me?" he said bitterly.

"I'm sorry, Charles. Truly."

"You'll change your mind," he said firmly.

His tone angered her.

"No!" she cried. "She is my cousin! I love her, too!"

With that, she fled, almost tripping over the skirt of her gown, not caring that the branches caught it, that she could hear the tearing. She ran for the house.

He did not follow.

She did not know why she went to the rose garden again that night. Or else she would not admit it. Charles had made his excuses and she was alone. She did not know where he went and she told herself she should not care—Chloe, Eleanor, it was really not her concern. Or at least it should not be. A walk would calm her. She had been warned, early upon her arrival, not to wander alone after dark. Since the rose garden was almost an extension of the manor itself, the interdiction would not apply here.

At night the rose perfume was even stronger than in daylight. It was clear and the moon had risen. A slight breeze ruffled the foliage. The quiet seemed a mask; there were sounds trying to get out—the low tap of a fallen leaf, a night creature slithering through the grass, tree toads and cicadas and crickets vibrating, crescendoing into the hoot of an owl.

She walked along the rows, coming back to the bench she had sat upon earlier in the day. Why, she thought, had she added the word *too* when she told him she loved Eleanor? Would he consider that an admission of her feeling for him? He must not. He must see it to mean that she loved Eleanor as *he* did *too*. He must see that; he surely must.

And what he said—their proximity, their sharing of talk, meals, caring for his children—well, it was just being there, so convenient, so close. These sparks flew up all the time between people thrown together. It was inevitable. The sparks could ignite—and consume.

Their proximity—it affected her too. Did he think of that? A small inner voice told her that likely he did. It made her so vulnerable, she groaned. It was not to her advantage to be here, husbandless, so close to this exciting man whose wife had abdicated out of misery. It really was a tangled web, and she was caught in it.

She was too restless to sit for long, and she roused herself, seeking out the rose bush where Charles had cut the flowers. She stood before it thinking idly how carefully he had selected the ones he would take and the ones he would leave, not to disturb the balance of the branches. In the basket he already had the different colors he wanted from the other bushes. She remembered the centerpiece on the dining-room table this evening. Had Eleanor fixed the flowers? Or Cicero? Or Joseph? She had stared at it, perhaps too long, and Charles had caught her eye. It seemed to please him that she had lingered on the arrangement.

She sighed. And then she saw him. As if she stood outside herself, another Jessica noted that there was no feeling of surprise that he was here. It was as if he were expected. He stood there silently, almost majestic in his tallness, the moon caught in the silver of his hair, reflecting off his high cheekbones, the long fine eyes lit up by moonbeams or some incandescence fired from within.

"I knew you would be here," he said quietly.

She stiffened.

"How could you be so sure!"

"I knew."

"I should not have come."

"Yes, it was right that you should."

"And so expected," she said meanly, flashing out at his self-assurance.

"Let us sit down for a while and talk."

She permitted him to lead her to the bench. It was pleasantly cool.

"I thought you were gone for the night."

"No," he said evenly. "I had some letters to write. You know the mail post comes tomorrow?"

"I have a packet ready to go."

"To your mother?"

"Letters," she said obstinately.

"Good."

He still wore his dinner jacket. His black-sleeved arm touched her own.

"We did not finish it, Jessica," he said.

"Finish what?"

"You know very well. What we were discussing this morning."

"There's nothing to discuss."

"There's everything to discuss.

"It mustn't be."

"It *has* to be."

"Do you get everything you wish?"

"Usually," he said.

"Oh?"

"If I want it enough, I do."

"There must be change sometime."

"I do want you very much, Jessica."

"For the moment."

"We're talking at cross-purposes."

"I have no purpose here, other than to fulfill my obligations—the children. . . ."

"Come now, Jessica. We're not talking of them at all now."

She stood up and he rose with her.

"We must resolve this thing," he told her.

"You must simply stop."

"How can I?" he said hoarsely, reaching for her. "I can't think of anything—anyone—else."

She was about to say something, but he kissed away her protest, tenderly at first, but then hard and long, his tongue probing at her tightly clamped teeth. If she thought about the pressure of his lips and the softness and then hardness of his embrace, she would surely melt, lose all her resolve. Again, as this morning, she broke free of his strong hold on her.

"Oh!" she gasped. "It's impossible."

"Do you not feel as I do? That it is wonderful between us? That it is all there waiting for us? To take, Jessica?"

"You have no right . . . I have no right . . ."

"You are such a righteous woman," he mocked.

Stung, she said, "And you are a wicked man." She did not really believe it.

"No," he said, knowing that she did not believe it. "We are just human, Jessica." He gently pulled at her hand. "Come with me . . . and let me prove to you how human, and feeling, we are."

She drew away.

"I cannot."

"You must put away your reservations."

"I cannot."

"Don't you know what you are doing to me? Don't you know how overwrought you make me?"

"You have your outlets," she said resentfully. "I am just a woman—with all the limitations, restrictions . . ."

"Not *just*—"

She wanted him to talk about love. He did not.

He reached for her again and held her so tightly she could not move away. He kissed her passionately again, their teeth grinding against one another until hers gave way and his tongue, this time swollen, was inside her mouth, probing and flicking and rousing her fully.

"Please," she groaned.

"You cannot tell me now," he said thickly, "that you don't want me."

She could not talk for a minute.

"No, I won't tell you that."

"Then, will you come with me tonight to a private place I have?"

"If we *try*, we can overcome this . . ."

He laughed wryly.

"Don't you *know* about men?"

"With will power and—"

"And what?" he said savagely. "Cruelty?"

"No!"

"What then? Is not denial cruelty?"

"I must have time to think."

"You have had time."

"Charles . . ."

"You came here, Jessica."

"Yes."

"You came here, looking for me, just as I came looking for you."

"Yes . . ."

He reached out his arms but she stepped back, shaking her head. She wanted him, very much, and his urgency and the good feel of him struck and resonated against the central nerves of her being, of her soul, her brain, her body, whatever a woman was—but still in her head were all the reasons why she must not do this thing, loving him. He must have seen the anguish, perhaps the rejection, in her eyes, in the tightening of her frame, for flushed and miserable, he flung himself away from her and this time it was he who left the rose garden first, stumbling off into the darkness.

Eleanor was not at dinner again the next evening. The meal was cleared, the children made their appearance and were taken back to their nursery, and Joseph and Cicero left. Jessica could not bear a repetition of the night before. She rose, bringing an expression of surprise and some pain to Charles' face. He rose, too, in automatic response to his training, and bent to kiss her hand goodnight. Listlessly she let him take it, but then he would not let her fingers go. He pulled her gently toward him, and his arms encircled her shoulders.

"I think I'm in love with you," he whispered, "and have been ever since you stepped out of the carriage that first day."

She could only look at him silently, her eyes large and luminous.

He kissed her deeply and long; she felt he was drawing her out of herself and into his mouth, his body. She leaned against him, trembling.

"No, no, no."

"Yes, yes, yes," he said, kissing her again and again. She held back at first, then responded passionately.

He led her out of the room into the hallway. Mindlessly she

followed him, lit by pleasure and passion, and only once half-listening for a soft rustle of a skirt behind the back stairwell. She was past caring for anything but the present moment and the moments to come, and she followed him gladly to his office in the front of the house. She saw vaguely the familiar welter of ledgers and books and papers flowing over his desk, and then, as he led her to an almost-hidden door in the back of the room, she knew before it opened that it would lead to a space of privacy and comfort.

"I've shared this with no one before," he assured her. "This has always been my retreat, my own special place."

He kissed the top of her bosom above the bodice of her dress and then slowly began to undo the ribbons and laces. Jessica's dreamlike lethargy began to leave her. She stirred in his arms and pulled herself reluctantly away.

"I shouldn't have come," she said unhappily. "It won't work, Charles."

"It will."

"It would give us pleasure for the moment. . . ."

"For more than a moment." He drew her close again, but she resisted.

". . . but it would only add to the misery of the house."

"Jessica . . ."

"Eleanor's my cousin, my kinswoman . . ."

"She need not know. . . . I . . ."

"But I would." She could not bring herself to mention Chloe.

"You want me just as I want you," he said firmly. She was silent. "Of course you do. Believe me, you will do Eleanor no harm. You have seen the way she is, and I love you all the more for what you have done for her." He lifted her chin so that she looked directly into his eyes. "You are not keeping me from her tonight. . . . I swear it!"

He pulled her close to him again and held her tightly, stilling her protests with his mouth, the deep kissing drawing her outside herself once more. She felt weightless. Charles lifted her in his arms and carried her to the bed, where he finished undressing her and stripped himself of clothes. At first they exulted in the vision of their nakedness. They made love. She lost all sense of thought about the act, she became pure feeling . . . a creature lost in responsive chords. Her need was urgent; and she strained to his thrust; he accommodated her until they found their mutual rhythm, and it was good, so very good. He found her most sensitive areas and played upon these until it was almost more than she could bear. She held him tightly as if she might fall away from him. She would spin off the bed and be whirled away into far-off regions of infinite space. Oh my love, she heard herself murmur over and over . . . and the feeling of surprise that intruded itself into her consciousness–no, Jason was her love, her own true love, but . . . I've been so lonely until you came, she heard him say, no one really to talk to, no one to understand. Now she whirled away. She could not think what the words meant: *oh my love* and *I've been so lonely until you came.* Not thinking, she could only feel now; nothing mental, only physical now. Later she might think . . .

They rested but her hunger excited him and they began again and the world continued to spin. She clung fiercely to him. He counted out the beauties of her body and went on to murmur that she was all he had hoped of her, and she felt the long lean weight of him upon her and its excitement and comfort. It was so long since she had been with her husband, and the contact with the body of a man felt so good, so very good, to her. She had missed this touching almost as much as actual fulfillment. But fulfillment was everything. She convulsed joyfully with him.

Chapter Five

For the next two weeks, Jessica floated rather than walked; she looked inward and seemed to be listening to the tides of her body; when anyone but Charles spoke to her she seemed to be coming back from a long way. "You're not paying attention!" Charlie protested in class. "Did we do something *wrong?*" "No, no, no!" she hastened to reassure him, "it's just that I . . . ." "Am woolgathering," Jenny said sharply, sounding like her grandmother.

She was surrounded by a soft comforting quilt that buffered her from the demands of the world . . . but not her own needs and Charles'. She sometimes thought it was as if his arms were warmly wrapped around her all the time they were apart.

She went over and over again in her thoughts what he had said to her the night before, or the night before that, and what he might whisper the next time they came together in their lovemaking. She dallied over her toilette. She bathed herself sensuously in the tin bathing trough they had brought to her soon after her arrival, touching herself here and there, down the length of her arms and legs, down her chest and her stomach and between her thighs, down her back and her buttocks, remembering the fervent words he had said in praise of her as he touched her here, there, everywhere.

"Miz Jessica, are you all right?" Billy asked her anxiously in the kitchen. "What . . . what? . . . oh, yes, Billy, I just lost my place is all . . . Sorry. . . ."

"Jessie, where in the world *are* you!" Eleanor laughed—was it coolly, Jessica wondered, then brushed the pang aside.

"Oh, just thinking . . . thinking. . . ."

It was a form of madness, love, if it *was* love that enveloped her. It seemed to her that her desire for Jason had had more reason behind it, the firmer base, or had she really not felt then the same way she did at this time? She pushed aside the intrusive idea. It had no place here; it was disloyal to Jason and to Charles. This was a thing of beauty, her own and Charles'; no one else had a place in it. No one but they themselves, she and Charles, she told herself firmly.

The heaviness of spirit she had had to dispel each morning after Jason was gone lifted from her. She awoke in her chamber, eager and expectant of the day. And of what it could, would bring.

Her body did not tire. She seemed to need less sleep. And though she drifted off into reverie, perhaps little waking catnaps of daydream, her eyes were more receptive. The world around her seemed ever more beautiful. She looked more carefully at the flowers, examined their petals, the intricacies and miraculous folds of the buds; she followed the birdflight, the song of the warbler. The colors of the earth became more varied, the trees and the grass showing green in every gradation.

"I will take you to a special place," Charles whispered to her when they met as the house silenced in the afternoon siesta. "We shall ride. . . . It will be as if I am showing you the fields and crops once again."

Then, after a proper walking gait, he set their mounts to a canter until they had skirted the cultivated ground. He tethered their horses and helped her down.

"Come," he said, still holding her hand and propelling her forward. "I want you to see. . . ."

It was quiet and cool, away from the glare of the summer sun, in the woods. Toadstools and jack-in-the-pulpits grew in the narrow path they followed, and looking downward to avoid stepping on fungi and wildflowers, she saw the droppings of deer. Their passage startled an animal, a doe she thought, and there was the quick brush of large wings, perhaps an owl disturbed from sleep. Squirrels scolded them in nervous chatter, tails upright in bushy fright. The path became ever more overgrown, and the tangling of foliage turned the blue sky green.

"Here," he said.

He parted long stands of rhododendron and they stepped over, inside and past them.

She had never seen a tree as huge. It must have grown for centuries. Its branches, which ended as close to the heavens as she could imagine, extended in offshoots almost to the ground. Again Charles parted branches and, as he led her still by the hand, they entered into a dim green-shimmering bower. No underbrush grew here; the shade of the thick leaves and the spread of massive roots had nourished nothing but soft velvet moss.

"It's like a house," she murmured.

"Yes," he said, "I discovered it when I was only eight, and it was my very own."

"Your very own?" There was a note in her voice she wanted to control.

"Yes," he said. "My escape, when the big house grew too much . . . too heavy. . . ."

"Yes," she said.

"As it does at times for every child," he finished.

"Yes."

He drew her into its very center, against the gnarled trunk, where its ceiling of branches was highest. Listen, he said, and you will hear the song of the forest. And she kept still, dropping to the ground beside him. She heard the insects and birds and the crack of dead wood breaking somewhere in the distance, a natural shedding, the drumming of a woodpecker, a tree toad pulsating in the heat. If she strained perhaps she would hear an acorn dropping, pine needles with a muted *s*-sound falling from their frond, a fern dancing in a current of air.

"My very own place," he said, "a refuge of my own. See, no manmade axe marks, no gouging of knives in bark. My very own natural tent . . . no one but Indians, many years ago before the settlers came, ever venturing in this space."

Chloe? she thought . . . with Chloe? . . . but she banished the name and the picture it drew.

She listened more intently to the song of the forest. To Charles' song as he intoned the joy of discovery of this hideaway, the wonder and joy of a child, then the wonder and joy of the man, a man with his woman, a man with his woman and with their passion.

It could never have been like this for him before, she willed. Never. He could never have been so wild, so consuming. His body could never have been so hot, burning female flesh; it could not have been.

But it was now and it was beautiful. "My dear," he whispered, "in my very own tent, all my own all my **own** . . . my own dear, dear love. . . ."

"I've never seen you look so well," Eleanor said, but not in compliment, Jessica could sense.

"It—agrees with me—the climate here—this country, the South . . ."

"It usually dries the skin," Eleanor said acidly. "You have no right to be so radiant."

"I am not yet long gone from the nurturing English air."

"English air? You've adapted very well . . . and very rapidly, I would say."

"Yes . . ."

"And nurturing?"

"The children are doing very well, don't you really think so?" Jessica said firmly. "The children, they've come a long way."

"Yes," Eleanor said at length, "they have. At least I have that to thank you for, Jessica, and I do."

They stared at one another for a time and neither dropped her eyes.

"And I am getting better, too," Eleanor said finally. "Stronger . . . stronger . . . Jess . . ."

"Children," Jessica said to Charles one night, as they lay together, arms and legs entwined. "I'm afraid, Charles, of having a child."

"A child? You're—not?"

"I don't know—yet. I am afraid."

"I would take care of the child—and of you, Jessica. I would, I would, you know that."

"I know that. . . . In different circumstances, I would want your child, but for us it would be too . . . too complicated . . ."

"I would never abandon you."

"But . . ."

"I would see to your needs."

"But you could not have us here in this house." *I am not Chloe,* she thought sadly. But she would not put that into spoken words.

"I would establish you in another," he said quickly.

"No, no, no," she said in sudden agitation. "We must be careful . . ."

"It's rather late . . ."

"Yes," she said. "I should have thought." I. I. He was not the type of man to scatter—she thought of the Biblical phrase—to scatter his seed on the ground. Her heart leapt to her throat, it seemed. In his passion, in his need, there was no staying him.

"You did not have a child . . . with *him,*" he said. "Perhaps you are not fertile." She did not reply. "I am a fertile man," he said proudly. "You do not have . . . a device . . . like some of the French women are rumored to have. . . ."

"Not only the *demi-mondaine,*" she cried more sharply than she would have thought possible. "Even the English women of the Court. . . ."

"Ah, Jessica, do not be cross. . . ."

* * *

Sometimes she managed to be on the entrance steps of the manor when he came from his inspection of the fields. She would watch him ride up the drive, seated so easily and so well upon his horse, held to a moderate gait. A stablehand would run out to take the reins, Charles would pat the stallion's mane—the sight pleased Jessica greatly, and a fleeting memory would stir, Charles stroking her long, tousled hair, his fingers twined in the strands—and then he would stand in the saddle, swing one long leg over the horse's rump, and dismount, refusing the groom's assistance. Then he would see her and his eyes would begin to sparkle.

"Ah, good afternoon, Miz Jessica," he would say formally, for the benefit of the groom and the little black children who had come scurrying at the sound of the horse's hooves. But she could hear the mocking lilt in his voice. "Nice day, isn't it?"

"Very nice," she would answer. "Very, very nice." Especially now that she could have this little visit.

"You are looking very well. Evidently the sultry weather is not too much for you?"

"No," she murmured.

She was feeling beautiful. It took a man's love and admiration to make real and reinforce the compliments she had gathered along the way from family and friends. In their times together Charles whispered of the curve of her cheek, the softness of her bosom, the firmness of her thighs, the sweep of her neck. She could not have enough of his praise and he was generous. It carried over into her walk—the way she held her head, higher. It made her features glowing, her movements languorous.

"And did you have a good day?"

"Yes."

Cicero would hover in the hall to announce luncheon in half an hour, and they would part with formal bows to prepare for it.

One night at dinner Charles announced that he wanted to take Charlie on a hike the following afternoon, when he returned from the fields. There would be a picnic lunch. Did Teacher want to come along? he asked, turning to her for once during the extended meal. She could provide another botany lesson. Charlie had told him about the little field trips they had taken and how he had enjoyed them so much.

Jessica flushed and nodded with pleasure.

"Eleanor?"

Eleanor put down her fork.

"What?" she said coolly. "Walk in the hot sun, at that time of day? You are both mad."

"Not really," he said equably. "We'll find a shady spot for our refreshment; by then we'll have taken to the woods."

"Pah! All those crawly things."

"Well, we'll bring you violets," he promised his wife.

"Why not forget-me-nots?"

"We'll try to find them," he said.

Jessica cast down her eyes.

Charlie was delighted about the unexpected outing. He could not wait for class to end. Jenny was petulant that she was not invited. Aletha looked sad but resigned.

"It will be a difficult and long walk," Jessica explained. "You must be at least as big as Charlie, in order to manage it."

Charlie puffed out his chest.

She asked Charlie to leave his silk pongee jacket at home and asked whether he had any cotton work breeches. He shook his head dejectedly; he was not permitted to wear them. They were only for the slave pickaninnies. "Then your riding pants," she said firmly. "They are fitted closely at the ankles and will not be caught by roots and underbrush and pebbles."

"Your skirts will," he said.

"Yes," she agreed regretfully. "I wish I could wear a pair of breeches."

They gaped at her.

"A teacher would not do that!" Charlie finally said.

"No. She would not." Then she reassured him. "I would not, Charlie."

She temporarily basted the skirt of her riding dress an inch or two above her ankles, hoping the household would not notice, and wore a wide straw bonnet, tied under chin with a large bow, as proper dress and protection from the sun. Charles nodded approvingly as she and Charlie joined him outside. "All ready, I can see," he said. Also waiting was one of the young slaves, Zeke, a few years older than Charlie, the picnic basket balanced on his head. He carried an unfurled parasol.

"What's that for?" Charlie asked. "For Teacher?"

"In case she needs it."

"I won't," Jessica said. "I'm already wearing one!" She tapped her brim, and they laughed.

They set out first in Indian file, Charles leading, then Charlie, then Jessica, with Zeke bringing up the rear.

Charles took them in a direction Jessica had not traveled before, away from the house and the cotton fields, away from their bower, across a wide field covered with wildflowers. Jessica asked that they stop for a few minutes while they gathered buttercups and daisies and Queen Anne's lace and clover that she could give to Charlie to draw in tomorrow's class, and, she said to Charlie, when they studied the stamens and calyxes or sepals and pistils she would help him diagram them all. Charles had brought a seedbag from the fields with him. It was strung from his shoulder and he obligingly put into it all the plants they handed him.

With the sun at its zenith, it was hot in the field, but no one seemed to mind too much. Yet it was a relief later when they reached the edge of a forest on a piece of rising ground not visible from the manor.

"This is where we also get our wood for slave quarters and logs for heating purposes," Charles explained to Jessica, as they all came abreast for a moment before entering the path that led inside the copse. "We have many wooded areas on the land. You remember I told you we lumber in the midwinter months when the cotton season is over and the hands are free?"

She nodded.

A whiff of pine came down from above, where the trees grew taller and closer together. Jessica sniffed appreciatively, thinking it was a cool smell. She slipped her bonnet off her head and tied the strings behind her.

"Good," Charles said. "It would only get in the way."

But his expression told her he liked her hair uncovered and flowing freely.

The trees were thick now, branches almost touching one another, cutting off the sunlight. This was a different topographical aspect of Charles' domain. There was even more variety to it than she had thought. The amount of acreage was amazing to her, even in view of her knowledge of private English parks and estates; she thought the size of the Sedgely plantation equalled that of a hamlet. Charles was really quite modest, she thought, when he spoke of his land.

Since they were walking singly again, it was difficult to talk. Rocks loomed up in their path, and she could hear Charlie panting as he lifted his short legs over them. It was easier for his father, she thought, so long-limbed and lithe. Not quite so simple for her, with her skirts still too long and the stones sharp and slippery. Some had mosses growing over them, and they were better, but her toes were beginning to feel bruised and battered in her light shoes. Zeke had fallen back—she did not wonder, with the heavy basket and his bare feet.

"Are you all right?" Charles called over his shoulder.

"Yes," she gasped.

"Ye-yessir," Charlie said uncertainly.

"We'll come to a rest soon," Charles promised.

At times the insects were dense, a humming of large flies and mosquitos, and sometimes clouds of gnats had to be brushed from eyes, their nostrils, their ears. They heard the drone of bees. Caterpillars fell from the trees, making Jessica cry out as one landed on her. A box turtle held them up as it slowly made progress across their right of way. Jessica saw some orange touch-me-nots (for Eleanor? she thought ruefully) and mushrooms at the bottoms of trees. She saw a hummingbird whirring like a top, pecking at seed pods, and darting away when they exploded.

"Is it much—further?" Charlie asked painfully.

"No, we're almost there—where we shall eat and rest," his father said cheerfully, scarcely looking back this time.

A higher climb now, over fallen logs that blocked the narrow road, so they could not walk around them, over a boulder that seemed a mountain to Jessica. She stopped to gather some lichen for the seed bag—more, to catch her breath and spare her legs.

When she thought that she and Charlie would certainly collapse, they came, dramatically, upon a clearing. It was a flat table of land, with bits of charred wood strewn about the ground.

"Well, son, what do you think?" Charles asked, turning to place his arm around the boy.

"Better . . . it's better."

"It's magnificent," his father corrected him. "Imagine clearing this ground."

"A fire?" Jessica asked.

"A deliberate one. Indians. They fired it to make a meeting ground where powwows were held—and where they could hide from enemies below, sometimes surprising them when they swept down upon them."

Charlie's eyes widened.

"Are there any Indians here now?" he asked.

"Not that I know of. But if we dig," he promised, "we'll find some more Indian arrowheads, I know. Many in my collection came from this spot."

"Oh, I will, I will!"

"Later," Charles said. "We'd better all sit down now."

They found low stones to perch upon. Soon Zeke came into view and they took the basket from him. After they ate, Charlie's eyes began to droop. Charles made a soft nest for him from the tablecloth that had been with the picnicware, and the boy was soon fast asleep. Zeke looked as if he too would soon be dozing. Charles spoke softly to the black boy, telling him that he and Miz Jessica would continue to hike for a while and no doubt return before his child awoke, but that Zeke should stay by his side and reassure him that they would soon be back.

"Come," he said to Jessica.

She left her hat upon the seedbag and gladly followed him. When they were out of sight of the clearing, he reached back and took her hand.

"I'll pull you up if need be," he told her. "There is another special place I want you to see—and share with you." He turned to kiss her hand, and she saw the youthful happiness in his face; she was so pleased for him.

It was an even more difficult climb than before, but now she tucked her skirt up higher into her waistband and made better headway. Charles grinned as he admired her legs and they laughed so hard they both lost their breath and had to sit for a while until it came back. "Oh, Jess, Jessica," he said, "I haven't laughed that way since I was a child!" and his saying that increased her happiness until she thought she couldn't bear it. She jumped up and danced about in the path, which had narrowed again past the clearing, until she was about to whirl into the trees but for the quick reach of Charles' arm.

"Come!" she cried, with excitement. "I want to see what you have promised."

A little later the forest lightened. They could see the sun. They were at the top now and only a few trees were on the crest. Charles drew her out upon a broad stone ledge. She drew back at first, fearful of the height and the drop below, but she felt security in the strong grasp of his hand. He found a place for them to sit—a natural slice in the stone that provided a back to lean against and a seat. He held her as they looked over the sweep of the land below.

"This is the Sedgely place," he said. "It is a wonderful heritage."

The manor seemed far off and small, the outer buildings toy houses, the fields different-colored patches of greens and yellows and mixtures of both, the animals and people moving dots. A panorama of blue sky was feathered by cloud wisps, and the fruitful earth meeting it at the horizon encircled them.

"I thought it was a mountain when I was a boy—it seemed so huge—but then I learned it was a hill, really a foothill. I would come here when I was troubled and try to think things out."

"You were troubled?"

"Yes."

"Did it help, coming here?"

"From this vantage point my problems seemed smaller. The beauty of the land . . . and the labor needed to keep it that way," he said evenly, looking into her eyes, "made it all come out right . . . under a benevolent system."

She did not answer.

"It has been in the family for generations," he said coaxingly. "I must keep it intact for my son. He is my heir. I must see that it prospers for him, as my father provided for me."

"Were you Charlie's age then?"

"When I would come here? A little older, I think. I was more robust than he—I ran instead of walked, I climbed trees instead of going around them . . ."

"He is a fine boy, Charles."

"Yes, he is," he said proudly. "And he cares for you deeply, Jessica. . . . Who could help it?"

"And I for him." She smiled. "Who could help that?"

"One day he will manage the place."

Again she was silent.

"He will love it as I do."

She stirred.

"But he will need more gifted tutors than I, Charles."

"When the time comes. He will go away to college. He will follow in my footsteps." He tightened his arm around her. "I so wanted to bring you here, so you could see—and understand . . ." He kissed the top of her head. "It's always so lovely, Jessica, to spend an afternoon with you. I have never forgotten that day we rode about the fields, in the beginning, when you first came. Do you remember?"

"Of course."

"It has been good, Jessica?"

"Very good."

They kissed, holding together for a long time.

"The children," she said finally, breaking away. "They might follow."

"They are probably fast asleep," he said, but he scrambled to his feet bringing her upright with him.

"Oh!" she cried, looking downward, then grasping him more tightly.

"That's right. Just look at me."

"I think we'd better go."

"Until tonight then." He kissed her again. "You have brought me much happiness," he told her.

And he had brought her much happiness, too, she thought, as she lay spent beside him. She looked at the curve of the lashes against his cheeks as he slept. She liked the remembered feel of them as they fluttered over her face, her throat, her breasts, her body. She had once thought of his lashes as hummingbird wings, but the feel of them—butterfly wings. And his full throat. And how he had to restrain his explosive cries, into the cleft of her bosom, into the bed pillow, to mute the sound so no one would hear. And she, too, in the hollow of his neck, careful not to bite, not to show the mark of passion. She stretched against his long form, so that every part of her could feel his skin, his muscle, his bone. She lay in a field of comfort and pleasure. Then slowly, against her will, she began carefully to draw away. It was time to leave. He did not stir. At the door she blew him a kiss and slipped into the darkness outside the room.

About four o'clock one afternoon, after the manor had roused itself from its lethargy, Cicero came to the cheerful screened side of the veranda where Jessica and Eleanor were having tea. He bowed formally and addressed Jessica. It seemed she had a caller, Master Duane Bellows, who sent in his compliments and requested the favor of her seeing him. For a moment Jessica could not remember who Duane Bellows was, and then the vision of the importunate planter from the neighboring estate came to her mind. She smiled as she recalled his disappointment when, at the ball, she would not accompany him outdoors.

"Why, how delightful!" Eleanor exclaimed.

"Whatever shall I do?"

"Ask him to come in, of course," Eleanor said. "Cicero, see to it!"

Cicero withdrew and Jessica could hear Charles' voice as he came from his office. He evidently had heard the caller and emerged courteously to greet him. Charles led, somewhat stiffly for him, Jessica noted, and Duane followed eagerly to where the ladies waited. He carried a package, tied with a ribbon and an elaborate bow, under one arm.

"How lovely and cool you beauties look," Duane said gallantly, going from one to the other to kiss their hands as Charles scowled behind the visitor's back. "You are a vision to my eyes."

He presented the package to Jessica.

"Toffies imported from England. I thought how you must crave them, being so far from home."

Jessica's cheeks flushed as she thanked him for his thoughtfulness and assured him she liked these special sweets.

Cicero brought glasses, and the two men sat with the women. Duane talked of the ball, how he had meant to call on the Sedgelys and Miz Coopersmith in the days immediately afterward, but important and urgent plantation business had intervened and he sincerely regretted the delay. Jessica and Eleanor both absolved him of bad manners. He had an ingenuous face, given to wreaths of smiles, and broad and pleasant features. Jessica noted how carefully he was dressed; it was obvious the call was a very formal one. His stock was wound tightly around his neck, despite the heat, and he wore a waistcoat that contrasted with the well-cut frock coat he wore on top of it. Beads of perspiration misted his nose and forehead.

Cicero came again, bearing cider that had been cooled in the well, for the men.

Small talk soon out of the way, Duane broached the purpose of his visit. Not only to pay his respects, of course, and to thank them for their hospitality at the excellent ball, but he would also like very much to ask Miz Jessica to ride out with him, for an hour or two, to see some of the countryside and to take the air.

Eleanor looked at Jessica sternly.

"You must, Jessica, you really must."

"Oh—I don't know—though it is most kind of you, Mr. Bellows."

"Do you not have work to do?" Charles asked pointedly.

"No, she doesn't, Charles," Eleanor cried. "You know that classes are over for the day."

"But—" said Jessica.

"No buts," said Eleanor, "you really need to get away from the manor."

"And," Duane said politely, "Miz Eleanor, you must add the pleasure of your company."

"No, no thank you. I don't take well to the afternoon sun."

Jessica noted Duane's beseeching eyes; he seemed so vulnerable, and she had no wish to hurt him.

"Very well," she said. "If we can be back within the hour."

"Of course, of course! Anything you desire, Miz Jessica . . ."

"You have a driver with you?" Charles asked sulkily.

"No, not with the little gig, and one horse."

"Well then," Charles said firmly, "we'll have Sally attend Miz Jessica."

Charles instructed Cicero to fetch Sally and have her bring Miz Jessica's bonnet and perhaps a light shawl.

Eleanor smiled wryly.

"How careful you are of our cousin," she said.

Duane beamed.

"And I shall be careful of her, too," he promised, "you can be sure of it."

It was most uncomfortable in the small carriage, with three full-grown people on the seat, side by side, Sally on the outer edge, trying to keep her hip from touching Jessica. Jessica wanted to suggest to Duane that they leave her at one of the outer slave cabins, but she knew she could not do this without possible punishment of Sally for remission of duty. Nor did she want Duane to interpret her feeling as a desire for intimacy. Oh, the trappings of proper courtship, Jessica thought impatiently. She thought her nose, like Duane's, must now be glistening with sweat, but her head and her body had to be covered so as not to be unseemly.

Duane was oblivious of Sally, who had closed her eyes and made barely audible humming noises. Perhaps she had really gone to sleep, though Jessica doubted it; the young woman's body was so consciously squinched to be as tight and small as possible.

Duane prattled away, talking about his land and how bountiful his tobacco crop was this year. He didn't take to Charles' ways; one day Charles would have to go back to tobacco, too. "When he rotates his crops," Jessica said. Duane shrugged his shoulders. "All crops wear out the soil eventually, is my belief. And tobacco is a good cash crop. Tobacco," he laughed contentedly, "is cash hereabouts. I am," he said most pointedly, "in a very good position, a bachelor with an empty house, filled with everything to make a lady's heart happy."

She decided not to comment on that. She asked him questions about the fields and pastures they passed.

Some were Charles', old Sedgely land, and some were his; he proudly identified for her those he owned.

"I should like to show you my house," he said, smiling broadly at her. "But another time, when Charles and Eleanor will accompany us."

She nodded.

"We do have time to take you to a small pond on one of my outer fields. It is noted throughout the county for its water lilies—you will like it, Miz Jessica, I know."

"That will be nice."

"It is beautiful," he said, and then gallantly and lavishly, "The petals are like the blush of color on your cheeks."

If she were seriously courting, she would have whipped open a folding fan, carried for these occasions, and simpered behind it, her eyes flirting, demanding more compliments.

But Duane was content for the moment to talk of the land, and when they arrived at the pond, it was indeed all that he had said. From her seat, she looked down on a sheet of water almost completely covered with pink and white lilies, their green pads overlapping on the surface. Birds were flushed at the sound of the cart, and a bevy flew upward in a spiral formation. She heard the plop of water and quick flashes of almost imperceptible green as frogs startled from their sunning submerged into the tangle of roots.

"Come," Duane said, jumping down and offering her his hand, "you and I will walk around it and see it close up. Sally," he said, "will hold the reins while we wander."

Sally immediately took control of the gig. She heard when she had to, Jessica thought fleetingly, and probably shut out whatever she did not care to know, or whatever had no bearing on her welfare.

It was a pleasant stroll. The flowers were perfect and looked like solidified cream, or the wax of ivory candles tinged with varying shades of rose. Coming closer, she could hear the buzz of bees and was glad of the hat and stole and cotton gloves she dutifully wore. But the bees did not trouble them and soon the birds returned, and she could see the swollen throats of frogs as their mouths opened for flies and swiftly snapped closed again. Or the sated ones who pulsated on the pads and occasionally gave voice to their hoarse, croaking cry.

"It is lovely," Jessica told Duane, "and I am glad that you brought me to see it."

So different in every possible way from the bower and the foothill crest that Charles had unveiled for her, Jessica thought, sad for Duane and glad for herself and Charles.

"It's time to go," she said gently. "My cousins will feel concern."

"Oh, they know me," he protested. "There surely is no harm. . . ."

"An hour is all," she said apologetically.

He made the most of it, and she found his conversation pleasant as they finished their walk and began the homeward journey, Sally dutifully handing over the horse's reins. He talked of how he had always lived on his plantation, seldom left it but to go into town, and never had traveled abroad. He would like to go to England one day, he said magnanimously; he had forgiven the British empire its trespasses. Particularly, he said, he would like to go abroad if he had a lovely and knowledgeable bride to accompany him.

Jessica made no reply and he went on to talk of his sister, married and living in Tennessee, who would come to spend the holidays with him. Jessica would like her, he was sure, and he would have a soirée when his relative arrived and Jessica would get to know her.

Jessica only nodded.

When they returned, within the allotted time, at the manor door, he handed Jessica down carefully.

"I shall call again," he said, not quite hiding the question in his tone.

Jessica, knowing the hospitality and courtesy of the South, told him, "My cousins and I will be happy to receive you," and thanked him for the pleasures of the afternoon.

"What did he say to you!" Charles demanded that night, his fingers tightly gripping her shoulders.

She winced.

"Harmless things, Charles." She tried to wriggle away from his grasp. "He's a pleasant man—that is all—"

"A dolt."

"—all he is or could be to me."

"You must discourage him."

"I tried."

"Not convincingly enough."

"I did, Charles. And Eleanor wanted me to go."

"You don't need to do everything she wants."

"No, but I owe her. . . ."

"You owe *me*. . . ."

"He could never be anything to me at all, after you. . . ."

"The next time you must tell him no."

"For Eleanor's sake? To rest her mind . . ."

"Tell him it is because of your husband," he insisted grimly. "Tell him you are still—"

"Yes, still . . ." she said ruefully. Even in the madness of this illicit love she had never forgotten Jason.

"Oh, Lord!" he cried angrily. "Must you always be free of guile, woman?"

"Would you change me, Charles?"

"No," he said thickly.

"Should I have guile, perhaps lead him on for Eleanor's sake?"

"No!"

"To protect us, you and me. . . ."

"I don't need protection," he said hotly. "I can take care of myself . . . and take care of you, too. I just don't brook interference."

Charles held her so closely the entire length of her body was pressed against him. It seemed to her she did not know where he left off and she began. The pleasure she felt seemed to come from both of them, surrounding them in a heated, shimmering cocoon, and in the twisting and turning of bodies she did not know which was her arm or leg and which was his. Her long hair wrapped around his shoulders and enveloped him and strands were on her lips and in her mouth. He covered her mouth as if he would swallow it, pulling her outside herself and into him. It was as if her inner core were being sucked from deep, deep . . . a long way . . . and she was gone all gone but for sensation. Charles was in her mouth, he was everywhere. A vision came of the frog on the lily pad pulsating, pulsating—and flowers everywhere opening and closing . . .

When Duane Bellows came again, this time bearing combs of honey, his face alight with even more smiles than before, she walked outside with him, after the tea and cider, to tell him why she could not ride with him this afternoon—or any other time. . . .

He crooked his finger into his silk cravat to loosen it.

"Why, why?" he asked and blushed that he must beseech her.

"We want you to continue to call on us as a neighbor," she told him slowly, kindly, in discomfort. "We value you as a good neighbor, my cousins and I. We enjoy your visits; we really do, and you would be—you *are,*" she amended, "an invaluable friend. And so you see, Mr. Bellows, we don't want you to discontinue your calls but I—I cannot—I shall not be able to ride out with you. . . ."

He was completely crestfallen.

"We could have a good life together. My plantation, like the Sedgelys', is known the full length of Virginia. It is quiet there now, but you could . . . we could . . . bring it to—"

"I am not free," she said.

She was not free. She was tied to him, Charles, waiting for his nod, the message in his eyes, his touch. She went through polite charades at table, in the drawing room. She made light conversation at the proper times, but she was forever waiting.

He wanted to make up to her those lost outings.

"We'll ride in the afternoons. Eleanor does not care to ride. We'll ride to parts of the grounds you've never seen."

And when they rode, he wanted her to know she need not miss the outside world.

"We have everything here," he said. "It's a little village in itself. We do not lack for people. We do not lack for things."

She thought of the busyness of London, the color and the variety of its streets, the bustle of the port city of Philadelphia, but she would not speak of them. Only for a moment she yearned . . . but she was not dissatisfied . . . he must not think—

"We have everything," he said. "Don't we, Jessica? I have everything . . . so long as I have you . . ."

In the bower of the ancient tree it *was* the complete world.

He brought her gifts, too. A good luck charm that he had carried since childhood. She was amazed and grateful that he would part with it. A little scroll, parchment, printed with tiny letters, a love sonnet he had written for her, his love. Scrimshaw, a song of the sea he had carved into the whale's tooth. Things not to show but to look at by herself and to cherish as part of him. She would take them out when she was alone and turn them over and over in her fingers like the ritual saying of beads.

"Are you happy with me?"

"Yes," she said.

"You find me good?"

"Oh yes," she said.

"You understand me."

"Yes," she said. "Oh yes, yes."

Duane called again. Not as a suitor—he did not ask Jessica to walk out or ride in his gig with him—but ostensibly as a guest of the family. She was surprised when she heard his voice inquiring of Cicero whether the Sedgelys were at home and receiving. Of course, in the best tradition, Charles came from his office, politely stating that in the late afternoon it was good to take a break from the tedium of work, and ushered the other man to the coolness of the screened veranda. The ladies were summoned. Eleanor, though languid, seemed frankly curious. For a few moments Jessica was tense but she relaxed as the conversation flowed.

She saw the reserve in Charles' face. It was the face she saw at table when she and Eleanor dined with him. He would not look directly at Jessica. He seemed to be staring above her, or if she asked him a question, his eyes traveled from a point over her head and then descended in an arc away from her. At first it rankled; then she knew he had himself in tight control. She had been offended by what she thought was a mannerism but now she understood it to be protective—not only of himself but of the two women.

She listened to Charles' voice. It always struck a responsive chord in her. Now it was tight and studied, but the deep timbre was still there. Now it was loosening, as Duane directed the talk from inanities and approached more serious matters of the land. A rich, melodious quality was permitted to flavor Charles' speech. And, Jessica thought, keeping herself from shivering, his sound reached its lowest vocal range in passion. She loved it, the throaty reverberating richness of it. It played upon her spine. She was always affected by speech and tones, outside of love too. And she tried conscientiously to focus upon Duane and what he was saying.

Duane's voice was pleasant. He was a pleasant man, she thought again, bobbing to the surface of consciousness and then withdrawing inside herself and then coming out again once more. Everything about him was pleasant. His face was constantly set in motion with the now-familiar smiles; this was not an expression only for the ball or for their outing together. The smiles expanded and receded but always reappeared. She studied his plain, bland features; Duane's were not so fine as Charles', but they were mobile, the muscles teased to upward turns as wide and curved smiles stretched them. It must be anxiety, she thought with sudden intuition—the desire to please. But his eyes, she noted, when they turned her way, said the true *please.* She looked away.

She concentrated on their words. They spoke of the havoc of weather; the planter was at the mercy of the storms and lack of rain. The men remembered when fields were parched and brown stalks drooped on arid land, spectres of a harvest reaped by a relentless sun. And rain that when it came fell and fell and drowned everything. Or unexpected wild storms, the rare tornado, funneling their fortune into the roiling gray-black sky. And unusual frost turning everything into a brittleness that turned dark and cracked away despite the smudgepots and the desperate labor to keep the hot smoke going.

"A planter's life can be very difficult," Duane said, addressing this statement to Jessica.

She was silent.

"But you would not give it up."

"Never." Duane was just as matter-of-fact as Charles. "It is a way of life, the only life I have ever known. And my people before me."

Charles nodded.

Jessica looked at Charles' hands resting at ease upon his lap. They were long and narrow. She had long admired them, even before she felt their touch. She had watched them at table, elegantly handling his fork, his spoon, his knife. And then the strength of them as he handled the horses. The delicacy and the strength, too, at the piano. The tenderness and the delicacy and the urgency and the insistent strength as he caressed her.

"I'm tired," Eleanor said suddenly, crossly. "If you will excuse me."

She rose, the men immediately getting to their feet. Duane bowed his thanks for his refreshment and her hospitality, and she went inside the house.

"The heat seems to be bothering my wife today," Charles murmured, looking after her thoughtfully.

"Yes, it is almost unbearable."

Jessica wanted to ask Duane to remove his coat but she thought, as she had before, that it would be a breach—of what, etiquette? or the distance she wanted to place between them? Probably that. Charles had come from the office in his work costume—a thin lawn shirt, finely tucked down the front—so carefully sewn by Chloe, Jessica thought darkly—collar open to bare his long muscular neck. Riding breeches and boots completed his outfit. She was struck again by Charles' singular handsomeness. She retreated inside herself again. At table he always wore a cutaway jacket despite the oppressive heat of the room. There were customs that must be observed as they had been in this house for generations. A swallow-tail or cutaway coat, while young black footmen or girls, supervised by Cicero, came on the hottest nights to stir up the still air with turkey-feathered fans attached to long poles. She thought of dinner on hot nights as a scene lifted from a play and set to music—a humming and swishing as animate objects pushed against the inanimate.

And yet the men were talking of change. The steam engine—the steam boat and the steam railroad—they would bring much richness to the land. They spoke of the railroads and the boats that were already operating in different parts of the country. They must bring them in one day soon, they were so effective, disproving the dire predictions of constant explosion and doom. "Yes, we should see about it," Charles said excitedly, the true man flashing outward for the moment. "I should like to see that kind of progress!"

"And I, too," Duane said seriously.

They talked of forming a committee to discuss ways and means, and Jessica felt stimulated by the new direction the conversation was taking. She liked it when Charles had these conversations with her, when he was teaching her about the land and not fighting her through it. She listened carefully. There would be many new facets to this land as it grew. Changes had to come. Life was full of change. Look at her own. A person and a land could not grow without change.

"Change is not easy; it can be painful," Duane was saying.

And joyful, too. Like life, Jessica thought.

She listened to the facts and figures Charles so readily presented. He had great stores of information. And knowledge. He is essentially a scholar, she thought. She remembered poetry he quoted to her in their times together, the times when he wanted them to linger, to savor, to anticipate, not to rush immediately into physical union. He gave her lines that came from Byron and

Shelley. And the ancient Greek poets. His range was wide. He used words to tease her, too. He would whisper, perhaps, from Thomas Gray:

" O'er her warm cheek and rising bosom move
The bloom of young Desire and purple light of Love."

"Well," Charles said ironically to Jessica that night, when they were alone again, "he is certainly your admirer."

"Not quite the dolt?"

"No," he said evenly, "but he is not for you."

"No."

"You are mine, Jessica."

She was silent.

He lifted her chin to look into her eyes.

"You are mine," he repeated firmly. "You are mine . . . always."

When she was alone again she thought sadly of that *always.* He could not answer *always* for himself, nor could she. Life—no matter whether it held change and growth—and because of it—was complicated. She fell asleep thinking of Jason and the vows they had exchanged.

Chapter Six

Each day she told herself she would discontinue the affair. She would not go to him tonight. It was impossible. She was doing injury to her cousin. She might even be hurting the children, though she thought not. And Chloe. She could not bear Chloe's eyes when they chanced upon each other in the hallways.

But it was even more than that. She was growing entrapped; she was loving him too much. When he took her hand and led her to his study, after an evening of playing for her at the piano, she could not resist. She did not want to resist. All he had to do was look at her in a certain sensuous way and she succumbed. Her resolve and her dignity fled. Her guilt was wiped out. Her other concerns diminished. All she knew then was that she wanted Charles, that their lovemaking was of the utmost importance, that she was a truly awakened woman after the long period of Jason's absence from her, and that Charles had set her on fire and she was afraid she would be consumed.

She knew he eventually must return to Chloe, and to Eleanor, too; the pull would be too great; the Southern mores of wife and mistress and slave all serving the master were too deeply ingrained in his consciousness. For the moment, she knew she was the only one; he would not have energy for anybody else these past few weeks since they had begun. There could be no other reserves of passion. But she would not be able to bear it when he changed. When the memories of Chloe and the sounds of her swishing skirts rekindled old memories and pleasures, and the duties expected of a husband to a wife who was trying bravely to fight her alcoholism pressed upon him, he would slip into his socially approved habits and parcel out the favors. She was overcome by horror at the thought. She must make plans to leave before that happened.

After Cicero and Joseph had finished clearing dinner away and returned to the cook house, and Jessica and Charles discreetly sat on in the drawing room when Eleanor had said goodnight and gone to her room, Jessica broached the subject.

"I'm thinking of going away soon, before the cold weather sets in," she began.

"Going away?" he said incredulously.

"To continue my mission."

"I thought you had forgotten *that.*"

"Oh no!" And realizing that she had hurt him, "It's a promise I made to myself a long time ago, to search for him, to find out . . ."

"I won't hear of it!" he cried imperiously. "I won't have it!"

"But it must be done."

"It must *not.* And you will *not.*"

"I *will not?*"

"No, Jessica. Your place is here now, with me, in this house, with the children. You belong here now. You belong to *me.*"

Her temper, not easily aroused, flared now.

"Belong!"

They both knew he had used the wrong word. The name of Chloe hovered in the air.

"I didn't mean it the way you think," he said. "I love you, Jessica. We belong together."

She tried to tell him that it would be better in the end, and that she must make some resolution, but he would not listen. He covered her mouth with deep kisses and carried her off, where her reason fled.

* * *

The next night she told him she did not approve of slavery and that her living in this house with him and the rest of the family, in the midst of slavery, was making the meaning of her life a lie.

"Do I mistreat the slaves here?" he demanded.

"No, as far as I can see, but . . ."

He told her sternly, this time with unrelenting emphasis—a liturgy—that he saw to the needs of the slaves, that they could not provide for themselves, that he was their protector. He doggedly went over again what he had told her before: that they had adequate shelter and clothing for their bodies, that he never separated families, and that he did not sell off the children or husband or wife. (Evidently Chloe's husband did not count, she thought bitterly.) They did work hard, and when conditions were good and crop prices high he rewarded them. There were extra rations and bolts of cloth and barn dances. Sex was encouraged—children were desirable. The hands had time for church. And besides the individual garden patches, there was the area of good land set aside for the slaves as a communal garden where they could raise fresh produce for their own consumption or sale—anything they wanted, except cotton. And he even raised a small crop of tobacco for their own use. What more could they want?

"Freedom," she said shortly.

"Yes," he said sourly, "freedom to starve." He lectured her on the economics of the South. The agriculture of the South could not exist except for slave labor—the most inexpensive labor to be had. There was still little industry in this half of the country—there was some mining away from the coastal areas and some of the poor white folk transferred their Old World skills to the New World in this work. But it was agriculture for the most part, and the stoop labor so needed for tobacco and cotton growing depended on many hands. The South would collapse without them. If the South were to expand, the building of roads—which were still insufficient—must continue with slave labor. But most of all, he repeated, the plantations would disappear and the land go fallow without this supply.

"And let me tell you," he continued, reiterating what he had said before, "the white plantation owner must *support*, must *feed* the slaves even when times are hard and there is a depression, which we seem to have here with great frequency. Oh, he could sell off a few, and he tries to do so—but then the slave market is bad when the general market is bad—and the plantation owner knows eventually things will change, so he'd better hold on to them and keep them in good health and strength; after all, they are his capital."

"And human beings, as well," she said angrily.

"It's not easy to be a plantation master," he said grimly. "It may be a poor institution, but it is the only way I can see for these large establishments to remain operable."

She heard him out, then she began to talk of free men and women and wages and cooperative sharing of plots of ground—not a limited garden such as he provided but large arable fields whose products could be sold competitively in the open market, even out of state. He hooted and said that even if certain large plots of ground were set aside for the common people and land rent paid out by work on the big farm, there would be a natural return to feudalism. "Look how Europe functioned as feudal states; Russia is still a feudal state; the serfs are no better off—even worse off!—than the colored slaves. And don't suggest," he told her coolly, "that the large plantations be divided and subdivided and we become a region of small farmers. It will never happen—the plantation owners would never permit this to happen. Oh, a farm here and there may be owned by a poor white, but the abandonment of plantations that had been in families for years, some since the first settlements? Never!"

The evening ended with his swooping her into his arms and telling her how much he liked arguing and talking with her. She stretched his mind; she was an exciting woman, soft and keen at the same time. It was so good to have her here, she must never think—*never!*—of leaving.

She was attentive to Eleanor in the afternoons, when classes were over and the children had free hours to play. For some time she had been urging her cousin to take more interest in the household and the slaves who served in it and in the fields. Jessica had heard that one of the cotton choppers who had just given birth to a new baby was doing poorly and thought perhaps they should go see her. Hadn't she been told that Eleanor, when she first came to the plantation, had paid sick visits to the slave quarters, that this was one of the duties of the plantation wife?

"Mistress," Eleanor corrected her icily.

The expression on Jessica's face did not change, though she felt an inner constriction.

"The duties of the plantation mistress. There are a number of ailing people, Sally has told me, and in most of these cases their own herbs and balms aren't doing any good. You do keep a supply of remedies, do you not?"

"Yes. They are locked in the hallway closet outside my room."

"Won't you get them out and make some sick calls, Eleanor?"

"It's been so long since—I don't know whether I can do it . . . it's so hot today and—"

"I'll help you, Eleanor. I'll go with you."

"I don't have the key to the closet anymore."

"Who has it?"

"Charles."

"I'll ask him for it."

"No. I will."

They stared at one another.

"Very well," Jessica said. "Do it, Eleanor. It's needed. Could you get ready tomorrow afternoon? We'll ask Cicero for a boy to carry the baskets. . . ."

Eleanor was in a cool, simple dress, not unlike the one that Jessica usually wore. Sally was adjusting the bonnet on Eleanor's head when Jessica, also bonnetted against the sun, came for her. Eleanor produced a key and they went together to the hallway. When she unlocked the closet, the interior looked like an apothecary shop. There were small vials and basket-woven containers, carefully covered with lids and neatly labeled in Charles' fine handwriting. Jessica peered closely at the names: calomel, paregoric, alum, castor oil, flaxseed, ipecac, spirits of niter, salts and spirits, blistering plasters and salves and potions and caustics she had never heard of before. She was fearful of the opium and laudanum and morphine that she saw in the closet, neatly labeled too, available to her cousin.

"So many medicines!" she said.

"Yes. Charles has been in charge of them for the past couple of years. I went to him this morning and he gave me the key." She smiled enigmatically at Jessica. "I'll return it to him at dinner. You need not worry."

"You've been doing well!" Jessica said warmly, impulsively taking her cousin's hand.

"Yes," Eleanor said drily. "So Charles said, too. He's delighted I am 'doing my duty.' Did he put you up to goading me on, Jessica?"

"Oh no, visiting was my own idea—and I knew you did it in the past."

Sally came to them with a young black boy Jessica did not remember seeing before. He packed the remedies into a basket, along with old linens Eleanor gave him, and followed them down the stairs. There Cicero had another basket ready, filled with loaves of bread and pitchers of milk and packets of other foodstuffs.

They kicked up dust as they proceeded down the path to the rows of slave cabins. The August sun was hot and the air heavy. A monarch butterfly fluttered in front of them, and bees droned in patches of clover. Eleanor took a folding fan from her reticule, more, she said, to brush away the mosquitos than to create a breeze. They passed the corn patch grown for the slave rations. Birds flew noisily about the rows. The scarecrow had fallen.

As they came to the cabins they became aware of a sudden rush of activity. The grapevine had been at work and their visit had been heralded. Old ladies were sweeping out their front doors and curtseying to the *grande dame* and her companion. Eleanor called a greeting here and there, "Howdy, Auntie Belle and Auntie Venus and Auntie Psyche, howdy!"

They went first to the cabin of Sarah, who had developed a postpartum fever. They needed to adjust their eyes as they came from the bright sunlight into the dim interior. It took a while before they could make out the corncob mattress set upon a row of logs in one corner. A young woman dressed in the blue-checked garment Jessica had noticed on the women in the fields lay miserably on her side. They could see an elderly mammy, a bandana on her head, hovering over her.

"First," Eleanor said, with an authority that surprised Jessica, "you must open all the shutters."

The old lady muttered but did as she was told. As the shutters swung away from the open, glassless, square cuts in the wooden frames that served as windows, some of the fetidness of the air lessened. "Now, Auntie Cora," Eleanor said decisively, "the patient must be washed." Auntie Cora went to the bucket, but Eleanor told her it must be fresh water and sent her out to the pump. Eleanor asked for clean cloths and Auntie Cora went out again to canvass the neighbors who were home. Eleanor rolled up her sleeves, and Jessica did the same. There was soap in the basket, along with the medicines, and they washed the new mother thoroughly and gently. Eleanor asked Sarah a few questions. The child, for she was barely sixteen or seventeen, answered in a frightened voice. They could see that she was bleeding, as was normal, and despite her embarrassment and surprise that they should touch her private parts, she endured their attention. Eleanor deftly kneaded her belly, and after an interval of pressure and massage the patient expelled several dark bloody clots. Eleanor nodded with satisfaction. The midwife, she complained, should have seen more properly to the afterbirth, that every shred of it had been taken from the birth canal. Eleanor washed the patient again and went to her basket, where she mixed a concoction from the different containers. She held the patient's head upon her forearm as she urged her to drink it down. Soon the young mother slept.

"I'll leave you the medicine," she told Auntie Cora, "and you are to give it to her three times a day for three days. Her fever will soon be gone, and you are to send word to me at the big house how she is each day until that time." The woman smiled, relieved. "And now," Eleanor said more gently, "let me see the baby."

From another dark corner of the room Auntie Cora fetched

the infant. He looked healthy, with plump little arms and legs, and now that his nap was interrupted he cried lustily. Eleanor, smiling, took him in her arms and rocked him. "There—there. He looks well fed. Is someone nursing him?"

"Liza come affuh she fees huh own chile."

"Good."

Eleanor sent for another pail of fresh water and this time washed the baby. Auntie Cora fetched a clean rag for his diaper and a raggedy but soft shawl that no doubt had seen its better day in the big house. Then Eleanor went to the baskets again and left food in the house and clean linen wrappings for the child. She told Auntie Cora sternly to keep the shutters open and to bathe the mother and child each day. Then they left.

A few little children had gathered at the door, and Cicero's page had kept them from coming inside. Eleanor found some treats for them in the baskets and they grinned shyly at her. One of them pointed to the remaining pitcher of milk. She had brought only one bowl. She poured the milk into it, and they took turns, at a loud command from the house boy, lapping it up.

Eleanor then led Jessica to some other cabins where there were elderly ailing men and women. Some of the cabins had dirt floors; in others, planking had been laid. On the way Eleanor had remarked that there was a lot of hookworm. The slaves, she said, had brought it in their intestines from Africa, and it spread in the colonies infecting the soil. "Don't ever walk shoeless," she warned her cousin. And the slave ships brought yellow fever, too, she went on, and malaria. All sorts of ailments here, she continued, but mostly they stay amazingly healthy, considering the way they work and the food they eat. Though conditions here, she said quickly, are better than most. Charles had made many reforms.

Some of the cabins consisted of only one room without any partitions. Some had a loft dormitory, reached by ladder. This was for the children. Only a few of the quarters had fireplaces, and these were for exemplary slaves. Altogether there was little furniture: some rough chairs and tables and a few shelves that the men had built in their spare time. There was no sawmill on the plantation; Charles wanted to buy more slaves trained as carpenters, he had once told Jessica—to fix up the cabins and to attend to the repair of the cotton sheds and tool cribs. He had a forge and a smith to shoe the horses. Sometimes, he explained, he hired slaves who had been trained as mechanics from other plantations, paying their masters a set fee for their services. After this year's crops, he would bring in some more of these journeymen specialists to get the plantation in first-class condition.

Eleanor spoke briskly with the invalids, leaving ointments and elixirs she mixed. The old people told her how much they had missed her, that it was good to see her again. Some said they had heard the screech owl call and so some poor soul nearby would die; turn your shoes upside down for us, they begged her. Jessica could see that most of them were barefoot. She had heard that they wore shoes only from November to April. Then somebody made a joke and they talked about the weaving tasks they had been given to do in the cabins, since they could no longer go to the fields, and the corn that they shucked for the cornmeal rations. And they did the spinning, too—they showed the stockings they were making for the field hands against the cold of coming winter.

The old people were surrounded by children too young for field work. With big round eyes the little boys and girls watched the mistress and came to look into her baskets, guarded closely by the houseboy. Eleanor usually found something for them before she left, and once outside they trotted at her heels until she shooed them back.

Jessica and Eleanor were tired as they left the quarters and headed for home. They stopped at the vine-covered gazebo to rest a while on its benches. Jessica stared at her cousin with admiration. This was the old Eleanor, really one who was even more competent than the gay English girl that she had been. Jessica tried to express the thought to her. Eleanor smiled and brushed away the compliments.

"When I first came I thought I could do so much good," she said. "I was appalled; I hadn't been properly prepared for slavery. We were rather sheltered girls, Jessica, you and I. But you had your father to educate you," she said wistfully. "He opened your eyes more to the world than anyone had opened mine."

"Yes, he did."

"I thought conditions could change here on this plantation. But it's hopeless, Jessica. Some things Charles made better, but there are limits. Even if you want to change, you can't. It's pervasive in the South. You can't run a plantation in this country, anywhere in the world, for that matter, without being a true master."

"But–"

"Slavery can only exist through force and through fear. How could it be otherwise? Who would remain a slave? And the planters have to be a unified force to prevent it all from falling apart. Some day they'll rise up and murder us in our beds."

Jessica thought of Nat Turner and his band of sixty rebels. She was sure that Eleanor knew of him, too.

"There are vastly more slaves than there are of us. No one here talks openly about rebellion, especially to the women, but there have been attempts, never successful, brutally suppressed–and they must be brutally suppressed or we are done for!"

Eleanor did not know that Charles had spoken to Jessica about insurrection. Jessica remembered vividly what Charles had told her about the Maroons in Jamaica and the uprising in San Domingo and the early uprising in Virginia. She also thought about what her father had impressed upon her. He was rabid on the subject of slavery and told her about the runaway slaves who had made it through the Georgia swamps, going on to Florida, where Spain used them as a buffer against the Indians. Some of them, in 1826, under their leader Garcon, settled around an abandoned fort on the Appalachicola River, captured a United States Army supply convoy, and burned one of its men. In retaliation, they were later wiped out by the Army's explosion of their gunpowder. In an English newspaper Jessica herself had read of the outbreak in Texas just five years ago, in 1835. A large Mexican force was reported near the Brazos River and the slaves apparently thought this could help them in their revolt. Their attempt was quickly put down; a hundred slaves were severely punished. Some were executed.

"But Charles is an enlightened master," Eleanor continued.

"He tries to be, I guess."

"You've seen that he's done away with an overseer. There

were too many excesses." She shuddered. "Jessica, you really don't know about the bestiality of some—and the flogging—and the maiming—and the women. . . . I've tried to tell myself it's different with the women, when there is affection and—possibly—love." It was apparent that it was difficult for her to say *love.* After a while she added, "And maybe that's even worse. . . . But in so many cases it's just plain fornication."

Jessica remained silent. She was becoming restless and alarmed that they were treading on dangerous ground. She wished they could go on to Sedgely Manor. But Eleanor wanted to talk.

"He just has the drivers—oh yes, they used to carry whips, too, but they were mostly for the sake of importance, the sign of authority; they never used them. And Charles says he has prohibited the whips altogether. And he always is giving extra rations and blankets and clothes. He even gives the women some sunshine time to wash their clothes. That's not a hard master, is it? Is it, Jessica?"

Jessica shook her head.

"He is a decent man. I've always known that. He can't help himself in some things, Jessica." Eleanor blew her a kiss, a light token of affection she had offered when Jessica was a small child; it wounded Jessica now. "It's the way men are brought up here. Maybe everywhere, I don't know. Only it seems to be easier here, a way of life. Sometimes," she said, "a wife has to be satisfied with the crumbs of a feast." Again Jessica said nothing. "I hate *her!*" Eleanor said venomously, her face flushing. "Oh, I hate Chloe—but she can't help herself either. She's part of the way of life here, too. But—I don't hate you," she whispered.

Jessica was seized by a feeling of panic. She felt her face flush and yet she felt cold at the same time. She had realized that Eleanor knew, but she had wanted no acknowledgment between them, no confrontation. She had done the unpardonable thing; this she had admitted to herself many times, as she did now—she was a guest who had injured her hostess. But, a mitigating inner voice insisted, Eleanor had already injured herself or had been hurt by others or by a manner of life. Yet no matter the extenuating circumstances that Jessica tried to keep uppermost in her mind, her reason always brought her back to the admission of a breach of conduct unthinkable in herself, or at least in the person she had thought herself to be.

She knew, too, that sooner or later she would have to come to terms with herself.

She did not think there was any purpose to this conversation, it could only hurt them both. She could not disentangle herself from Charles at a moment's notice—nor did she really believe that Eleanor was serving notice upon her. Her genuine affection for her cousin surfaced through her anxiety.

"I'm sorry, Eleanor."

"It's all right." Eleanor's face had now grown pale and tight. "I tell myself you're taking him away from *her* and then I'm *glad!* And I can fight you, because you're so much like me, Jessica; we're equal—only I'm more equal than you, because I have privilege—I am his *wife.*"

"Yes, you are—and," Jessica continued, though it pained her, "you should make the most of it. You are his wife and you should act like it. At the ball you did. Today you did. I was proud of you today in the quarters. Charles would be, too."

"You've helped me," Eleanor said, reaching for her cousin's hand, "even though you've hurt me, too. It was difficult, oh so hard, almost unbearable at first—hell really—cutting down on the brandy, the whiskey, and finally giving them up. . . . I hope for good—" she shuddered "—but who knows? I saw the way the children look at you . . . and Charles . . . I don't know if I can really forgive you Charles," she said bitterly. "I don't know. . . . But you've put the strength in my backbone that Miranda always said was missing."

"You did it yourself, Eleanor. You can't put into another person's character what already is there. You'll be all right, you'll see. You'll involve yourself more and more in the affairs of the plantation and in the children. . . . And don't worry any longer; I'm going to leave. I've already decided that. I must be on my way to complete my search . . ."

"Leaving?"

"Soon."

"*He* won't let you go."

"That is for me to decide."
"No, it is his way. He holds on to all his women."
"I am not chattel."
"He'll never let you go."
"I must go—and I shall, Eleanor."

Leaving was uppermost in her mind as she went through the work of the following days. As she taught Jenny and Charlie their lessons, she looked at them intently, wanting to soak in their beautiful little faces so that she would remember them always as they were now. They were so eager to learn, and bright and dear. Jenny was forever throwing her arms about her waist and hugging her. Charlie, who thought he was too old and that it was not manly to act in this way, did cartwheels for her approval instead, or literally stood on his head, and brought her bunches of flowers for the classroom vases. Or he brought sketches he had drawn of the birds he saw on their bird-watching walks, or rabbits they had flushed, or squirrels nibbling on acorns. Aletha, who now was regularly inside the door, observed everything. She looked longingly at Jenny's golden curls and tried not to giggle when Charlie went through his tricks, and when Jessica read from the storybooks she was riveted to attention, carried off into a world away from the big house. It would be difficult to leave the children, Jessica knew. It was not the bearing of children that made them so precious; it was the being with them day after day, being part of their lives and their lives part of hers. Oh, she would miss them.

While she was teaching Joseph and Billy in the kitchen house one part of her mind split off from the other and wrestled with the problem of how she would do it—how she would go. Joseph and Billy were progressing so well, like their younger counterparts. They were now reading almost unerringly from their simpler books, without her prompting, and she could only think what intelligent young men they were. And, the thought came to her, how she would like to have them help in her journey.

How would she leave, she asked herself over and over. She had little money. She had come to her cousins as a guest and would not take payment as a tutor; her work as tutor, she had firmly settled before she had arrived, would pay for her keep. All she had was the income from a small annuity left her by her father. She would never agree that there was an estate of Jason Coopersmith, for that signified he was no longer alive. The little house they had owned stayed vacant. In any event, there was little else; the pounds he had left for her own expenses on his journeys away from home were long gone. She had few precious objects, other than the ring Miranda had given her and the ring with the Coopersmith crest. She would only part with these, especially the Coopersmith ring, under the most extreme circumstances. How would she manage?

She would have to take a carriage. Surreptitiously. She did not like that. She would have to provision the carriage. By stealth. She did not care for that. She would have to leave in the dark of night. Like a cutpurse or a slave running from his master. She did not wish to hurt Charles or Eleanor even more by taking their property. But perhaps she could borrow the carriage and the food. She could repay the Sedgelys later when she found Jason and they had income once again. Still and all, borrowing was just a euphemism—it still would be taking without permission. They were past the point where Charles, so adamant about her staying, would place her in the post coach; it was so different from the time when she had arrived in one.

She could write to her mother or to Uncle Josiah Barrows for funds. But that would take too long—by the time one letter crossed the sea in the months-long journey and the return voyage elapsed—no, then it would be six months before she could stir from this place. She must go soon. The longer she stayed, the more difficult it would be. The children . . . Charles. . . .

"Billy," she said suddenly, interrupting his recital, "have you ever driven a carriage?"

He looked shamefaced.

"No'm. Mum'n me, we had no money for such things. I never did."

"I know how," Joseph said. "I handle carriages good."

"Well," Jessica corrected him automatically.

"I handle carriages well. I is—am—good with horses."

Julia, working with the pastry dough at the table, looked up.

"Thas not his job, miz, tis Willum's," she said. "Don yall membah? He done fetch yall fum de coach."

"Yes, I remember."

"I kin drive good as he kin!" Joseph said hotly. "Drive *well* as he kin!"

"Ummm," Jessica said, thinking. "Do you know the roads around here?"

"Not much," he admitted, as shamefaced as Billy had been.

"You haven't been away from the plantation?"

"No'm."

"But I know the stars," she murmured aloud.

"I know the *Nawth* star!" he said proudly. "All the hans here know 'bout the Nawth star and where it is and where it leads to, Miss Jess'ca."

Julia shooked her head at them.

"Ssh!" she warned. "Don tawk so loud."

"The North Star!" Billy cried, then clapped his hand over his mouth and began to whisper. "But you have to take me with you, Miz Jessica. I'm still bound to Cap'n Northrup and I figger that means I'm bound to you, too. If I'm ever to go back to 'im, the cap'n, you must take me with you, Miz Jessica. I won't stay here without you!"

"Who-all is tawkin of takin en leavin en goin affah de Nawth Stah?" Julia said quietly.

"I'm just asking questions, that's all," Jessica said, thinking she had been very indiscreet. "After all, one day I must be going on. But when, I don't know."

She knew she had disappointed the two boys, and what she had done to Julia she was not completely certain.

"Well, back to our lesson," she said. "Joseph, please read from the bottom of page twenty-two. . . ."

She lay in his arms savoring the afterglow of lovemaking. In the darkness his white hair glowed like a mass of moonlit cloud, and she rested her head against his shoulder, her fingers tracing the muscles of his broad chest and arms.

"Charles," she said softly, "would you lend me a carriage?"

"I would give you a carriage, the world, anything you want."

"No, seriously, I would like a carriage."

"Why, you little hussy! Are you growing worldly and vain after all?"

"I would just like to borrow the carriage and supplies for my trip through the States."

He raised himself on one elbow and looked sternly at her.

"This is no time to talk about foolish things."

"It's not foolish, Charles. I cannot stay here any longer."

"You are a strumpet! That's not what your body has been telling me for the past few hours!"

"Oh, my darling! My body tells me I should stay—God, I want to stay with you—but my reason tells me I must go."

He was sitting entirely upright now.

"I won't hear of it! I told you that before!"

"I know you did, Charles." She tried to bring him down against her again, but he had grown rigid. "But I'm going to do it. I could steal away when you don't know about it, if I must. But I love you too much for that!"

"If you love me," he said passionately, "you would not want to leave me!"

"It's not that simple."

"If you think you're going to find your husband, you are misleading yourself. He's dead, I tell you, dead!"

"He is not!" she said stubbornly. "I know it. I feel it."

"You feel *me!*"

"Yes, I feel you, too, Charles. It's possible to love more than one person, you know that."

"Women love only *me*!"

"Charles, I will not steal your carriage. I want your help—and your blessing."

"Blessing," he said bitterly. "Are you teasing me, are you leading me on, are you playing the harlot!"

He flung himself upon her and took her viciously. He seemed to take pleasure in showing his strength. He thrust in anger. He did not spare her the weight of his frame. His teeth were in her neck, in her nipples. He scratched her back as he turned her on top of him. He held her in a steely vise. When he fell asleep his legs were heavily upon her and she could not creep away. He had never made love—made hate, she corrected herself bitterly—in this fashion. This was the way the masters took their slaves, rape, without love. But it was not his way with Chloe, she knew that; they had been children together and awakening lovers and then mature ones. And Eleanor . . . oh! it was a great mess! A sad, tangled web. She began to cry quietly. Later he awoke. At first his expression was anger, then it softened. "I'm sorry," he murmured. "I'm sorry, Jessica, forgive me. It was the thought of losing you that—oh. Jessica!"

She crept back to her room, tired, sad, hurting in body, more in spirit. Other nights she had flown up the steps, scarcely touching the carpeted boards, once safe in her room forgetting how she had reached it, her mind preoccupied with remembered words and touches and visions of his face, suffused and finely stretched in passion. Where before the lightness came happily without thought, now she had to caution herself about quiet movement, quiet shutting of the door, quiet coming to rest. With trembling hands, she removed the unfastened clothing she had hastily thrown over herself before leaving him. She was too shaky to place her things in the wardrobe, and she left them where they fell. She slipped into a nightdress and threw herself upon the turned-down bed—she had just glanced at the pitcher and basin; she would wash later—and lay there shivering, as if in fever.

There was a dread sick feeling within her. With her declaration that she must leave she had stretched almost to the breaking point a precious bond whose strength she had not realized until she had tried it to its limits. This man had such claim to her, in every way—physically, yes, her imagination, yes, the desire to love, to be loved by a man, this man. . . . She felt responsible for his anger, his cruel behavior. She had brought him to this point. It was her doing. She could have avoided it, she might have waited another day or week or been more circumspect about it. Then an inner rage consumed her, at first at herself, and then it turned, directed at

Charles. It bounced back and forth, leaving her even more miserable and tired than before. Determinedly, she closed her eyes, but she could not sleep.

She heard the grandfather clock in the center hall below strike the fourth hour. She would miss the sound of its chime, she thought sadly, along with everything else. She could not bear to think of all that she would miss.

She heard footsteps outside her room and, startled, she half-raised herself. Trembling—it seemed she had never stopped since she came upstairs—she lit the candle on the stand by her bed, and shadows rose in grotesque amplification on the walls. For a moment she fixed on them, mesmerized by the shapes and their movements, the expansions and contractions. Then, with a quick shake of her head, she came back to the reality of the moment.

She had never thought to lock her door; she did not even remember whether there was a key. A gracious house, nothing and no one in it to fear. She was overwrought. She calmed herself. Then she pictured Eleanor's accusing eyes that afternoon at the gazebo after their nursing mission, when she had let Jessica know that she was aware of her liaison with Charles. Perhaps it was Eleanor who had come from her room, to see whether Jessica was in hers, to listen over the bannister perhaps for sounds from the floor below. Stricken, Jessica thought about the nights when Eleanor must have lain awake, hoping desperately that Charles would come to her, perhaps hearing in the quiet of the night a sound that told where he went. Jessica remembered, too, in a bitter flash, her own feeling when his footsteps had gone down the hallway to the master bedroom—and to Eleanor. She cringed at the thought of two women—no, three; Chloe must have sharp, pained ears, too—who waited on the tread of one man.

The footsteps had not gone past her room. There was a presence there—it was almost palpable—outside her door. The door was too well hung for her to see the darkening of feet at the fitting, and yet she looked for it, a smudge, a different shade of blackness to tell her someone was there.

She could sense the indecision. There were no footsteps going away, in one direction or the other. Whoever was there was waiting, lost in uncertainty for the moment, not knowing whether to proceed or retreat. It must be Eleanor. Or possibly Charles? He would not be so rash. He had never come to her room, too prudent and sensitive to cause unneeded upset to the family, so close by. Or could it be Chloe, a desperate Chloe, not caring for her safety?

She must not wait. She must spring out of bed and open the door herself, confront whoever it was. She swung her legs over the mattress but could not bring herself to stand. She wanted to call out *Who is it,* but she restrained herself; it would be wrong to rouse the household.

In the flickering light of the candle she could see the doorknob move now. Slowly at first, and then more surely. The other's decision had been made, and it galvanized her to action. She stood before the door when it opened.

It was Charles.

"Jessica," he groaned.

She held her finger to her lips.

"Ssh," and shook her head as he came into the frame.

There was no denying that he would come inside the room, and she turned to let him pass. He gently closed the door and reached for her, the haggardness of his face bringing an ache to her throat.

"Jessica," he groaned again. "You cannot leave. Tell me that you did not mean it—or that you've changed your mind. . . ."

She was silent, though she clung to him. The thought that it could have been Eleanor, or Chloe, only stressed the urgency of her being on her way.

"Jessica," he said painfully, as though he felt her resolve, "you must not—*please?*"

She tightened her arms about him.

"Let's talk about it in the morning," she whispered. "It's so—so unwise—for you to be here."

"I could not stay away. I had to see you. To tell you—to *ask* you—"

"We'll talk tomorrow. . . ."

"To *beg* you—Jessica, you'll have your own home. I have more land not far from here—separate—everything you need—everything you could want—I've promised you already—I keep my promises to you. . . . Make me a promise, Jessica. . . ."

"Oh, Charles—"

"A staff to care for you—"

"Charles—"

"And I'll wait on you every day . . . every night. . . ."

"It could not work, Charles."

"It would. It *shall!*"

She was silent.

"I've never *begged* before."

He looked exhausted. His features were taut. There were dark hollows under his eyes. His pain became her pain and she shuddered.

"I cannot bear it if you go away. If you leave, even with all the people here, I'll be so lonely, so desolate."

"No," she said.

"I know otherwise," he said harshly. "No one to talk with—"

"You will, Charles. You'll learn to talk again . . . with Eleanor," she said, not able to restrain the jealousy.

"I need *you,* Jessica. Don't you feel my need?"

She had never wanted to hurt anyone, she thought dully, least of all to hurt the ones she loved. And yet life was full of hurt and pain. To live fully one had to experience it. To avoid it entirely meant not living at all. She had hurt herself coming to love this man. If one hurt others, one hurt oneself, too. Yet she did not regret loving him. If it had caused pain, there had been the pleasure and the gloriousness of it, as well.

He rested his head on her shoulder. It was heavy on her now. She stroked the thick hair. She murmured endearments.

"Promise me," he said quickly, raising himself to look at her.

The words came before she could stop them.

"I cannot. The cold will set in if I wait. I must go, Charles. I *must!*"

His tears fell upon her upturned face, horrifying them both.

Shock went slashing through her. She had never before seen a man cry. And Charles, who was so strong. . . . She began to cry, too, great, wracking sobs, muted (Eleanor, the children must not hear), the sorrow tightly binding her chest. Her throat must find release—she cried quietly—he cried quietly. . . .

They lay upon the bed together, beyond passion but not beyond grief. They lay holding one another, and slowly the sense of their bodies touching brought about a communion of comfort and for brief periods they fell asleep. A few minutes and then he would come awake with convulsive movement. A few minutes and, sighing, she would open her eyes. And then again they would slip into oblivion, for only a few seconds it seemed to them, half-waking to feel the reassurance of the other still there.

Then the grandfather clock tolled the fifth hour and roused them more fully. Jessica could see the lightening at the window and gently she tugged at Charles to bring him to his feet.

At first he would not look at her, overcome by embarrassment. His face flushed, then went pale. He clamped his lips together tightly. His eyes searched the floor, the walls around them. And then it passed. He turned to her. He took her hand warmly and brought her to the door with him. Before he opened it, he kissed first one of her hands, and then the other, on the palms and on the outer sides. She reached for both his hands and did the same, kissing one and then the other. They clasped their hands together to reaffirm a bond, and then quietly he was gone.

He made love to her once more, three nights later, but she knew that he had been back again with Chloe or Eleanor, she did not know which, or possibly with both. But it was loving love. Afterward he told her they must have this to remember, that it had been ever this way, with love and affection. Only that one time they must forget. And tomorrow, after dinner, they would talk. Her tears came again—she thought they had been gone forever with Jason—and she held him close. Oh, God, what had she done? It was like Eleanor's brandy; she was giving him—it—up, and it was so difficult, so damn hard, as Eleanor had said. She stroked his beautiful head, she ran her fingers down his elegant and arrogant nose, along his cheekbones and the strong jaw, over the rims of his long oval eyes. "I'll never forget you, Charles," she whispered, "never!"

They talked almost matter-of-factly the next evening, as he had said.

"I'll give you a carriage," he told her, "and two horses to draw it. Billy is your servant, really, and he may go with you. I would put you on the stagecoach, the way you came, but I know you want to look about you more and follow some of your leads. And I do have a few for you—stops you can make along the way, plantations where Jason did business."

"Thank you, Charles," she said. "I should think one horse would be sufficient."

"No," he said, "I'm giving you a pair, because there will be an extra passenger, if you are willing."

"Oh," she said, surprised, "who?"

"Aletha."

"Aletha?"

"As she grows older, life will be very difficult for her here, Jessica," he said sadly. "She is my daughter, as you well know—and everyone else does too. She would have a half-existence here. Would you take her—and raise her?"

"Oh, Charles!" she said, wanting to throw her arms about him, but he did not seem open to this now, "I would treasure her! She would be your gift to me."

"She has grown to love you as her teacher."

She was surprised that he should have known, but then she realized he was back again with Chloe; she would have told him.

"But her mother?"

"She wants you to take her. It was her idea. But," he said sincerely, "I can think of no better solution for Aletha. I'll provide for her. We'll always be in touch, won't we Jessica?" he said, permitting a note of wistfulness to enter his voice. "By post, at least? We won't lose each other? Not completely?"

"No. We shan't ever really lose each other, Charles."

"And she could pass—pass for white—up North or in England.

Her color could be Spanish or Sicilian—an Arabian princess," he said proudly.

"Oh, she is so beautiful and has such a quick mind! I love her, Charles, as I love Jenny and Charlie. I would take her without any conditions, even without the coach, without help from you, if I had known that Chloe would let her go—that you would be willing."

"I am—and her mother is, for the child's sake."

"Thank you, for Aletha. I promise to love her as your child, Charles, and to make her my own."

"Without hating her mother?"

"Yes."

"Certainly not her color? No, not you."

"Never."

He sighed.

"And you will be supplied with maps and everything for your comfort."

"I won't have to depend upon the North Star."

He looked at her grimly.

"I'm giving you Joseph."

"Oh!" Her hand flew to her throat. "You would not punish him!"

"What? By giving him to you? Will you be that hard a task-mistress?"

How had he known? Chloe? His old mammy Julia? Was Eleanor's fine hand behind all of this?

"Oh, Charles."

"You will have his papers. Everything will be in order. And he drives as well as William—well, almost. It will be good for you and Aletha to have him along. Even with his papers, you will need to be extremely careful, however. There are many bounty hunters around, and sometimes they don't care about papers at all. Sometimes they have been known to tear them up and smuggle a slave out of his owner's hands and into the slave market again."

"Oh," she said, horrified, "whatever will we do?"

"Are you sure you won't change your mind about going?" he asked wistfully.

"I'm sure."

"Then just be careful. I'll give you arms and I'll accompany you part of the way, to the main road that you will follow . . ."

"Bounty hunters," she said.

"Ask Joseph about them," he suggested grimly. "The hands all know about bounty hunters. They know everything there is to know about running away. It's such knowledge that keeps them in their place."

She looked at him questioningly.

"Joseph is a good young man."

"Yes," he said. "He is Julia and Cicero's son in every sense of the word. I am glad that he and Billy will be there to see you and Aletha safe—as safe as can be under the circumstances. . . . Oh, I want to keep you here," he lashed out savagely. "I want you here, Jessica!"

"But there's Aletha, too."

He brushed his hand over his forehead.

"Yes," he said. "Yes."

They were to leave quickly, the next day, before any rumor, fed by unexplained excitement, about Joseph and Aletha might spread among the hands and the countryside. Charles worked with cold efficiency. He called Joseph and Billy to his office and asked Jessica to attend. The young men stood at attention; Jessica he directed to a chair beside his desk, where he presided.

"Joseph," he said directly, having no time or inclination for preamble, "you now belong to Miz Jessica; I have sold you to her and the papers are being drawn up."

He looked sardonically at Jessica, and her heart quaked. He had drawn her into his circle, which she thought to be base, and had made her a slave owner, too. But his voice changed when he spoke of Aletha. "I'm providing papers, too, for Aletha." He would brook no more conversation before Joseph and Billy about the child. "Joseph, you are to be a good boy, do everything Miz Jessica tells you, understand?"

"Yassuh."

"Mind you now. And Billy, you have paid your keep in good labor, I am told, and you are not bonded to me—so you are free to go. You are also free to bear arms, which Joseph is not, and I am providing you with a handpiece, which you must use if necessary. Can you shoot a gun, Billy?"

"Captain Northrup taught me, sir."

"Good."

"Thank you, sir."

"I have drawn maps that you both are to study and take with you. You may come stand beside me at the desk and I shall point out the route. The stops at night are marked. The route takes you to these plantations where I am known and where you will be safe. You must look out along the way, Joseph, for the paddy rollers." Joseph bobbed his head. "They are on the prowl, often stealing slaves to sell elsewhere. You know that, Joseph, don't you?"

"Yassuh."

Their heads were bowed over the maps as Charles traced his markings with the point of his quill. He went over them again and again, not expecting the boys to read them but telling them familiar landmarks to look for as they went down this road a way and then as they turned here, there would be a church, here a river, here a country store, and so on.

"I have routed you all the way to Boston, if you decide to continue from Philadelphia," he said to Jessica, then turning to the boys again. "The maps will be entrusted in the care of Miz Jessica, of course." Then, more gently, "Joseph, you go spend some time with Mammy Julia–she'll miss you, you know; you are excused from your other duties, now that," he said sardonically again, "you belong to Miz Jessica–unless she has other duties for you this minute?"

"N-n-no," she stammered.

Joseph bobbed his head dutifully, not looking directly into his ex-master's eyes, thanking him.

"You, too, Billy. . . ."

Charles having dismissed them, they went quickly.

"And Aletha now will be yours–legally and in every other way, Jessica."

"I will treasure her, Charles."

"I know you will."

He rose from the desk and drew her up from the chair. He placed his arms around her.

"This will be our last private farewell," he said softly. "There will be much activity about the house tonight, preparing the child."

And soothing the mother against her sorrow, Jessica thought with a pang.

She nodded.

"I'll accompany you part of the way tomorrow, but I want to tell you how much you have meant to me, Jessica. I love you very much, in my fashion." He kissed the top of her head. "There are different compartments, in my mind or in my soul, whichever it is—you know?" She nodded again, and her arms went up around his firm, full neck. "I did not like the idea of losing you, and I still do not, but knowing you will take the child and raise her so that she can live a full, free life has made it easier." He kissed her, on the mouth now, and for a few moments they clung silently together. "You have no sense of sin?"

"No."

"Nor do I. Value what we have had, Jessica."

"I shall."

"You have brought much goodness to this home."

"And you have been good for me, Charles."

"And for that one time . . ."

She shook her head.

"Don't speak of it."

"You will write?"

"Yes, but not of us, Charles."

"But of how you are and what you are doing . . ."

"Yes."

"The letters may fall into the wrong hands. When you write of Aletha, please call her by another name."

"I shall write of her as Charlotte."

He nodded gratefully.

"That's gracious."

She looked at him longingly, then resolutely looked away.

"There is much to do. Sally is waiting to pack my trunk."

"Yes. But let me hold you for a minute longer . . . Jessica, my dear . . . my love . . ."

She went into the cook house to take another private farewell, of Julia and Cicero. Cicero looked very woebegone and his wrinkled hands trembled.

"Ahll nebbuh see im agin," he said sadly, to Jessica. "Mah younges boy, mah son . . ."

"But he'll be gone way up Nawth," Julia said softly to him. "Yall wan dat foh owah chile, don say not, Cero."

He nodded but could not smile.

"I'll set him free, just as soon as the proper time comes," Jessica whispered, and Julia drew her to her ample bosom.

"Yall be good ta ma boy."

"I will," Jessica promised. "I will."

"But the junney's so danjus," Cicero fretted.

"Et's danjus heah," Julia said firmly. "Kine ob boy he am he'd only come ta trubble heah. . . . Aletha," she asked of Jessica, "she will be yo chile?"

"Yes, Julia, I promise that too."

Julia hugged her. Then the smell of biscuits browning set her scurrying to the woodstove. She brought out great pans and told Jessica she was fixing a large hamper of food for the travelers; Master Charles, she said, had so instructed her. And she winked her eye at Jessica to let her know she would have done so anyway if he had not. Jessica came to kiss Julia as she was fussing with other pots and pans. Julia took an amulet from her bosom and pressed it into Jessica's hand for safe travel. Jessica nodded and kissed her again. She then went to Cicero and took his hand. He jumped as though she had burned him, but she shook his hand nevertheless and thanked him for everything he had done for her.

She almost bumped into Joseph as she went out the door.

"Well, Joseph Joseph," she said quietly, "we shall be on our way to the North Star tomorrow."

* * *

It was difficult to say farewell to Jenny and Charlie. She sat with them in their nursery as they were served their supper. Jenny wailed and did not want to eat. At first she was angry at Teacher for deserting her, then sad. Charlie was more manly, the way he was taught to act when he was in pain—not to show it. For a while he became withdrawn.

"You will be a great artist some day," Jessica whispered to him. "Keep working. Draw everything you see—people, animals, flowers, as you have been doing, Charlie. Keep a book of them to show me. Some day we shall meet again and you will have a big collection for us to share. . . . And you, Jenny, you shall be a great beauty, and you must read every book you can put your hands on—both of you—so that you learn about the world and how to think for yourselves. Hear?"

Both children nodded solemnly.

She hugged them both and their tears intermingled, even Charlie's, for he could no longer keep up the pretense of not caring.

"But none of this tomorrow morning," she warned them. "This is our private time. Oh, I shall miss you both so much . . . !"

She sat with Eleanor in her room before dinner. Jessica looked at her approvingly. Her hair was carefully coiffed and her dress elegant and spotless. So different, she thought gladly, from the way Eleanor had looked the first time she had seen her in this house. The fine furniture tops were not so cluttered. The chamber was orderly and sweet-smelling. Jessica could see no container of whiskey—but then it could be concealed.

Eleanor saw her looking and laughed grimly.

"It's gone, Jessie," she said. "Maybe not for good. I hope forever, but who knows? It's so easy to backslide. . . ."

"But you'll try?"

"Yes, I'll try. Jessica, I've weighed it all—you've done me more good than harm, in the end . . . and so I must be glad that you came."

"Oh, Eleanor—"

"Especially now that you are leaving."

They both laughed, though it was no jest.

"I fell into the trap of being a southern woman," Eleanor said.

"Not all southern women . . ."

Eleanor ignored that.

"And you," she continued, "you fell into the trap of simply *being* a woman."

"Perhaps."

"Yes," she said. "I shan't say that I shall miss you, but I am glad that you were here and I love you as I always have—well, I love you—and I am grateful to you. . . ."

"Grateful?"

"Oh, for many things. And now especially for taking that child away. It will be easier for me not to see her all the time."

"Yes," Jessica said sadly.

"Perhaps one day Charles will send away her mother . . ."

Jessica remained silent.

"Perhaps," Eleanor said. "Probably not. But perhaps . . . good fortune go with you, Jessica, and may you be safe and find what your heart is set upon . . ."

* * *

Jessica and her party took their leave just before dawn. Charles had provided a coach hitched to a pair of mature sorrel horses. She would never be able to repay him, Jessica thought, as she looked at the fine conveyance. She had thought of a surrey, but of course that had been unrealistic—she realized that now. They could never have made the long trip in a light rig. This one had a sturdy look that gave her confidence, and she trusted that it would be more comfortable than the stage in which she had arrived.

William had already stacked her trunk, and Chloe's little carpetbag and Billy's and Joseph's small possessions tied in kerchief sacks, in the storage area. The food hamper was inside and the maps safe in a case that she carried. Charles, astride his favorite stallion, circled the coach and inspected it from every angle, tested the horses' cinch straps and reins, and handed them to Joseph who, with Billy, had already scrambled aboard the driver's seat. Charles gave careful, last-minute instructions about the grooming and resting of the horses at night. He looked into the buckets of oats tied under the springs. He shook the shaft, making the horses neigh nervously, but found it steady. He nodded to Jessica that it was time to go inside.

She took another long look at the Sedgely plantation house. She would never forget the graceful columns and the broad veranda sweeping around the building surrounded by stands of magnificent trees and lilac bushes and bountiful green shrubbery. She glanced upward to the portico where Eleanor was standing in her dressing gown, red hair streaming gracefully to her shoulders. The women raised their hands to each other in salute and farewell. Under the catalpa tree, a few feet from the driveway, Charlie and Jenny stood with Sally. Julia and Cicero were with them. Julia was twisting her apron and Cicero's hands still shook.

Charles turned in the saddle and looked to the doorway of the manor house and beckoned. Chloe, her long dress swishing around her graceful form, came walking out with Aletha, who clung tightly to her. Her face impassive, but her dark eyes large and moist over her high golden cheekbones, Chloe approached Jessica. The two women's eyes met and held for a full minute. Chloe's were proud but yet full of supplication; there was grief but yet there was joy. Jessica stared at her first in jealousy, but that quickly vanished in a rush of compassion.

Chloe pressed her lips to the top of the child's head, loosened her hand, and placed it in Jessica's. Aletha trembled, with so many people standing before her, all staring soberly at her. Then, looking up at her teacher, and knowing the happiness of the hours in her classroom, Aletha smiled tremulously at her, and Jessica kissed the top of her head, too. Chloe vanished inside the big house. Then William took the child, before she could notice what he was about to do, and placed her upon the seat inside. Jessica waved once more to the somber group, fixing them forevermore in her mind and her heart. Jenny began to wail and Sally saw to her. Swiftly Jessica entered the coach. Joseph spoke to the horses and handled the reins. Charles' mount came into the postilion place. They were off.

Chapter Seven

They had traveled for several hours and Charles, despite his stated plan to leave earlier, continued to ride with them. Still holding Aletha's hand tightly in her own, Jessica could see through the coach window his mount's rump and part of the tall figure of the man. Charles had bypassed the post highway and had directed them on a seldom-used road. The going was difficult. There were ruts and gnarled roots and rocks in the hard sunbaked soil and the coach rolled and jarred and jolted as they proceeded. Jessica thought of all the traveling she had done in the past six months, and she decided the sea voyage, despite her seasickness at first, was most pleasant of all. Captain and Mrs. Northrup and Douglas Graham had been so kind to her and Billy. She would have liked to travel along the coast, but Charles had said that this would be very impractical—that the waterways they would need to pass were better traversed by boats but while these craft would save time they were not safe at all for a lone woman traveling with slaves.

She stared down again at the maps in her lap. She looked at the lines Charles had carefully drawn. It seemed to her the way he routed them north was indirect and at times almost circuitous, but she imagined good reason had decided this. Charles knew the location of swamplands and where the paddy rollers, whoever they were, were most apt to lie in wait and which plantation areas were best to avoid. He had told her in a calm voice, not to alarm but to inform her, that several women had made journeys from the North to the South with the sole purpose of transporting slaves away from their masters to freedom on their return swing. There had been great anger when these forays were made known. One of the women had been apprehended, and the scalawags who had caught her had been hard on her and the people in her carriage. What had they done? she had asked. But Charles had simply shaken his head and looked grim. His expression had made all the horror stories she had heard race through her mind, and for a moment she thought of them now. Rape, flogging, murder. She shuddered involuntarily, and Aletha looked at her questioningly. The expression of fear on the child's face made her more resolute. She smiled calmly at Aletha and looked out at the trees and their canopy of green through which they were passing. Much of the path—she could scarcely call it a road now—was through uncleared ground, and she wondered who had made the swath through the forest. Indians? Fur trappers? The Indians were gone now for the most part. Charles had told her of the Virginia troops that last century had fought the French and Indians after raids in the state. There had been a steady migration after that, and the Indian population had grown smaller and smaller. There was the movement of Indians to the West and to Florida at the bottom of the South. Charles had said there were still some small Indian colonies left near Virginia cities, where the families came to trade. They did not make good servants, Charles had said. Efforts to enslave them, years ago before the African slaves had been brought to the country, had proved futile.

The coach halted and Charles withdrew from her vision as he approached the drivers. After a lengthy pause, as she listened to the sound of his voice talking to Joseph and Billy, he wheeled around and approached her door. She jumped up and opened it, preparing to leap down. But he shook his head at her as she stood framed in the aperture. He had not dismounted. He was very erect in his seat.

"I must take leave of you," he said evenly. "You will reach the Avery plantation before sundown. It is marked on the map. Soon you must make a rest stop. I have told Joseph. Give him the map but keep the notes I have written to the plantation masters. The notes were placed in the same packet as the maps." She nodded; she had seen them. "You will enjoy Southern hospitality. I have explained the children as your servants—Aletha and Joseph as your slaves—and you must keep your papers with you carefully at all times."

"Yes, Charles. I shall."

"And keep the maps with you at night."

"Yes, Charles."

"Well, then—"

"Goodbye?"

"Yes."

He raised his head and looked over Jessica's shoulder at the child clinging to her dress.

"Goodbye, Aletha," he called. "Be good. Listen to your new mistress. Some day perhaps I'll come North to see you both."

The child smiled. Even she, Jessica thought dully, knew that he would not come.

"Thank you for everything," Jessica murmured.

His face was pale.

"Have a safe journey."

She nodded, unable to talk.

"I must go back," he said, so low that she could scarcely hear him. "I shall miss you."

"And I shall miss you too, Charles."

He wheeled his horse around sharply and dug his heels into the stirrups. The horse set off at a gallop. Charles was soon out of sight.

Jessica, desolate, stood in the doorway for a few more minutes, not wanting the child to see her tears. She had just brushed them away when Billy came to talk to her.

"Joseph has the reins," he reassured her. "Master Charles said there's a clearing just around the bend."

"Good," she said briskly, "that's where we'll pause for lunch."

Billy grinned.

"We all need to stretch our legs, Miz Jessica. You comfortable back there?"

"As comfortable as can be expected."

"Joseph tries to miss the holes."

"I'm grateful for that."

"When you close the door, we'll start again."

"Oh, yes," she said, "Sorry . . . I . . . very well." She withdrew and sat down again beside Aletha. Billy slammed the door and soon they were on their way again . . . on their own now.

She had no time to grieve. At lunch break they all disappeared behind bushes, discreetly far from one another. When they reassembled, brushing their clothing, Joseph unpacked the lunch hamper.

"Is this all for one meal?" Jessica asked, astounded.

"Yassum. Mammy has done us proud," he said, spreading a large white cloth on the grass. He then opened a napkin full of fried chicken, another of biscuits, and a basket of sweet potato pies and apple pies and mince pies, and removed the tops of stone jars filled with apple cider and milk.

"Perhaps we'd better keep some of this for tomorrow," Jessica suggested.

"Oh, they'll pack another basket for us to take in the mornin, Miz Jess'ca," Joseph told her. "No one leaves a plantation wiv—wi*th*," he smiled at her, "without vittles for the day's trip."

"Better food than on the ship," Billy said.

"It wasn't so bad." She looked at him; he too must have thought of Captain and Mrs. Northrup as they had begun their journey.

"Oh, the biscuit and brandy and cheese were good," Billy said, remembering the galley, "but all that salted fish—" he wrinkled his nose.

"Joseph," Jessica said, seeing him get up with a napkin of food, ready to leave the group, "stay here with us."

He looked uneasy.

"I dunno . . ."

"We all stay together—and especially when we picnic. Join in the feast." She gestured to a tree stump nearby that would serve as table. "Sit down, please."

He seemed uncertain, but he was hungry, and soon he was biting into a drumstick as enthusiastically as the others.

"Julia is certainly a fine cook," Jessica said appreciatively, wiping her fingers daintily on a napkin. "Joseph, did you often have food like this back at the Sedgely plantation?"

"Mammy always done took cayah—care—of the house slaves. Wiv . . . *with* fieldhands, it's diffrent." He swallowed his food, then laughed. "No hog jowls fer—" *"For,"* she said automatically. "—for us." He then went on to tell Jessica and Billy, who listened attentively, and Aletha too—although her eyes were fastened on the flight of a butterfly—that the hands mostly ate pork, not those parts high on the hock, and corn grits or mush, sometimes rice, sometimes rice and beans mixed together, and sometimes collards and okra and other greens they were permitted to grow behind their cabins. And sometimes they trapped coon and possum and rabbit. "Oh, thass good!" He said sometimes there was a party in the quarters when the trapping was bountiful. Lots of eating, lots of singing and dancing and, as a special treat, there were goobers.

"Goobers?"

"Pindahs . . . pinders," Joseph corrected himself.

"Mamma says they's peanuts," Aletha said. She had been quiet until now and Jessica smiled at her encouragingly.

"Do you like peanuts, Aletha?"

"Yassum."

"We'll get you some when we can."

"And fish sometimes," Joseph continued, "when they can cotch 'em."

"Is it difficult to be a fieldhand, Joseph?"

"Spozed to be bettah . . . *better*," he was trying to sound all the consonants of his words now, the way she had taught him, "to be a house slave, but it's mo . . . more joyful outside. . . . you kin—" "Can," Jessica said. "—can talk and joke and sing long as you pick or hoe the cotton." He looked down at his hands. "Long as no mean overseer's aroun . . . around."

"Not at the Sedgely plantation?"

"No, miz."

"Master Charles is a good bossman," Billy said. "Not like stories you hear about other places."

"Tell me what you know about the bounty hunters."

"Theys like paddy rollers, Miz Jess'ca. Bad men. They come with dogs and look for runaways. They gets five dollars a day or more—"

"That's a lot of money!" Billy said.

"An extra when they cotch a nigger. . . ."

"Nigra," Jessica said automatically.

Joseph repeated they were bad men. He said they often did not honor the pass system, even when the master gave written permission for the slave to travel from one plantation to the other. Sometimes, Joseph said grimly, a bad master could even give a slave a note that told the paddy roller to whup him. The paddy roller would then beat the unsuspecting slave and bring him limping back to his plantation. Some plantation masters found it easier—and sometimes funnier—to punish slaves that way.

Jessica noticed the fear that was gathering in Aletha's face and wished she had not begun the discussion.

"Well," she said authoritatively, "they would not dare to trouble us. We're from the Sedgely plantation—that in itself is a guarantee."

"And I have the pistol that Master Charles—" Billy began.

Jessica shook her head at him, looking pointedly at the child, and Billy understood.

"They would not dare," he said lamely.

They ate the pies and drank the milk. The cider and the large amount of leftover food, Jessica decided, should be kept for later in the afternoon. As she gathered up the napkins and sent Aletha off to a clump of daisies to pick a bouquet, Jessica talked quietly to the boys. She would give them the maps to study the path ahead. Then they must return them to her as they approached the Avery plantation. No one should know the boys—and especially Joseph—could read. Joseph must be very careful to conceal that fact. He nodded. He knew well the trouble they all would be in if it were apparent he had been taught the meaning of printed words. And Aletha? Joseph and Billy asked anxiously. Jessica said she would tell the child the same when they were back in the carriage. She would try to keep Aletha with her as much as she could at the plantation.

"Yes," Joseph said sadly, "or she will miss her mama."

Aletha slept, with her head in Jessica's lap, as they continued on their way. She is my charge now, Jessica thought, as they all are. The boys were so young, but they were her protectors too. Charles knew that Joseph was strong and practically full-grown and that Billy, though younger, was wise in the ways of the world. Charles had provided well for her safety. She was not one of those brave and vulnerable women missionaries who must flee from the master, as they took his slaves, and from the bounty hunters as well. With Charles behind her, and the owner's papers in her hands, she was relatively secure.

The Averys, remembering Jessica from the Sedgely ball, were gracious hosts as they greeted her. They sent Aletha to the kitchen but agreed she would then go to her mistress's bedroom to see to her lady's clothing and turn down the bed. The boys were directed to the stable to tend to their horses.

At dinner Jessica talked of Jason. The Averys revealed that they had met him once; he had done some factoring business for them. It was very sad he had disappeared, but Jessica was a young woman and must look for another husband. They had a cousin, a charming young man on the neighboring estate, who had just lost his wife and had small children who needed the hand of a genteel lady. A new eligible Englishwoman appearing in the South always sent flurries into the local gentry. . . . Mrs. Avery smiled playfully at Jessica, tapping her with her fan. Jessica smiled, too, and tried to direct the talk back to Jason.

"He was an excellent factor," Donald Avery said. "He certainly knew the cotton business well. I like direct trade with Europe and he understood that. I still don't know why my imports from the European markets must come from the North. Damn nonsense to boot why so much of our cotton, too, still goes to Europe through Boston. . . . Yes, he was a very astute man, Jason Coopersmith, in some ways and not in others."

Jessica raised her eyebrows.

"Others?"

"Rather rash in his statements."

"Not very discreet, don't you know," Faith Avery said. She brushed imaginary crumbs from her watered silk gown.

"All his talk about the new territories—how all new land annexed to these United States should be free." Donald Avery became indignant thinking about it. "And Jason not even a citizen of this country. Damned impertinent!"

"Well," Jessica tried to placate him, "with the laws against the importation of slaves he may have thought conditions were changing. . . ."

"It cost him dear to be so bold."

"Cost him?" she said fearfully.

"Well," Faith said, "we don't know for sure. But word gets spread around and tempers are high. . . ."

"All of England's press gangs and—" Avery sputtered—"this holier-than-thou attitude!"

"You think—?" Jessica turned to Faith.

"Well now, my dear, there may be room for doubt, but—"

"All the felons and thieves they sent us!"

"That's not the issue, Donald. It was his—"

"A man should tend to his own business. He knew the cotton industry well, I warrant you that."

"You would deal with him again when he reappears?" Jessica said testingly.

"If he appears."

"Oh."

"Yes, I would deal with Jason; his prices were fair. Prices have slumped miserably, my dear. I often wonder how wise I was to follow Charles Sedgely's example of planting cotton. . . . If Jason set a low price, I would know the market was glutted, not that he was trying to make a miserable deal."

"He should not have talked about slaves in that fashion," Faith said sharply. "The way we have to look after them, so expensive to keep . . ."—Jessica had heard that before from Charles; it must be the common cry in these parts, she thought wryly, and yet the slaveholders still kept the slaves—". . . and nobody buying the surplus. And yet ten years ago this state was exporting six thousand nigras annually. Good breeding stock—who cares about foolish laws forbidding importation from Africa! We raise our own here at home. It would be better now to ship the extra hands to new territory or to the turpentine fields further south."

"Well," Donald said heavily, "I shall hold on to my hands until the trend turns upward. If the railroads are ever developed here, as Charles and I believe and hope, we shall have industry after all."

"Oh, yes," Faith said scornfully. "Then what would the nigras do? Can you imagine them working in the factories! And the white trash are just as bad. Don't forget the white-trash labor groups that sprang up ten years ago and had to be put in their place—which we surely did!"

"Well, we're in the 1840s now and they learned their lesson."

"We hope," Faith said tartly.

"Did Jason speak to many people about the territories?" Jessica asked cautiously.

"Well," Donald said disapprovingly, "his reputation as an antislaver was spreading. Damn foolish, a man in his trade, dealing in this part of the country. And his trips to the North, selling there; that didn't help either." He coughed. "People could mistake what his enterprise really was."

"Most indiscreet," Faith joined in.

"And so if he has disappeared from this earth, it is a fair assumption to make that someone helped him from it. I'm sorry, my dear, but you are a young woman and should—"

Jessica shook her head. No one had expressed an opinion so bluntly.

"I had thought he could take care of himself."

"Can't you see the heat that slave talk gives rise to? Even here, in our home, Miz Jessica, and we are generally peaceable people. . . ."

"And perhaps you should take a lesson from it."

Jessica looked incredulously at her hostess.

"Lest you be tarred with the same brush," the other woman continued.

Jessica shivered.

"Now my dear," Donald said, changing his tone, "we've disturbed the lovely lady. Perhaps we could take our coffee and brandy in the drawing room and let our guest tell us of the poets and theater of London. . . ."

Jessica retreated to the guestroom as early as she could. She made certain the door was locked, then raised Aletha from the pallet on the floor to share her bed. The child snuggled against her and in her sleep cried out to her as Mama. Jessica put her arm lightly around her and wished the hours would fly, that it would be morning and they could take to the road even before breakfast. Faith had sent a chill down her spine. The woman had a malevolent look about the eyes that was not matched even by the coldness of her husband's. On the surface they were the gracious receivers of a guest and her party into their home, in accordance with the mores of Southern hospitality, but their conversation had taken an ominous tone. Jessica did not have to search very deeply to sense they condoned whatever misfortune might befall Jason. They were a rigid pair. There was a right way to talk in the South among the plantation owners and a wrong way to talk. And a right way to think. And yet Charles had deemed the Averys safe or he would not have sent the travelers to them. Jessica dreaded the encounter at the next evening's destination; perhaps even Charles did not know his neighbors, farflung as they were, as well as he should.

She would have tossed and turned but for the presence of Aletha. She looked down at the lovely young face. She was a beautiful child, Jessica thought, quick to learn and easy to love. She would keep her as her daughter, she vowed; Jason would approve and would love her, too. But suppose a posse or some paddy rollers with their dogs surrounded him and had done him lethal harm—whipping, burning, hanging—oh dear God, she could not face that! Before tonight his disappearance had been an emotionally charged but still vague happening and she had firmly believed that her search would be fruitful and she would be happily reunited with him. Now the certainty was faltering. There was more evil in the world than she had been aware of—or else she had had an acceptance of evil in the abstract sense. Now it was a living, blazing, destructive force that any speech or encounter could set into ineluctable motion.

She watched the black of night at the window give way to shades of indigo, as she had that time not so long ago when, set aflame by Charles and what could be between them, she could not sleep. She had loved him. She still did and perhaps she always would. Perhaps in time he would fade in her imagination. It did not disturb her feeling for Jason. She still loved Jason and always would. Perhaps he too in time if there were no reunion would fade in her mind. But she had learned that it was possible to love different people at the same time, and to do so did not lessen the love for either one.

The child stirred in her arm. Her hand had fallen asleep and gently Jessica withdrew it. She rose quietly from the bed. Without waking, Aletha cried out for her mother again, and Jessica stared at her, empathizing with the little girl. And she thought of Chloe and what she must be suffering this night, sending her child away never to see her again. Jessica's own mother had sent her daughter off, too, on a perilous journey, but it was different. Her mother, Jessica thought tenderly, could join her if she chose—and if she were strong enough for the long voyage—but Chloe had no such choice. What a loss she must be feeling, the child gone from her forever. Was Chloe lying awake weeping? Jessica imagined Charles was there with her to comfort her. And perhaps Charles must take comfort from Chloe for having sent away his elder daughter, fruit of his first passion. He, too, must feel a sense of great loss. She forced herself to hope that Chloe could give him solace. Jessica sighed. She had never dreamed that she would be part of an uncomfortable relationship, a sisterhood nevertheless, she and Eleanor and Chloe, bound together by the love of, and for, one man.

Jessica walked to the window and looked down. She thought she heard a rustle in the foundation plantings below. She tried to block out every sense but her hearing. Nothing came again. Perhaps it was a squirrel or a bird or even a cat or dog. She may have seen a shadow, or she may have imagined it. Her nerves were on edge this night; she would be so glad, she thought again, to quit the house.

The azure light at the window and the ornate French ormolu clock on the fireplace mantel indicated now the propriety of leaving the room. Relieved, Jessica roused Aletha, who looked about her in bewilderment for a few minutes, her eyes brightening when they lit upon Jessica. They made a hasty toilet, the child modestly turning from the woman as they each tended to themselves. Quickly Jessica placed the night things into her heavy damask bag. She gave it to Aletha to carry, for the proper appearance of mistress and slave, kissed the top of the child's head before they left the bedchamber, grandly walked down the winding graceful stairway in the center hall, and shooed the little girl off to the kitchen quarter.

Faith eyed Jessica narrowly as they sat at the table.

"You look a little peaked this morning," she observed. "It would be better if you rested here a day or two."

"Thank you," Jessica murmured, "but I must go on."

"The way really to see the country is to tarry a while in different places."

"Well, perhaps the next time," Donald Avery said, helping himself to a large slice of ham from the silver platter served by the houseman, dressed in satin knee breeches and jacket, a powdered white wig sitting askew above his dark head.

"If you would stay for a while, we would give a ball in your honor."

From the changed, wistful tone of Faith's voice, Jessica realized she was a lonely woman.

She murmured her thanks again and said that she wanted to travel while the weather was still fine. Otherwise she would have stayed longer at Sedgely Hall.

They talked safely of the fine Sedgely house and Charles' setting the example of turning from tobacco growing to cotton and how the soil had benefited. Though, Donald Avery amended, sooner or later they all would have to rotate to something else again—perhaps wheat, already popular as an alternate crop—to prevent recurring soil exhaustion. Ah, the lot of the poor farmer, he sighed, while Jessica kept her eyes on the fine china plate set in front of her.

Later, they walked with her out of the house, to see her off. They admired the carriage and Donald Avery commented on the good physique of the driver.

"Yes, a fine young buck," Donald said. "Good stock for breeding. Must borrow him from Sedgely when you send him home. We'll give him a broadwife here."

"Joseph is now my property," Jessica said calmly, though the words were abhorrent to her. "I purchased him from Charles and of course have his papers."

"You bought him?"

"Yes. When I set up my own household in Philadelphia, I shall need a general houseman and butler. And Aletha, too, as my personal servant. I shall teach her to sew."

She looked nervously at the coach. She noted that the horses looked rested; even more, they seemed eager, and Joseph kept them on tight rein. Jessica's eyes caught Billy's, and he jumped from the box to open the door for her. She was relieved he read her so well.

A large slave woman, reminding Jessica of Julia, came out of the cook house carrying a huge basket of food. Aletha ran at her heels. In the child's arms were loaves of bread whose ends peeked from the cloth wrappings.

"Well!" Faith said wryly. "I really didn't get a good look at the little pickaninny last night. Good-looking little thing, ain't she? You can see whose by-blow she is! Well!"

"Get into the carriage, Aletha!"

Jessica's voice frightened the child and she scrambled forward, letting Billy boost her upward and inside.

"Well," Faith continued sardonically, "she has good hair, but you can't say she's just a little sallow, too much coffee in the cream. She could be a Moorish princess or a—"

"She's a good little handservant . . . and I shall teach her to work hard," Jessica said evenly.

"Eleanor must be happy that you have bought her."

"Aletha will fit into my house staff very well," Jessica said coldly.

She hurried her thanks and her goodbyes and Billy had only to touch her elbow and she was into the coach as if on a tight spring. She waved from the window to her host and hostess and could feel her face burning as she rode away.

A few hours later they stopped for an early lunch. The road Charles had set for them was still as rugged as before, and when she had descended from the coach and the children looked away she rubbed her sore bottom and her legs and made a few dancing steps. She stretched and it helped. She grinned at Aletha who, like a puppy, was running around in place. The field they had come upon and had chosen for their picnic was sunlit and still. But Jessica suddenly stood there, with her head to one side, listening. She noted that Joseph, watering the horses, was doing the same.

"What is it, Joseph?" she called.

"I dunno," he said slowly, and she came closer to catch his words. "Somethins gone on not too far way." He patted the near horse's rump. "Queenie knows bout it too." Both horses pawed the ground.

"Do you think it's wise to stay here?" she asked the boys. Billy had joined them.

"I dunno," Joseph said. "We maht—might—run into it effen—if—we go on."

"That's true. You think it's a storm coming up?"

Joseph looked at the clear sky.

"Not that kina storm."

Her hand flew to her throat.

"Trouble?"

"Mebbe."

She saw Billy touch the sidepiece that was tucked in his belt, take it from its place, and hide it inside his clothes.

"Well," Jessica said, taking charge, "let's have lunch and then continue on our way. I don't think we should go off this path unless we must, for fear of getting lost. We shall see. . . . Let's try the goodies the Avery cook provided us."

But lunch was not the jolly picnic of the day before. Joseph went off a short distance away to eat alone, and Jessica did not stop him this time. She played with her food, not hungry, and listened carefully.

"I thought I heard a dog bark," she said quietly to Billy.

"Yes'm. I did, too. And a thrashin-about sound, maybe many horses' hooves."

They listened intently again. It was not quite like a high wind blowing; it was the low steady hum of energy coming closer.

"Let's get back into the carriage," she said suddenly.

Without question, they each assumed a task, quickly gathered the remaining food and packed it, harnessed the horses, resumed their former places on the box and inside, and were about to set off again.

A dog bounded into view. It howled and another dog followed him. They startled the horses, and Joseph had difficulty keeping them from rearing. Aletha clutched at Jessica so as not to fall off the carriage seat. "It will be all right," Jessica murmured to her, wishing that she had more conviction that it would be so.

Joseph did not attempt to move the coach. Now they all clearly heard the approaching horses, and it was evident to Jessica that Joseph knew it would be useless, and perilous, to try to outrun them. Before they could guess, or acknowledge to themselves, who rode the horses, the riders came at a gallop.

A group of rough-looking men in rough clothing circled the carriage, pointing their guns at the two boys on the box seat. They cried out some coarse words to them and then came behind their leader to the carriage door. Trying to still the trembling of her hand, Jessica opened it.

"Howdy, ma'am," the leader said to her, tugging at his hat. "Sorry to detain ya but we're lookin fer a runaway slave. Slave patrol—by order of th' county."

"Joseph is my slave and so is this girl." She pointed to the cringing child. "I have their papers if you must see them, but if not please let us go on our way."

"I know bout Joseph an the gal," the man said insolently. "It's a bigger wench we're lookin fer. A runaway from the Avery place."

"We've just left the Avery plantation."

"I know that, too, ma'am. Master Avery tole me. Beggin yer pardon, we'll jes look inside fer the varmint."

"I didn't steal any possession of the Averys!" Jessica cried, enraged.

"No one said ya did, ma'am. Sometimes they stow away . . ."

He dismounted and came inside while his men kept their guns on the carriage. He asked Jessica to stand up for a moment. She was tempted not to cooperate but he had a frightening look and she was not going to invite disaster if she could help it, for her own and the others' sake. The man opened the two seats, which had inner storage compartments that Jessica had not even been aware of. She held her breath. Could someone, unknown to her, possibly have . . . ? But there was no one there. In disappointment, the man slammed down the cushions. He glared at Aletha and she began to cry. He slapped her, and Jessica was about to fly at him but she restrained herself in time.

"I can chastise my own slaves myself," she said icily, amazed at herself that she could speak at all.

"See that ya do! Snivelin brat!"

He left the coach and Jessica could see him walking slowly all around it, looking underneath it, on the innersides of the wheels. Then he roughly pulled the boys from their perch, so they fell at the horses' hooves. They did not resist. They just scrambled to their feet, not dusting themselves off, and standing tensely still. The man opened the box and looked in there as he had in the carriage seats. Evidently no one hid inside, for he banged down the box lid. He jumped down with the buggy whip he had snatched from its holder.

"We'll keep this," he said, standing close to Joseph. "We need this fer niggers."

"Yassuh," Joseph said, keeping his eyes on the ground.

Billy remained motionless. Jessica hoped he would stay that way and not think about his iron piece.

The man mounted his horse again and rode once more to Jessica's open door.

"All right," he said. "Mine yall, helpin an escaped slave is a serious oh-fence in this here state and man er wumman it makes no difrence, we punish both the same."

"I have no escaped slave," Jessica said wearily.

"We'll fine her," he said, tapping the whip butt smartly against the carriage side.

"And when you do, you'll take her back to the Avery plantation?" Jessica asked anxiously.

"She'll wish she never been birthed."

Jessica stared at him in horror, but he was soon gone from her sight. The dogs leading, the men on horseback dashed out of the clearing into the green thicket through which the path led.

Now Jessica permitted herself to shake. She felt the great chill of shock, and when she looked at Aletha and saw the livid imprint of fingermarks across her cheek, Jessica felt a wave of anger engulf her so strongly that her eyes misted and she could scarcely breathe. It will fade, it will fade, she told herself, until she recovered. Then she clasped the child to her and allowed herself to cry.

She soon grew aware that Joseph and Billy were standing diffidently at the door. She let go of Aletha and sat back once more upon her seat.

"You both did very well," she told them. "I'm proud of the way you handled yourselves. I hope they'll outride us and we won't come upon them again."

"They evil," Joseph said quietly. "Slave catchers hahred—hired—by plantations. They do it for money—and for po—pure—spite."

They set off once more at an easy trot; Joseph seemed to be judging the distance between the carriage and the patrol and was determined to keep that space. Jessica studied Charles' maps and was dismayed that there were so many blank spots in them. There were few roads and they could be in trouble if they did not follow the route he had outlined. Nevertheless, the wavy line of a small creek off to the west of their route, not more than a few miles or so she would judge from the small scale Charles had meticulously included on the paper, captured her attention. They had been near no water on their way, and here they might finish their interrupted lunch. Much more important, which resolved her decision to make the detour, was the idea that they would be out of the way of the patrol on its return. No doubt the patrol would use the same road they had all traveled before, since there was no other in this section. She rapped on the ceiling of the coach and Joseph stopped the horses and ran to her window.

She showed him the creek on the map and asked whether he thought he could find the turnoff that would lead to it. Would there be a way to get through? He thought for a while and said he and Billy would watch the road carefully and maybe they could find one. If there is water, there must be old Indian paths leading to it, he told her. Would it be wide enough for the coach? They would see, he said. They seemed to be of one mind, wanting to avoid the posse.

They crawled along slowly now so that Joseph could search the path for an adjoining branch. The sides of the path were so dense with shrubbery and foliage that it was difficult to see what was beyond them. A few times Joseph stopped the carriage and jumped down to part branches, like curtains, and look through them. He peered around carefully, and Jessica imagined he was searching for animal tracks. Perhaps they might come to a deer crossing, she thought excitedly, that would lead the way. And ten minutes later they did. Joseph found the deer hoofprints and droppings and they led inward through the brush. He disappeared through the bushes and they could hear his triumphant cry. He ran back and told them he had found it. And it was just big enough for their carriage. Maybe hunters had brought sleds through, or Indians portaging their canoes or dragging their *travois,* or litters, bearing their animal hides and clay pots and baskets. All he and Billy need do was to rip out the undergrowth that shielded it from view and blocked it. There was the hatchet in one of the pails under the carriage, and Joseph and Billy took turns chopping away at the dense shrubbery. At last they cleared enough to get the coach through. As an afterthought, Joseph pulled to a stop again after they had bumped over the uneven sidebank; he quickly jumped down, ran to the aperture, and filled it again with the cut-down foliage to camouflage the gap. Then they slowly went on again.

The carriage walls brushed both sides of the new path and foliage colored the windows green. A filigree of myriad shapes was etched upon the rippling glass. Jessica felt as if she were traveling underwater, and she could see Aletha's big eyes grow even larger in wonder. At times the horses balked; the branches must be scratching them. But Joseph urged them on and, miraculously, it seemed to Jessica, they persevered. Perhaps they smelled the water. Suddenly the path widened, and they came upon the bank of a wide creek.

They all left the carriage. Joseph unharnessed the horses again and tied them, on a long rein, to a tree. He would water them later when the heat of their bodies, raised by their exertion, had subsided.

They decided to rest here for a while and have an early supper. Jessica felt it was better this way, even though they would reach the next plantation at sunset. The longer they stayed, the better the chances that the patrol would have returned to its headquarters.

Jessica brought some pillows from the seats and they stretched out in the sun.

"The girl," Jessica said to Joseph, "she must have been very brave—or very foolish—to run off."

"Evbody wanna run off," Joseph said flatly. Jessica knew their relationship was one of trust, and for this she was thankful. When she had jeopardized herself to teach him in the kitchen to read, the bond had been firmly cemented. "That's the dream of evvy slave."

Billy and Aletha were listening carefully.

"Back home we sing a song—*Follow the Drinkin Gourd to Freedom*—when the master cannot hear."

"The drinking gourd?"

"The one in the sky."

"Oh, the Big Dipper!"

"Follow it to freedom. We all knows—know—that song. For a long time, Miz Jess'ca, I've been listenin to the way the white folks talk while I stay in the dinin room and serve them. I wanna speak that way, when I am free in the North, when I go to Canada."

"Canada?"

"Scuse me, Miz Jess'ca. If yall ever free me—"

"Of course I will!"

"—free me, I'll go on up to Canada—where there is no slavery. Even if I freeze there! The Queen Victoria is mammy to colored folk; she'll pertec—protect—me . . ."

"Where did you hear all this, Joseph?"

"They talk bout it all the time in the quahters. News bout runaways who've got away," he was becoming worked up, "go round the quahters from one plantation to another. In whispers. Thisn got away, thatn got away. Some even go south—not me, I'd never go south. But some went to Nawth Carlina and hid in the swamps. They still there, no one kin cotch em" (he was so excited his speech slipped back momentarily) "an sometimes they comes out and raids the plantations for clothes and food. . . ."

"Amazing."

He was so wound up he began to tell her the information the slaves back home had gathered about escape. How sometimes the slaves used the water as escape routes. There were boats from Richmond to Philadelphia and black people on the run occasionally were able to get aboard and hide in coal bunkers and barrels. He had heard of a slave who was packed in a box that was then nailed up and shipped to Pennsylvania. Sometimes the captains of the boats helped the slaves. Often they did it for money.

For money? How would they get it?

The master sometimes let his slaves sell the extra chickens they raised or barrels they fashioned on their own time or a passle of fish they caught on Sundays. Some masters, Joseph told her, let their slaves work for small farmers on Sundays and keep the change. Not all, he said carefully, just some.

Jessica had never comprehended that a slave could have some cash—maybe they could exchange goods, work for barter, but not have cash. She had only seen the small children scramble for pennies. The day of the ball she had seen them besiege the guests' carriages when they arrived, and laughingly the arriving couples had sprinkled coins at their bare, dusty feet. Charles frowned on that.

Some boat captains made a business of it, Joseph continued. They charged from thirty to one hundred twenty-five dollars apiece. Sometimes it was the stewards and deckhands who stowed the fugitive aboard, without the officers knowing about it. They charged the same fees as the captains.

"Don't they get into trouble?" Billy asked.

Sure, Joseph said. If the boat people were caught they were put in jail for years, or the posses might get them, but it went on. So there was that hope—if a slave had the money. Sometimes, even on land, a slave could find someone—black or white—to lead him out of the South, for money or without money, maybe for two dollars or so. But it was risky. They—the leaders and runaways—were almost skinned alive and more often actually hanged or shot or flogged to death if caught. And sometimes, he said, mean colored folks pretended to help and then turned the runaway in for reward.

"It's best to trust in yourself," said Billy. "Look how I came to find Miz Jess'ca."

"Yall came unner a carriage," Joseph told him, "and that's the way a lot of runaways travel. It's awful, runnin, they all say," Joseph continued. "Often they caint—can't—get food and they jes starve. The snakes an screech-owls scare em out of their wits and sometimes bein away from their mammies or their wummins is jes too much an dey turn dem—they turn themselves—in. But not me," he said staunchly, "I can bear bein away from Mammy an Pappy, but I do miss em awready." Jessica thought she could hear him swallow the lump in his throat. "But," he said, "I would go on—on—all the way!"

"Where can they hide?" Billy asked.

"Sometime inside hollow trees," Joseph said to his friend, "or behine cornshocks or in haystacks. Or in a church belfry or unner a mill wheel or a woodpile. Course yall pray the dogs won't sniff yall out."

"You'd get so dirty," Aletha said, turning up her nose.

Jessica thought Aletha must not associate this running away with herself.

"Sure," Joseph said, "so dirty, Aletha. They say that when a runaway come nawth an fines someone to hep him, he has to stay out of the house til he's cleaned up. He smells too bad. Hear tell they sets out tubs of hot water and soap in barns where folks can strip off their rags and soak off the crust and then get into clean clothes the good people fines for em."

"Pooh!" Aletha cried.

Jessica found this talk unsettling and it made her decide to bypass the second plantation. She did not want to see more people like the Averys. She asked Joseph and Billy whether they thought it would be safe to camp out here near the creek for the night. They talked about it, while Aletha went off to gather black-eyed susans that grew wild and in abundance in the field. Jessica had been relieved to see the fingerprints on her cheek had faded considerably. They watched the child as they made their decision. They would stay; another day and they would probably miss the continued furor of the hunt for and perhaps capture of the runaway slave, and they could then return to the path Charles had drawn.

"It's the only route we know," Jessica said thoughtfully, "probably the only one we can take outside the post road and the waterways." The boys nodded their heads in agreement. "Though we'll have to travel extra tomorrow to make up for time lost"—now she was thinking aloud—"so we can get to the third plantation on our route. Otherwise we'll run out of food."

"There's plenty here," Billy said. "We still have some of Julia's pies left, besides a good part of the Averys' hamper."

"Good. Then there's nothing to worry about."

They were unprophetic words. A shrill cry came from Aletha that set them running.

Aletha was down at the water's edge, and first they thought it was the sight of a snake that had rooted her, pointing and hollering still, to the spot. Jessica folded her into her arms, the child squirming and pointing into the water.

"Someone's in there," Billy said.

Joseph and Billy scrambled down the gentle dip of the bank. They saw what looked like a bundle of rags clinging or caught in the branches of a bush overhanging the stream.

"I . . . I . . . saw a . . . a . . . hand!" Aletha cried, then buried her face in Jessica's skirt.

"What is it?" Jessica asked the boys.

They were trying to unfasten the bundle, but it seemed to be tightly stuck—or resisting. They pulled. Part of the bundle twisted and turned, and then there was a contorted black face in view. The eyes blazed furiously and, as they watched the ragged body turn again, they could see the hands holding tenaciously to the shrubbery.

"Cmon outa deah," Joseph said, reverting to slave talk. "Yo haf-drownded awready, gal. Yo safe wid usns." The girl would not let go. "We gots vittals; ainchall hongry?"

The head, tied in a dirty wet kerchief, bobbed.

"Leggo den."

She did, and Billy and Joseph pulled her from the shallow water and hoisted her to her feet on the bank. Her knees seemed to buckle and the boys half-supported and half-dragged her toward Jessica.

Jessica's spirit had sunk. She was certain this was the runaway slave from the Avery plantation. The shadow she had seen under her window in the early hours of the morning as she had waited for the sun to rise. If she had thought their predicament risky before, now she knew it was downright dangerous.

She let go of Aletha.

"Get the lap robe from the coach," she directed her and went forward to see the fugitive.

The girl was shivering. She had a thin small frame and Jessica guessed she could not be more than fifteen, possibly even fourteen. Pools of water formed at her bare scratched feet. She had mud all over her.

Aletha had come with the blanket.

"Take off your clothes," Jessica said peremptorily, "or you'll catch your death of cold. . . . Here, I'll hold it spread out before you so the boys—and I—won't see. . . . Joseph, Billy, go to the carriage and get some food. . . ."

The fire in the girl's eyes had gone out and obediently she stripped off the rags. As she kicked them out of her way and stepped forward toward the blanket, Jessica wrapped it tightly around her.

"What's your name?" Jessica asked her, in a softer tone.

"Mandy, miz."

"All right, Mandy. We won't hurt you. You can trust us."

The girl still looked at her fearfully.

"You saw me at the Avery plantation?"

"Yassum."

"I was just a guest there—you know that—not part of the family."

"Don sen me back!" the girl pleaded. "Dey'll flog me . . . an ah'll run way agin soon ez ah kin walk!" she cried defiantly.

"Don't think about that now!" Jessica said, not wanting to promise her anything before she could think it out but knowing she would never willingly turn the poor thing over to the patrol or the Averys. "The first thing is to get you warm again and to feed you."

Jessica had given Mandy a cloth to wipe her face and wherever else she chose. Then Jessica searched her trunks and found one of her morning dresses. It was too long for the girl, and Jessica simply tore away the bottom flounces so it would not drag along the ground. The girl's face brightened at the feel of the soft material, such as she had never worn before, and she seemed to grow prettier by the moment before Jessica's eyes. Jessica peeled off the rag on the girl's head and saw the nicely shaped skull, with its close cap of hair. With her high cheek bones and proud profile she was a little beauty. Jessica groaned inwardly. The danger was even greater: not only a slave, but a nubile little beauty that a plantation owner or overseer would want for his bed. She wondered whether that was what had set the child running.

She brought Mandy from the carriage, where she had dressed, to the picnic the boys had spread. Mandy's eyes widened when she saw the napkins of food and the half-full jars and Jessica could feel her salivate. The child would not look at the boys as they spoke to her or even answer Jessica. She kept staring at the food as she swallowed painfully.

Immediately Jessica set out a jar of milk for her and a pan of cold ham and potato salad and biscuits and honey, and Mandy snatched the tin plate from the picnic place where Jessica had placed it. She ran away to a tree several yards from them and began to eat ravenously. They did not call her back; they could only watch her with morbid curiosity. The girl had been in flight, in mortal terror, for about twelve hours and evidently had had no nourishment in that time, and perhaps not for a longer period, before she had brought herself to make the escape. She ate greedily with her fingers and stuffed in her mouth whatever they lit upon, tearing and scarcely chewing what she swallowed. She drank thirstily from the jar Aletha shyly brought to her, exposing a long graceful neck as she tilted her head backward. Jessica had never seen food disappear so quickly. Her instinct was to refill the pan, but she did not, knowing it would only make the girl sick.

The others then had their picnic. They tried not to stare at Mandy, though Aletha could not help it, and she kept a running commentary on what the runaway was doing—not much now that the food was gone, but she was watching them from her distance. When Jessica looked at her for a minute, she could see Mandy's amazement that they were all eating together.

Jessica rose from the grass and went over to the girl. She took her hand and brought her, almost having to pull, to join the group. Jessica sat down, bringing Mandy beside her. She gave the girl a cookie. Mandy snatched it from her hand. Aletha came, bringing her a flower.

"Where were you headed, Mandy?" Jessica asked, and then when the girl did not answer, "Where were you running to?"

The girl hesitated now only for a moment.

"Nawth!" she said with conviction.

"That's a long way off," Jessica said sadly.

"Ah do et!"

"Yes, you want to do it, but you will need help."

"Yassum."

"We'll try," Jessica said, with a sigh. She sighed because she knew there could be no question about aiding the girl even though it jeopardized them all. There could be no question, she thought wryly, but there could be an abundance of trepidation. "You must trust us."

"Yassum," Mandy said. "Yo sho yall won sen me back?" She looked around nervously at all of them. But she had taken Aletha's flower and had gratefully patted her hand.

"Miz Jess'ca won't do that," Joseph said, more careful of his speech again.

Mandy looked at him suspiciously.

"Don yall mess wid me neithah, niggah!" she spat at him, turning to include Billy too. The boys' mouths flew open in amazement at her fury.

"They won't," Jessica promised her.

"Calm down, gal," Joseph finally said. "Nobuddy's gonna hurt yall."

"Tell us how you got away," Jessica said gently.

At first it was difficult to get a few words from Mandy, but once she began they flowed more quickly and fully. She had not planned it, but things had grown so bad–she did not define "things" and no one pressed her–that she could stand it no longer. She did not even say goodbye–her mammy and pappy had been sold away to a far-off plantation many years before and she had not seen or heard of them since. There was no one to say goodbye to anyway except for cook and a few of the other older women slaves who had befriended her. One thing she did do, though, she said proudly. She knew all about the dogs and she had heard talk in the quarters about what to do to prevent being trailed. She had taken time to go to the barn and put together a mixture of cow manure, some snuff one of the old women had given her and that she had never used, and the hairs of a dog's tail–old Rover, he didn't mind too much–and she had rubbed it over the soles of her feet.

They all stared at them now, but the water had cleansed them.

"Some folks rub jimsonweed over their whole selves," Joseph offered.

But she had not trusted that entirely. She had walked long and hard, and when she heard that same noise far off that they had, she had found an opening in the undergrowth of the path. When she came to the water she could not believe her good luck–"Fo-chun," she said–and when she heard the lead dogs bark, far away as they were, she had lowered herself in the water, holding on to the brush. They would never get her scent that way, she said defiantly.

"And when you heard us? You did the same?"

"Yassum."

"All the time we were here you were in the water?"

"Yassum."

"You must be chilled to the bone."

"Yassum."

"Put the blanket over your dress then."

"Yassum," the girl said, complying.

They camped out for the night, Jessica and the two girls in the carriage. Billy, so much smaller than Joseph, curled up in the box seat, and Joseph slept on the ground atop a pallet Jessica fashioned for him from a large shawl and other soft garments from her trunk. Beforehand, Jessica and Billy and Joseph had had a conclave. They would take turns, each sleeping four hours and keeping watch for two hours. Six hours would be enough, and then they would start out again, even if it were not yet light. Mandy must lie on the floor of the coach as they traveled, they decided. Jessica would cover her with the cape, so that if anyone should peer inside the window he would—they hoped—see only a garment carelessly thrown on the floor.

Tie her face up with a bandage, too, Joseph advised, as if she had a toothache. That might be a good idea, Jessica thought; then no one would see how pretty she was if the covering should fall away or if they dared to descend from the coach. She would reserve that for later, when they were farther on their journey. She prayed the path would skirt the towns all the way. The newspapers she had seen at the Sedgely plantation—the *Virginia Gazette,* the *Spectator,* even occasionally the *Natchez Ariel* from as far away as Mississippi—had advertisements offering rewards for runaway slaves, describing them minutely down to their birthmarks and height and weight. Some of them read "Wanted—dead or alive." She shuddered.

* * *

The night went slowly. During Jessica's watch she looked at the stars and the shadow of the wagon on the grass. Fortunately the moon was on the wane and just a small sliver lit the sky. At times the horses snorted in their sleep. She listened, too, to the lap of water as an occasional wind ruffled its surface. She wished the next few weeks had already passed and they were settled in Pennsylvania and free territory where she would have help to call upon. She had heard of the societies that had been formed to assist runaways.

When Joseph came to relieve her at the end of her stint, she lay down on the inside seat of the carriage. First she had covered Aletha, who was sleeping on the other seat. She was afraid to touch Mandy under the cape on the floor, to pull the material over her exposed feet, for she knew the girl was trigger tight and would spring up terrified.

She wondered what Charles would say if he knew she had endangered Aletha's chances, Joseph the slave he had given her, Billy, the expensive coach and the horses. Would he think she had abused both his and the Averys' hospitality by carrying Mandy with them? Jessica had used the word possession when she denied to the patrol leader taking anything from the Averys. It was an explosive word. Perhaps in itself it explained the entire slave system and why it had lasted over the centuries. To the Averys the girl was property. To Charles, too.

She slept poorly, dreaming of the slave patrol and their men putting her in shackles along with Mandy and taking her, a slave too, to the slave auction, putting her on the block; she watched all the cruel calculating eyes upon her as the bidding began.

In her dream the remaining bidders, now only two, became Charles and Jason. She saw their faces clearly and cried out to them. The girls stirred. Jessica sat up, knowing she had actually spoken. She tried to rest again, but it was impossible. She left the coach to sit with Billy on the third watch. He would not go back to sleep again, as she implored him to do, and they talked quietly about plans for the coming day. It would not be wise, they decided, to go to the third plantation on their list now that Mandy was with them. They would be careful with the remaining food, making it last as long as they could, and perhaps if they came upon an out-of-the-way farm or—but Billy shook his head. Better to fish from some stream or pick berries or apples.

They were on their way before daylight, safely through the aperture, Joseph having dug away the camouflage of branches so they could pass and then running back afterward to put it back in place.

The morning journey was uneventful. The horses fresh, they traveled steadily. Occasionally Mandy half sat up to relieve the boredom of lying flat on the floor of the coach. She would stretch painfully, for the bouncing of the carriage was making her sore. Aletha would at times come from her seat to sit with her. They talked in whispers. Jessica could not make out what they said. So far Mandy had not giggled or laughed, no matter how Aletha tried to cheer her. Then Aletha would climb onto Jessica's seat and place her head on her lap and ask questions about Chloe, her mother, and whether she too would follow the North Star and come after her to be her mammy again. Jessica would not answer that and instead hugged the child warmly.

They had almost completely relaxed after a few hours of quiet travel. The road, so much a secondary one, was evidently not much in use and they had not passed anyone at all that morning either on horse or wagon or afoot. Jessica was about to knock on the carriage ceiling and ask Joseph whether he would not look for a good place to stop and take an afternoon break. Joseph himself, however, stopped suddenly, pulling on the horses with such sharpness that Aletha fell from her seat and Jessica, by holding on, barely kept her own. Mandy had slid down the floor, cape and all.

Jessica hastily opened the door.

"What—?" she called, and then stopped.

Two men on horseback were in front of the coach. Their rifles were pointed at Joseph and Billy. They were rough-looking men, even rougher than the men on the patrol. Jessica quickly descended from the carriage, hoping they would not look inside.

"Come down fom theah, boy!" one called, as he pushed his wad of tobacco in one cheek so he could speak.

Joseph seemed frozen in place. It was evident the man meant him.

"One minute," Jessica said, coming to the head of the carriage.

"Howdy, ma'am," they both said, not taking their eyes from the box.

"Joseph belongs to me. I have his papers."

The second man turned lazily in Jessica's direction and spat at her feet.

"We done heah tell of this fine young buck in yer pahty."

"He belongs to me. I have the papers from the Sedgely plantation, where he was born."

"Now ma'am, he belongs down souf; we need im ta till the soil an poplate the earth."

"The black earth," the other said, laughing snidely.

"Let us pass!" Jessica said icily. "Or the law will go hard with you!"

They laughed.

"He'll fetch a good price," one said to the other.

"Uh-huh."

Paddy rollers, Jessica thought fearfully. They'd take Joseph and sell him, papers or not.

"I need Joseph to drive this carriage, and he is rightfully mine!" she insisted, trying unsuccessfully to keep the quaver from her voice.

One of the men reached up and Joseph once again was yanked from his seat, this time pulled so forcefully that he fell heavily down on the ground. Jessica screamed, seeing the pain and terror in his eyes. Billy, his face pale and set, struggled to keep the horses still.

"Don't touch him!" Jessica screamed.

"Up on yer feet!"

Joseph, still stunned by the fall, could not move.

"You done heah me, boy?"

Jessica could not even reach Joseph's side. Not only the men, but the horses blocked her way.

"Please!" she begged. "I have a little gold–I'll–"

Not enough, she knew, not equal to what Joseph would bring on the market, even the illicit market. "Please–I need to get on!"

"Mebbe we'll take that, too," one man said nastily.

She was lost, she thought dully, and Joseph fallen to a dismal lot, far worse than the Sedgely plantation, when a rustling was heard in the underbrush. A shot rang out. She looked at Billy. It was not he. One paddy roller was holding his shattered right arm with his left, the gun fallen from his grasp. The other, distracted, turned to aid the howling man, and now Billy quickly brought out his piece. He took aim and rapidly fired. He caught the second man in the shoulder. Joseph, in the commotion, had rolled away from the horses and now stood up. He gathered up both fallen rifles.

"Yall hang fer this!" snarled the paddy roller from the ground where he had fallen, as soon as breath came back. "A buck niggah bearin arms–yall hang!"

Joseph paused. In that one second Jessica could see him begin to move the rifle upward. His eyes were blazing. And then, just as suddenly, he brought down his hand.

The bounty hunters' faces contorted in agony and hatred. Puzzlement, too. Cursing, when they regained their feet and their balance, and stomping to relieve their pain, they told Billy and Joseph in graphic terms what the patrol, which they would bring back in full force, would do to them. Jessica covered her ears in horror. Billy sat shocked but in seeming impassivity, holding his rifle pointed at the men.

"Should I kill em, Miz Jess'ca?" he asked, without turning his head.

"Billy, no!"

The bounty hunters, sweating, twisted about to look at Jessica.

"Did she fahr the fus shot?" one asked the other.

"Ah dunno. Chris, ahm bleedin lak a stuck pig! We gotta git halp!"

"She musta done et. We'll fix er good, too!" Then in the next breath: "Kin yall bine up our wounds, miz?"

Jessica told herself she must not faint. Her head felt light and spinning and she leaned against the coach. She could hear a low whimpering inside, and she told herself sternly she must keep Aletha and Mandy's presence hidden from the bounty hunters.

And the shot. Her bewildered thoughts were swirling around that too. The rustling. Someone had been there in the brush. Who was it? Her heart beat uncontrollably. Could it be Charles? Could Charles have been following them the past two and a half days and come to their rescue?

She snapped to attention as she saw the man inching away from Billy.

"Stay where you are!" she ordered peremptorily.

"Yall gotta rag ta bine us?"

"No!"

They loudly cursed her, and the boys brandished their irons at them.

There was a stirring behind the trees that grew close to the path. Birds flew out of the disturbed brush accompanied by a chattering of squirrels as they leaped from swaying branches. A rabbit was flushed; grasshoppers jumped and butterflies flitted into the sun.

A horse snorted, and they all stared as a stallion came into view bearing a large man. A woolen cap covered the man's head completely, so that no hair was visible, and a kerchief hid the lower part of his face. He rode carefully to the bounty hunters' horses and methodically removed their reins. Then he smacked their rumps and they dashed off into the woods. Billy could scarcely keep the coach horses still and manage his covering rifle at the same time. Joseph, a cut in his face bleeding, sprang up into the box to help him.

The man on the stallion waved his rifle at the paddy rollers.

"Be off!" he ordered harshly, brandishing his rifle in the opposite direction that the coach must travel. "That way!"

"Wivout hosses?"

The man fired a shot at their feet.

"While you still can walk," he said icily.

"Niggah lovah!" one spat at him.

The man fired another shot at their feet.

They set off as quickly as they could manage, each one supporting a useless arm with the other. There was silence among the remaining group as they disappeared. Then Jessica and Billy and Joseph all began to talk at once. The man would not let them thank him. He shook his head and told them they must proceed at once.

"It will be better to travel at night and sleep during the day," he advised. His voice seemed vaguely familiar to Jessica. It was not Charles' voice, and yet it could be. Maybe he was disguising it. She had heard it before. She wanted him to be Charles.

But she had no time to wonder.

"Please," he said to her, in gentler tones, "get back inside. You must be under way as soon as possible." He turned again to the boys. "Today you must ride day and night to beat the patrol and the paddy rollers. You have a start and you can outride them—you can rest only tomorrow evening. I shall have fresh horses waiting for you along the way. Leave the tired ones in their place."

"Where?"

"I'll find you."

Jessica still had not entered the coach. The man dismounted and came to her, offering his arm to help her inside. It was long and fine, she thought dazedly. He was the same height as Charles. She searched the cap for the distinctive hair but could see nothing beneath it. She tried to look into his eyes, but he averted them. Oh, she wished it were Charles who had come. But her fingers on his arm had informed her of one fact. The man was not Charles.

Chapter Eight

The party had traveled all through the past night. Fresh horses had been waiting at a deserted bend of the road, just as their benefactor had promised. The mare and the stallion, sleekly brushed and chafing at their reins tied to a tree, whinnied as they caught scent of the tired animals pulling the coach. After the switch, Joseph had advised against lighting the lantern and they had made their slow way over the rutted, dark ground. There was a cloudy sky and the stars were hidden; the sliver of the waning moon penetrated the cover only occasionally. The boys had to urge the beasts on as best they could. Occasionally they stopped to rest them, but mindful of the paddy rollers' attack, they pressed them onward as steadily as possible through the night.

The condition of the narrow roadway was so poor that their short rest periods were less than adequate. Occasionally Jessica and Aletha and Mandy descended from the coach and walked behind it to spare the horses. Jessica held Aletha by one hand and Mandy by the other, and as they stumbled over the roots and rainholes she told them fairytales from the brothers Grimm. Mandy shouted in amazement through the telling and had to clap her hands over her mouth as Jessica shook her head at the unwanted noise. Jessica thought of herself as the child she had been when her father had read her the stories, recently published, translating from the German as he went along. She, too, had cried aloud. Mandy's amazement was no more than her own, she remembered.

It was even more amazing, she thought, that she should be here in this strange country, walking through back country roads with two girls not blooded kin and of different color but for whom she felt a growing kinship. And for Billy, who had also jumped from the seat to lighten the horses' burden and brought up the rear. And for Joseph, who managed the journey so well.

She joined the girls' hands together and dropped back to talk to Billy for a few minutes.

"We're not out of Virginia yet?" she asked, hoping he would say yes.

"No," he said. "We're takin the long way out. Master Charles wanted to keep us away from settlements—especially along the big waterways, where we'd have trouble with the coach." They both thought of the rickety bridges they had passed over and of the streams they had forded. The boys had had to use every bit of their strength to get the horses and coach across. "We're goin up through the middle of the state, and we'll touch on West Virginia, accordin to the map he gave us." She nodded. "But we'll cross over into Maryland soon."

"How soon?"

"Another day or two."

"Oh."

She tried to hide her disappointment, smiled at him, and went back to rejoin the girls. They had persisted until the first graying of the sky and made camp before sunrise. They were too tired to eat. The boys saw to the horses, picking their hooves, watering and feeding them. Joseph volunteered for the first watch, and soon the others were fast asleep.

They had been on the road again since noon. Jessica was worried. The food had run out. Aletha had developed a blister on her heel. They had let her ride on the box with Joseph, and she loved that; sometimes she rested her head affectionately in his lap.

Jessica wondered whether it had been part of Charles' thinking when he assigned Joseph to the group to guard against Aletha's homesickness. The child had known Joseph since birth as an older brother or uncle figure, and both were closely connected to Julia and Cicero. Certainly, too, Charles had added Joseph for their safety.

The others walked behind the coach once more. Jessica had drawn her long skirt and petticoat through her waistband, as she had done on the hike with Charles and Charlie and Zeke, until her legs were free from the knees downward. Billy had looked at them once, blushed, and quickly looked away. She had also braided her hair and pinned the plaits to the top of her head so that the branches that overhung the road would not catch, as they had the night before, in her loosened fall. Her face was dirty, she knew. They had not paused at any brook or lake the past twenty-four hours, and every drop of water they carried with them was precious. When she saw still another new set of horses waiting for them in the bend of the road, tears of gratitude rolled down her cheeks.

Going forward to pat the restive animals, she found two baskets that had been left out of their reach. They were filled with napkin-covered plates of sliced chicken and there were jars of water and milk. Fresh fruit and pies were mounded on top, and as she replaced the checkered cloth coverlets she could only shake her head in wonder. A note had been pinned to one of the handles. In simple lettering it instructed that the tired horses be left now at the same spot. This was as before. Then the new horses would be picked up the next afternoon and fresh ones provided. She worried how their benefactor accomplished this, where he found them, and how much money it cost him each day. There was nothing else—no signature.

Joseph and Billy expertly made the switch. Jessica was almost reluctant to leave the area when they were ready to go again, for she felt their benefactor, as she called him, must be somewhere close by. He must be watching them, she was sure. He would give them only a few minutes to be on their way and then he would gather up the horses, not leaving them for any paddy roller who may still be on their trail. Was he—the benefactor—following them? She thought so. She had the feeling of a benign presence in the bush. Perhaps it was not just intuition, she thought sagely. Maybe her ear picked up an unusual swish of the grass or a thud that could be an unseen horse's hoof. Or perhaps, she thought tiredly, it was just wishing it were so. Like the Grimm fairytales. The Good Spirit, with all the different labels. Was it Charles? Could it possibly be he? She wanted to think so. But the eyes, though she had not seen them closely, had been different—she was almost sure of that. And the feel of his arm through the sleeve—she would never forget the special muscle tone, what it was like to touch Charles. If it could not be Charles, who else could it be? Who would risk his neck for her? And for her party? Was it an emissary of Charles, sent to do battle for her in his name?

For the next few days their trip was uneventful. At sundown fresh horses and food were found in a secluded turn of the road. There were picnics, travel by night, a creek where they could bathe—Jessica and the girls first, then the boys—and wash their clothes. There were times to talk when they rested, and Joseph and Billy, and even Mandy—who had grown more relaxed each day she shared with them—told stories about their lives. Jessica could only shake her head over the hardships of Billy's and Mandy's childhoods—the poverty of Billy's and the cruelty of Mandy's. Joseph's life had been easier, sheltered by the valued status of his parents, but poisoned by the mental shackles of slavery. She, in turn, told them of her life at home. It was difficult for them to believe she was not wealthy, especially when she described the two houses she had lived in—the house of her parents and the house of her husband—and she decided that if they wanted to believe that the riches she had enjoyed, all the books and the love and the little surrey and old horse, were indeed wealth, she would give them that pleasure.

The paddy rollers had evidently not found the posse, or if they had, Jessica's party had successfully eluded them. Perhaps the two bands, joined together, were still hard on their heels. She hoped not. When they passed a marker that indicated they were leaving Virginia, she trusted they were leaving the pursuers behind. Though paddy rollers, she had been told, did not respect state boundaries. She knew they were not out of danger yet, but she felt relief that at last they were in Maryland. They would not come as far east as Delaware and would travel from Maryland to Pennsylvania, through Hagerstown and Gettysburg, and make their way to Philadelphia.

There was no reason to relax their guard in Maryland. There were many plantations in this state, Jason had once told her, and Jessica had later learned that though there were some sympathizers to the manumission of slaves among isolated individuals in the Maryland towns, the prevalent feeling of the day was proslavery. While legislation had outlawed the importation of slaves from Africa and the islands, in Maryland there was still brisk business in the buying and selling of slaves brought in before the law was passed, or born in bondage, not affected by the law. It was just like Virginia's attempt in 1832 to cause a legal halt to slave trade—at the same time the Virginia planters were doing a vast export business of slaves themselves. It came in waves, like the economic periods of depression and prosperity—in a depression, sell them off; in prosperity, when more hands were needed, hold on and buy more. No matter that the Averys—or even Charles—said they cared for their slaves in hard times.

Different societies had been set up in various places to consider the plight of the slaves; perhaps these groups would get stronger as time went on. Perhaps in Pennsylvania she would learn more of the abolition movement. Perhaps she would even get in touch with Charles Finney at Oberlin College in Ohio. He was head of the abolition movement; she had read that in a newspaper found in Charles' library. The paper damned Finney and his insistent group, including Theodore Dwight Weld. She wanted to remember those names.

She thought again about Jason and how his antislavery conviction must have grown and turned away from his early excuses for the plantation owners' needs. This conviction could have become more emphatic—and perhaps even reckless—since the days when they last spoke of it. Where was he? She knew that their nighttime travel and flight from the cities did nothing for her search for him. She had thought the plantation people might have little bits of information that she could string together, and now she had cut herself off from these possible sources.

And where would her search take her? She was already bone-weary, and now, if need be, she must go on through New England and—possibly—to Canada.

As they made their way farther into Maryland the path took different turns, widened, and led them through tiny towns and cultivated farmlands. One evening, in the basket of food that was left beside the fresh horses as it had been every night except the first, Jessica found a second note.

"You can resume your travels by day now," it said. She turned it over and over in her trembling hand. There was no signature. She yearned to be close to this man who was their faithful supplier, defender. Part of her wanted to think she alone was heroically leading the little group to safety, but it was he—the stranger, the benefactor—who was making it possible. She smiled to herself. It was a joint effort. She was working in tandem, in cooperation, with this man whose identity she did not know.

She dreamed it was Charles, but the color of his eyes was wrong.

She dreamed it could be Jason, but if it were he, he would have revealed himself immediately; he could not have controlled the joy of reunion. She knew it was not Jason. The color of his eyes—the build—everything was different from Jason, her husband. Her husband, she mused. The word had a strange association in her mind; it was gradually fading—almost like the vision of Jason's face behind her eyelids—from familiarity.

When they traveled during the day again, she had less time to dwell on her thoughts, for there was so much to see, to do. She welcomed the sight of people busy at their work, women in groups as they went about their chores with their baskets, the farmers in their markets, the men in the fields tying up the drying cornstalks. The path of the coach was an easier one. No more fording of streams, with the horses balking and needing to be coaxed across the water and Jessica gathering up her skirts and wading across. When the water was too deep, they had sat atop the box, Aletha clutched in her arms, as the carriage floated across with Joseph and Billy and Mandy swimming beside it.

Now there were decent ferries and bridges—though their route for the most part had avoided the vast waterways, taking the longer way around not to come upon them. She had held her breath on the ferry lest someone ask for Mandy's papers, but fortune was with them and no one made such a move. She remembered stories she had heard about boat captains in Ohio who carried runaway slaves through the Great Lakes and the St. Lawrence waterways into Canada and freedom. She looked at the ferryman with interest and noted a man speaking with him who looked vaguely familiar. Her heart skipped a beat. Perhaps it was the benefactor. Though it was not yet cold, the collar of his frock coat was pulled tightly about his chin, and his hat came down to his eyes. His body frame was large and he rolled with the motion of the vessel; she noted that his legs, in their tight striped pants, were slightly bowed. She felt a moment's agitation. What was the block? What was she trying to recall? Who?

She still avoided the inns, though they passed several on their way, the bright painted board signs beckoning gaily to them. They set up campsites in wooded areas early in the evening, before sunset, and picnicked from the ample baskets. The last few nights Joseph and Mandy had disappeared after supper, when the coach and horses and empty containers had been attended to, and had not reappeared until the first watch was established. Billy would sit glumly with Jessica and Aletha, and Jessica would be hard put with stories of England and folksongs from back home to bring him out of his funk. Then Joseph and Mandy would reappear, hand in hand, a glow on their faces, and Mandy would come to curl at Jessica's feet, as if to bring her the present of her happiness.

At last they passed the marker that said they were in Pennsylvania. Young surveyors, Jessica thought, probably looking like George Washington and working in his time, had measured off the lines. She smiled to herself, liking the tie to history and this new country, which, whatever its faults, she still liked for its excitement, beauty, and promise of growth. "Pennsylvania!" she shouted with joy and relief to the children, and they all whooped loudly, knowing it would be easier for them here—that in this state, as Jessica had told them, and as Joseph already knew, the abolition movement had a strong base and was growing, that the Pennsylvania Quakers were a strong force for good, that there were state laws for emancipation, and that the manumission of slaves in the area was a fact.

"Are we almost home?" Aletha wistfully asked Jessica.

The word *home* agitated Jessica, for she realized she had not looked that far ahead. Oh, yes, she had had a nebulous idea. She had dreamed that she and Jason might settle for a while in Philadelphia, the city where she had landed with the Northrups. She had liked what she had seen of it, a bustling port city, with gracious buildings and red brick homes—especially the ones she had glimpsed on Walnut Street—and Jason had spoken kindly of it. But *home* still had meant London. Now she was not so sure. She had not yet accomplished her mission. She had not found Jason.

Even her letters about him to the newspapers had brought only a few guarded replies—and clippings of small notices, among a welter of other notices of missing men, and women, too. William Cullen Bryant had written her a kind personal note expressing his sympathy and enclosing a feature published in *The New York Evening Post* about individuals who vanished, leaving no trace behind them, in various regions of the country. "There are so many," he had stated, repeating the theme of the article, and she had despaired.

But she knew she would take up Jason's mission, wherever that would lead, for she now was convinced that he had taken an active part in or stand on the slave question. She was determined, after her experiences, to carry on.

"Yes," she told Aletha, with as much positiveness as she could muster, "we'll take lodgings in Philadelphia. It will be our home base."

"I'll be with you there?" the child asked anxiously.

"Of course!" Jessica hugged the child.

"Forever and ever?"

"Of course."

"Maybe my mammy Chloe and mammy Julia could come too . . ."

Jessica could only look sadly at the child.

"You'll always love them," she said gently, "and they will always think of you with love. But we are here together, and we shall love each other, too." She could make no false promises about those left behind. "I already love you very much, Aletha, and always will."

Aletha placed her arms around Jessica's neck. As Jessica patted her long, thick black hair, she tried to work out a plan. She would seek out lodgings, just as she had said. Perhaps a little house, if the gold Charles had given her was sufficient, or if she could sell Miranda's ring and the carriage and horses—though idly she wondered whether the horses now belonged to the benefactor or whether he had traded them, as she had imagined, all along the way—would the final team be hers? Though he deserved them, she thought resolutely, as his own. Then, if she had a house or even rooms—though a house would be better with Billy and Joseph and Mandy to accommodate as well—perhaps the Friends—the Quakers—would engage her to teach in one of their schools. Would she earn enough to make ends meet, she fretted. Well, she would see. She could have her mother, through the solicitor, sell the house she had lived in with Jason. The thought seemed a final knell to Jason's and her relationship, however, and she firmly set it aside to consider at another time.

Jessica saw, as she looked at Charles' map, that he had drawn a line from Hagerstown on the Maryland side—which they had already passed—to Gettysburg in Pennsylvania. They were not very far now from Gettysburg, and from there the route continued north with very few detours. It had taken them more than twice as long to make this journey as it had by the stagecoach south when she had come to Charles and Eleanor, but all the factors of the back inland roads had accounted for it. It had accounted for their relative safety, too, and Jessica did not begrudge the extra time, though she knew the children's bodies, as well as her own, were exhausted from the bone-rattling, teeth-gnashing travel.

Later at a relief stop she gathered wildflowers—black-eyed susans still grew—to place in the empty baskets for the benefactor. When they reached the waiting fresh horses and the full hampers, she realized he had already been there and saw another note pinned to the top covering cloth.

"A woman who has important news for you will come here at daybreak. She will take you to her home, where it will be revealed to you. Trust her. Follow her."

She was completely mystified. It was difficult to pass the hours intervening before the meeting would take place. During her watch that night she wondered what part the woman had to play in her life. Was she a friend of Charles'? Had he come after them and would he be waiting for her in the woman's house? They were almost at the end of their journey—why this sudden mystery?

She was very weary, not only from the coach's bouncing but also from the nights spent curled up on the uncomfortable bench and from her anxiety for the safety of her charges and herself, for the man following—or preceding?—them, her sense of not having accomplished what she had set out to do, her uncertainty about what her life would be like in Philadelphia. She found herself in an unaccustomed and terrible rage. Her emotions swept wildly through her, and she railed silently against fortune for having tried her so cruelly, for taking away her husband whom she loved, for placing her in the arms of a man she wanted very much but knew she could not keep, for putting her life in danger from scallywags and hoodlums, for making a world where there was so much injustice.

But as quickly as the storm had come, it passed in the relief of tears. She should count her blessings, she told herself. She had been married to a fine and loving man, she had enjoyed the passion of another, she was surrounded by young people who looked to her with affection mirroring her own, she had family who cared for her, and she had a purpose, no matter how fuzzy it seemed in the making—a principle to work for. She had lived—and would live. She had loved—and would love.

She would not let Billy or Joseph take turns at watch this

night but saw it through alone. They sensed she must do it and did not insist. They seemed to know that the coming end of the journey was as difficult as its beginning.

The woman, on horseback, seemed very tall. She had high cheekbones and seemed part Indian. She nodded curtly to Jessica, who had stood beside the coach awaiting her, and did not dismount.

"You are Mrs. Coopersmith," she said.

"Yes."

"Please come—please follow me."

"I must bring the others."

"Very well."

Without further explanation, the woman wheeled her horse around. Jessica nodded to Joseph, then climbed into the coach where the girls were waiting, and they followed the woman. She led them to a small, neat farm, carefully fenced and tended, far away from the road and reached through a long, meandering lane. She dismounted, quickly gave her mount's reins to a young man who was waiting, and came to Jessica. When they stood side by side Jessica could see the woman held herself very straight and was not much taller than she.

"I want to prepare you," she said, gently now, "before you go inside. . . ."

Jessica blanched.

"What—who . . . ?"

"I have nursed a man for a long time—"

"Who? Is it—a long time . . . it must be . . . is it Jason?"

"I did not know who it was until the other man came—"

"The man—what man?"

"The man who has brought us together."

"Oh."

"He . . ." she paused, "your husband, I am told, your husband had been gravely wounded. He was more dead than alive when my son and I found him—"

Jessica's hands flew to her throat.

"Jason!"

"It is a miracle he has lasted this long—"

"Take me—"

"—and he cannot last much longer. Perhaps he knew some day you would come. . . ."

"Why—why?"

"He never regained his memory. We never knew who he was until the man came asking for him; he had heard of this poor soul . . . We found him, across the Maryland line, with the body of a slave who had been burned. . . ."

"Oh, God!" Jessica cried.

"Come," the woman said. "Brace yourself. He will not look like the man you once knew . . ."

It was as if an old man lay in the clean narrow bed. The cheeks were sunken, the eyes were far back in their sockets. There was scarcely any hair on the feverish head. But the shape of the prominent skull, the high forehead, the cheekbones, even the wreck of his mouth—all were his. She sank to her knees beside him and gathered his thin hands into her own, looking at his fingers and remembering how they once had caressed her. She whispered his name and thought she saw the vein in his temple twitch. "Jason!" The eyelids opened and a light seemed to come into his eyes. "Jason, I'm here now, it's Jessica!" Did he hear her? The fingers plucked at hers and seemed to tighten their frail hold.

She sat there for hours—perhaps, she thought tiredly later, a day. She heard the voices of the others—the woman, her son, Joseph and Billy and Mandy and Aletha—in the kitchen. Sometimes the woman came and went, with a tray, a wet cloth for the invalid's forehead. He could take no food. The woman wet his lips with a teaspoonful of milk. Some penetrated his mouth; most dribbled onto his chin—all across the clasped hands of husband and wife.

"It is a miracle," the woman said again, whispering. "He must have waited for you. The doctor cannot explain it."

She went away and came again after another interval, with more wet cloths and cotton teats of milk.

"He recovered from his wounds, but there was the great fever—the body pushed beyond its limits," she murmured to Jessica, who still held fast to him.

The house quieted. It must have been nighttime and everyone bedded down. No sound came now from the other rooms.

She began to talk to him—to tell him how glad she was to find him, how grateful she was that he had waited for her, that they would take leave of one another if they must, but that she wanted to tell him how much she had loved him, that their time together had been precious, and tender, that he had always been a fine man and that he had left his mark forever upon her and upon the world.

"I could not lose you that way—gone, without a trace—never knowing. A man . . . lost in a war, a casualty. This was a war, was it not? To hold you . . . to say goodbye."

He was beginning to shiver. It racked his frame. He must be cold. She did not know where there were extra blankets. She would not wake the woman. She would warm him. Without loosing her hands from his, she slipped onto the bed and fitted her body around him. Once they had slept like this, like spoons he had said, after making love. His body had been so different, so beautiful; now it was reduced to a husk, a shell, but it still contained the feeble flame of Jason and she would nurture it until it finally went out.

The shivering stopped and he seemed to fall into a peaceful sleep. The weariness of the journey and the past hours overcame her and she fell asleep beside him. She awoke only when light flooded the window and the woman came and touched her shoulder. She gently helped Jessica untwine her fingers.

"You know he's gone," she said softly.

Jessica nodded.

"I know."

Mrs. Danby gave her tea in the kitchen. She was blessedly quiet. At first Jessica was numb, then the tears came. Mrs. Danby tiptoed around the room and let the storm overtake her. Jessica knew she wept for the many emotion-laden experiences of her life. She wept for Jason, that his life should be cut so short, that the idyll of their first years together should be so brief, that the good cause he had wanted to further was now without the physical presence and effort of one good man. She wept, too, for the death of her father and the realization that her mother was growing old and that perhaps they would never see one another again. She wept that she had left her mother country and that the determination to settle permanently in this new one was a frightening challenge. She wept for Charles, who, welded to his plantation in the South and to Eleanor and Chloe, could never be a permanent part of her life. For Eleanor and Chloe. For Aletha, who must forget her parents and Julia and Cicero and accept her, Jessica, as her very own. And her grief, making its cycle, returned to Jason—that he was gone, that the hope for reunion was over, that the new life with him in the new land had been snuffed out, that she could not rescue him, that the will no matter how strong was not omnipotent. For a moment guilt stirred. Perhaps it was a punishment; if she hadn't been with Charles—but she quickly banished the thought as unworthy of reason. She had not sent Jason into the path of danger. If she took paths of danger of her own, it would be her own doing, too. There was no guilt. Jason had spun out the thread of his life, and hers was still unwinding. Some of her tears were for the fear of what lay ahead and what she must do.

When she had calmed herself, Mrs. Danby talked with her. She told Jessica that her great-grandmother had been a full-blooded Nanticoke who lived in the land that the white folk called Delaware. She was the wife of a squaw-man, turned out by his people who scorned his way of life, joining with the Indians. After her great-grandmother's death, her people migrated because of the pressures of white settlement, and her great-grandfather stayed behind with the child. That explained, she said to Jessica, smiling proudly, the cast of her cheekbones and the ruddiness of her skin. Sometimes it skipped a generation, depending on the mix; her son Seth had the strong bone structure of the face, not the color. She and Seth worked the farm. She was a widow.

Seeing the question in Jessica's eyes, she explained again about finding Jason. How she and her son had nursed him, how the doctor she brought to see him had given him up in the beginning.

"But me? Bringing me here to him?" Before she could ask it, Mrs. Danby understood her need to know.

"Your friend," she said—and Jessica's eyes grew wider—"had heard from a way-station in Philadelphia . . ."

"A way-station?"

"We are setting up houses along the way," the woman explained gently, "to help escaping slaves and others who need refuge."

"A safe house?"

"Yes," she said, "a few people who belong to the American Colonization Society in Delaware who believed in more than manumission splintered off and formed their own little antislavery group, joining with the Friends in Pennyslvania. . . . There are houses of refuge along the way. This," she said, in an offhand manner, "is one of them. We have had others, besides your husband, here."

In her emotionally drained state, Jessica took a few moments to organize her thoughts.

"But my friend you spoke of, who is he? And how did he know of the connection between us?"

"Your friend is here," the woman said carefully. "He is outside working on the pine box—the coffin—for your husband." She paused, to lessen the shock of the words. "Your friend will come in soon with my son, who is assisting him."

"My friend."

"Who went to fetch you."

Jessica shook her head; she was confused.

"He saw a ring on your husband's finger," the woman continued slowly, "that reminded him of the one you wore on your own. When he saw your husband and took his hand in his, he said he knew immediately who he must be."

Jessica looked at her hands. She wore the ring with the Coopersmith family crest. Jason had given it to her when they were married, and she had never removed it. His had belonged to his father; hers, to his mother.

"The ring is still on his finger. I saw it. It pressed into my hand . . ." she said sorrowfully.

"You will want it," Mrs. Danby said firmly.

"To send to his family."

"Yes."

"And who is my friend?"

"Don't you know who brought you here?" Mrs. Danby said in amazement.

"He has not shown himself."

"He has not?"

"No. But he saw to our safety. We called him . . . called him . . . our benefactor," she said nervously. "Where are the children?" she said suddenly, "Aletha and Billy and . . . Joseph and Mandy . . . ?"

"Seth gave them chores to do around the land; we thought it best to keep them busy, while we make arrangements here."

"Yes," Jessica said sadly. "How will it be done?"

"The men and I will take care of everything." She rose to go to the window. The hammering had stopped. "They will be coming soon," she said.

Seth entered the kitchen first, but Jessica could only stare at the man behind him. Another great shock went through her. Of course! She should have known! The very blue eyes. The large frame. And now without the hat she could see his hair. It was less blond than she had remembered it in the bright sun reflecting from the sea; it was more a sandy-colored shade.

"Douglas Graham!" she cried.

"At your service, ma'am."

He came to her quickly.

She wanted to thank him for all he had done, but before she could stop them the words flew out, "Why? Why the secrecy?"

"I wanted you to see your husband first. I didn't know how badly off he was. I still had no right . . . You needed to see him first. I'm sorry that he's gone. . . ."

She sighed.

"All you did for us . . . the way you provided . . ."

He shrugged.

"You didn't return with Captain Northrup!" she said, amazed.

"No. I couldn't leave the country with this . . . this question about you dangling in the air."

"Poor Captain Northrup–you and Billy–"

"I saw the ragamuffin. Almost cuffed him."

"You didn't!"

"No." He grinned lopsidedly at her. "For doing what I wanted to do? For going with you. . . . Oh," he said contritely, "I must not talk this way with your poor dead husband in the next room, but. . . ."

Mrs. Danby and Seth had quietly left.

"When I came to this house and saw him," Douglas said, now sitting at the table beside Jessica, "and I saw the ring and I *knew*, I rode on to the Sedgely plantation to tell you. You had just left, and Charles Sedgely sent me after you. He charged me," he said, looking obliquely at Jessica, "with your safety. Luckily I found you when the paddy rollers did. When you found the slave girl, then I knew you were in more trouble than ever."

"How did you know of this safe house?"

"After you left, I stayed in Philadelphia for a few weeks. I joined the Society of Friends," he said humbly. "I admire what they are doing, the way they conduct themselves . . ."

She nodded.

"I have settled there."

"And your farm in Sussex?"

"I am selling it to Captain Northrup."

"Really?"

"Yes. I gave Captain Northrup notice and stayed with him until the *Elizabeth* left for Boston. I did not leave him, like Billy, without telling him first."

"I'm glad. . . ."

"And he promoted the second mate, a good man."

"Good."

"And the captain gave me his blessing." He smiled at her.

"You arranged for the farm then?" she asked incredulously. "How did you know what you would do?"

"No," he said. "Of course not. When he returned from the sail to Boston, before the return voyage to England, by then I had joined the Quakers and knew what I must do . . ."

She closed her eyes.

"And you are working, too, in the cause against slavery?"

"Yes," he said simply.

"I knew it," she said wryly. "Warning me not to take up the fight–"

"I would worry for you–"

"But not for yourself."

"I am an able man."

"And I am an able woman."

"You are that," he conceded. "It's easier to be in peril yourself than to see those you care for in danger. . . ."

"And what are you doing?"

"I have bought a farm in Germantown–north of Philadelphia . . ."

"And you have a safe house there, do you not?" She seemed already to know it as a fact.

"I am just setting it up. I was in the midst of it when I heard word of this wounded man who had lost his memory, found near Hagerstown together with a mutilated slave."

Douglas explained carefully, knowing the state of shock Jessica was in, that one of the projects of the antislavery group he was with was to keep track of the brave men and women who made forays into southern territory to bring out what slaves they could. Part of their work in Philadelphia was to arrange assistance along the way, arrangements for scouts who knew the territory, food, money and secret lodgings. There was a network not only of people and housing but of information as well.

The antislavers in Philadelphia and in other cities exchanged lists of individuals injured or murdered in these endeavors. Bad news always traveled and was eventually–if slowly–relayed to the recordkeepers.

"Good travelers who stopped here at Mrs. Danby's on the freedom route knew the details of how Jason was found and the black man with him–and reported them to us. Of course we have never learned who the slave was, poor soul; he was so disfigured, destroyed. . . ." Jessica shuddered. "That would have helped, perhaps," Douglas continued gently, "matching the slave with the man who had befriended him."

Douglas went on, describing some of the methods of the information gatherers. He and other members of his group had tried to match Mrs. Danby's patient with people known to be working in the South—not only from Philadelphia but from other cooperating societies throughout the country—but they had turned up nothing. All their people, their angels of mercy, could be accounted for, either dead or imprisoned or safely returned to their homes. No one had reported a missing associate. Of course there always were cases of people of good intention, acting individually, who were not known to them. Jason could be one of these. It was not knowing who the sick man was that raised his hope. Perhaps it was also intuition; he shrugged that away. He had been driven to find out—anyway, to see what assistance he and the antislavers could give to Mrs. Danby.

"Oh. And you dropped everything—"

"Yes. To see him—and then to find you."

"And who was to do your good work back home?"

"I left a dependable Friend in charge."

"Oh."

"But he must return to the needs of his own land and his family, and his work in finding stations along the way. . . ."

"The way?"

"Even beyond—to Boston, to Canada. . . ."

"Oh," she said.

"Think on it," he said suddenly, "though this is no time to make decisions, before the thing"—he paused and she knew he meant the burial—"is done. Let me take you and your party to Germantown. All of you—and especially Joseph and Mandy—will be guarded there from harm."

"Why . . . why?" she said wearily. "It is not your cause. It is not even your country. Why?"

"It was not Jason Coopersmith's country either."

She nodded.

"That's true."

"Through the centuries my people rose from poverty. They lived through feudalism. They were slaves of another kind," he said simply. "It angers me to see human beings owned—controlled, misused by other human beings."

"Yes."

"You must be tired," he said quickly, noting her pallor. "Why don't you rest now? We're going to have a simple ceremony and burial at sundown."

"Where?" she asked quickly.

"In the Danby family plot—at the edge of the farm."

"How good of her."

"She gave him excellent care, Jessica."

"I could see that."

"Do rest now, Jessica. There is a bed for you in the borning room, off this kitchen."

She nodded.

"I'll send Mrs. Danby to you. Will you be all right?" He began to reach his hand to her, then thought better of it, withdrawing.

She smiled at him gratefully.

"Yes."

The small group stood around the open earth after Douglas and Seth Danby had laid the pine box in it. Mrs. Danby gave the short eulogy, that Jason Coopersmith had been a fine man who had worked in the cause of justice, leaving his dear wife and a torch to be taken up by others. No man is free, she said, so long as another is in bondage. Aletha clung tightly to Jessica, searching her foster mother's face for tears; there were none, only a tight, tired look that frightened her. Billy stood next to Douglas and Seth. Joseph and Mandy held each other's hands. Then each one of them threw a flower into the open grave, and Mrs. Danby led Jessica and Aletha away as Douglas and Seth, with Billy and Joseph joining them, began to move the black earth back into the hole.

They spent a quiet evening, first in meditation, Mrs. Danby giving testimony at times to the bravery of the man in his suffering.

Seth had a homemade zither, and he held it in his lap and began to play Elizabethan songs. Jessica wept now when he sang, "Make my bed soon for I fain would lie doon. . . ." When he had finished and struck a few chords, Mandy broke in with old hymns, revealing a fluid, rich contralto voice. The others could only stare at her in wonder. Joseph then joined her, counterpointing in bass. Then Joseph swung into the black work songs, with the grunts that signified the wielding of a pickaxe or a hoe or a hammer, and Seth adjusted his chords, sometimes trailing the singer, sometimes ahead. "An if they aks you wuz I runnin . . . and if they aks you wuz I runnin. . . ." They all joined in softly, letting Joseph lead. "Jes tell em I wuz walkin, jes tell em I wuz walkin. . . ."

At times Jessica felt numb, at times keenly anguished. The brutalizing of Jason's body at the hands of murderous slavers was too much to bear. She could only put meaning into his suffering and loss by vowing to pick up his work. She would fight his murderers by helping however and wherever she could to bring about what they feared most–the end of slavery. Even in the numb times, she knew it was right to know the truth as it was, that Jason was forever gone, that she could keep their good times intact, that she had been with him in the end and that now she must pick up the threads of her life and make that life meaningful.

She looked at the faces around the table. The curtains at the window had been tightly drawn lest some unfriendly intruder see the dark faces there, though it was unlikely that anyone would come to this isolated farm far from the road. She was immeasurably strengthened by the supportive roles all these people had played; how much they meant to her! Mrs. Danby and Seth were new friends, but their care of Jason and their response to her own needs endeared them to Jessica forever. And the perilous journey they had made together, Jessica thought as she looked at Billy and Joseph and Mandy and Aletha and Douglas, had created a bond that never could be destroyed no matter how their lives might change.

Douglas said quietly that the party would be on its way come daybreak, and everyone nodded. Hazel Danby told them breakfast would be ready just before the light, and they dispersed wearily, each to his pallet or bed. Aletha, troubled by Jessica's sadness, asked whether she could come into her bed. Jessica agreed, smiling at the child, realizing with a pang that Aletha had called her mama, just as Jenny had sometimes, slipping into it naturally in the classroom. For a moment she thought of the two children, and Charles, left behind, and Eleanor too, and her mother. She was overcome. She felt bereft and needed them here beside her. But she rallied quickly. She swallowed and placed her arm around the child's waist, saying brightly, "We'll soon be home—in Philadelphia."

The remainder of the journey was taken at an easy pace. The two nights they were on the road were spent at Friends' houses known to Douglas. There were secret rooms, their entrances cleverly concealed, for Joseph and Mandy. Joseph could have gone openly, as Jessica's legal slave, to the barn, but he chose to stay with Mandy and they went together joyfully.

Jessica was astonished at the safe houses. Was there a chain of safe waystops from the South to the North, she asked Douglas? Not completely, he told her. There were still many wide and serious gaps. Eventually there would be an uninterrupted chain. He was sure the movement would grow. Not every house was a Friend's house; there were many different people involved. And not every Friend was an active antislavery worker. No idea or movement was uncomplicated. She smiled at him. He had begun to sound like her father. He asked her what amused her. She only shook her head, looking at him delightedly.

Douglas had traded for an extra horse, and sometimes she rode beside him, leaving Aletha with Mandy inside the coach. The weather was pleasant, with just a bracing touch of autumn in the air, and she liked being outdoors again, in the sunshine, feeling no threat to their safety. Douglas filled her with confidence. She admired the way he rode—so well for a man of the sea. Douglas explained to her that when he was a boy on his father's farm he had worked the horses, and sometimes even those old beasts of burden, the drayhorses, seemed to take wing for him as he had ridden them unhitched over the meadows at daybreak or sunset or on holidays, their day of comparative rest. It was the same freedom he had experienced then, racing over the fields, that he had felt on the ocean, over the waves. "There is a strong affinity between land and sea," he said to her, and then, looking at her obliquely again, as he seemed to do from shyness when moved, he added, "as between man and woman." She remembered, smiling, how she had stood before the mirror aboard Captain Northrup's ship, looking at herself, after Douglas had spoken with her and she had felt the stirrings of her womanliness, the need. She had not taken sufficient note then, she thought in wonder. She had not been ready.

And, she reflected, he did not have the impetuousness of Charles. Each man had a quality of his very own; it was his hallmark, his individuality, and it was to be cherished.

He walked with her when they called a halt and rested the horses.

He told her more about himself, about going to sea when he was less than Billy's age. How he had missed his people but slowly learned to be on his own. How he sent money home so that his brother could stay on the farm and take care of it and his parents, and marry. Now the family was self-sufficient and he was not. He could not or would not speak further, and she could only smile at him and nod her head in understanding.

Sometimes he spoke of Captain and Mrs. Northrup and the admiration he had for them. "A loving couple," he commented. "Wherever the captain goes, he takes her." Jessica nodded.

Sometimes he talked about how much he liked this new land. Rough in spots, and with its problems, but beautiful in the wilderness areas—and there were so many of them—and the richness of the soil, and the plenitude of fish and animals and variety of plantlife. She nodded.

He liked the farm he had bought. She would, too. The house needed fixing, he said anxiously, but he was a good handyman and craftsman (becoming prouder), and it could be made beautiful with a woman's hand to give it the homey touch.

She nodded.

And he liked books, too, he said earnestly. On all those lonely voyages, he had spent much of his time reading, learning. . . .

She nodded.

He was not so young as Jason or so handsome as Charles . . .

She looked at him curiously and found herself flushing.

But he was a steady man, a one-woman man, he said evenly. A man to depend on.

She nodded.

He had explained to her that they would bypass Philadelphia and skirt around the city to come to his place in Germantown. If she wished to stay in Philadelphia, at an inn, he would take her there. But he wished that she and the boys and the girls would accept his hospitality. There was a special look of pleading on his face that touched her.

"I would like that very much, Douglas," she said softly, "and I think I speak for the others, too."

He laughed with pleasure.

"We'll see to your comfort," he promised.

"We?"

"There are tenant farmers," he explained, "the Baileys, who have a cottage on the grounds, and they are paid with an equitable share of the crops, and cash money besides."

She smiled. He seemed anxious to explain that he was not exchanging one form of slavery for another.

"They will be glad to see you home again."

"Yes, though they are accustomed by now to my absences."

"You leave frequently?"

"I have not been at it too long. When needed . . . I have promised. . . ."

"Oh? Should I ask . . . ?"

"I trust you with my life," he said huskily.

"You have risked it for me, and I thank you."

"We have set it up. I take southern runaways from Philadelphia to Trenton, to a place of safety, and from there someone else takes them to New York, and then on. . . . It will grow. More people will join us."

She should feel amazement, she thought, and yet she did not. It was so familiar, first her father, then Jason, then Douglas. They acted, as so many people did, upon their convictions. As she did herself, she acknowledged proudly. She could have returned, alone, safely on the post coach to Philadelphia. She need not have brought the others. And Charles—for whatever his motivation, she must give him credit, too—he had sent them; he did not need to. Life could have been picked up at the plantation with no losses, no investment, exactly as it had been before she had come to it.

"I would like to take part in it, too," she said quietly.

"If you marry me," he said eagerly, "we could work together. . . ."

"Is that a proposal, Douglas?"

"Is it too soon to ask?"

She shook her head.

"But first we must talk of love, Douglas."

"I could speak of it now . . . but I will court you," he said feverishly, almost pulling his horse up short, not thinking of the others following behind. He caught himself in time. "I'll court you, Jessica. I'll stay at the Baileys' and call on you every day!"

"You need not."

"But I want to! I want you to know the depth of my feeling."

"I've come to know it."

"I want you to know me as I am."

"I think I know you."

"I want you to know me better," he said doggedly. "I want you to know how much I value you as a person, as a woman, as my future wife."

It was late afternoon when they reached his place. She liked its spread and the low stone wall around the fields and the solid clean lines of the stone house that had been built on a rise of ground. The farmer was bringing the cows to the whitewashed barn for milking, and he raised his hand in greeting as he saw Douglas and his party come down the lane.

"Welcome home!" he called. He left the herd to come to Douglas, to shake his hand and bow to Jessica. He looked quizzically at the two heads popping out of the carriage windows and the boys upon the driver's seat. "Do we have new tenants for the safe room?"

"No need of that. Mrs. Coopersmith has papers for Aletha and Joseph and we can get some, I reckon, for Mandy."

"We have extra papers," the man agreed.

"They can stay in the house with Mrs. Coopersmith."

"Mrs. Bailey was making a big pot of stew for supper."

"Good," Douglas said heartily. "We have a tired lot of people here, as you can see, and a good meal would be most comforting."

"I'll tell her!" Bailey said and warmly shook Douglas' hand again. "It's good to have you back."

They settled into a comfortable routine. Douglas and Joseph and Billy worked on the land with Jeremiah Bailey, and Jessica and Mandy took charge of Douglas' house. Aletha helped wherever she could. Jessica found pleasure in cooking again, but with the large meals for the extended family she was in need of Mandy's and Aletha's hands. Sometimes Aletha, taking a turn at stirring a batter or grinding corn, slowed them down, but the child took such satisfaction in sharing the chores with them that Jessica thought the time waiting for her was not wasted. The meals were jolly ones, with everyone at table. Curtains were drawn for protection, as they had been at the Danbys' place, though here too the house was far enough from the main road that they doubted any proslavers or bounty hunters would be on the prowl to spy on them. Mandy and Joseph were shy at first, as before, but their shyness wore off after the first few minutes. Everyone helped fetch and carry, and soon they were inviting the Baileys for company meals. The nights they were alone Jessica held class again for the young people; she set special preliminary exercises for Mandy, but she was sure Mandy would learn from Joseph and would eventually catch up to him. After the lessons, when Aletha went to bed, the house quieted and she and Douglas had time alone to get to know each other better.

Douglas and Jessica took long walks around the dark land, and, returning chilled from the night air, they sipped a hot toddy that Douglas carefully prepared. He pressed his suit in gentle fashion, holding her tentatively and then not so tentatively in his arms. He kissed her warmly, but with reserve—she could feel the tight control he kept upon himself. She knew it was difficult for him. Each night he left even more reluctantly than the night before for the room reserved for him at the Bailey house.

Some evenings he busily built the shelves she asked for in the kitchen, a cupboard in the dining room for the china and silver plate she would send for from her house in England. He liked the activity; it was a release for him. They planned to widen some of the fireplaces. She walked about the house happily, thinking of which piece of her furniture would go well here, or possibly there. She would commission her uncle to send them in Captain Northrup's ship. She would commission him, too, to sell the house that she and Jason had lived in together. It pleased her that she was not coming to Douglas as a penniless bride, though she knew it was of no importance to him. She would order bolts of cloth to decorate the Graham house and lengths of fine goods for dresses for herself and Aletha and Mandy. She was carried away, humming happily, and Douglas looked at her with joy.

She would ask her uncle to have Captain Northrup bring her mother for a visit, or to stay if she wished. Douglas agreed. And if her mother felt the voyage was too much for her, she and Douglas would take passage on Captain Northrup's ship and go to her. Douglas was agreeable to that, too.

At times she thought sadly of Jason. The dear man, whose life was too brief. She wrote long letters to his relatives and to her mother, who had loved him, too. She also wrote a letter to Charles to tell him she had arrived safely in Philadelphia and all was well, so they would know, he and Chloe, about Aletha–and Julia and Cicero, about Joseph, too. She had asked Douglas to see about selling the carriage and horses. At first she planned to send the money from the sale to Charles, but then she decided to place it in a trust fund for Aletha. When Aletha was older, she would send her to England for more education; the money was only a fraction of what would be needed. Perhaps Charles would help at the proper time.

"Let's not wait too long," Douglas begged her.

What a dear man he was, too, she thought, remembering all the things he did for her–the big things, his concern for her and his bringing her safely to this place, and the little things (yet not so little in themselves), bringing sweetmeats from the markets, posting her letters to England with the first vessel setting sail. He carried Aletha about on his shoulder and made her toys of wood that he whittled.

"I'm ready," she told him, happiness welling up in her.

They were to marry in the Friends' Meeting House. Before the Sunday designated, however, Joseph and Mandy came to them one evening. Papers for Joseph's manumission had already been obtained, and when they had been given to him, tears had streamed down his face. Jessica, deeply moved, had clasped his hands and Douglas had put his arms around Joseph's shoulders.

Now Joseph stood before them, seeming torn. When Douglas asked him and Mandy to sit down, Joseph shook his head. Quickly, in a rush, Joseph said that he wanted to go on—to Canada, to follow the North Star of his dream—and he wanted to take Mandy—if they would permit it—with him.

Douglas and Jessica said, in unison, so that they had to stop to laugh, that if that was what they really wanted. . . .

Joseph and Mandy nodded.

"You know you always have a good home here—and work with wages?"

"Yes," Joseph said, "and we are proud to know it, but—"

"You want to go."

"Yes."

Douglas, nodding, looked at Jessica. She nodded too.

"And so you shall."

"Together," Joseph persisted. "Mandy and me—we—"

"Yes," Douglas said.

It was done quickly, a few days later, though the leavetaking was painful. Aletha went into a fury. Billy was glum; he had never fully recovered from Mandy's usurping most of Joseph's attention. Jessica and Mandy clung together for a minute. Then Jessica kept shaking Joseph's hand and finding more supplies for him to take along. Douglas quickly hustled them out into the darkness of the night and hid them under sacking cloth in the farm cart. Though technically Joseph was a free man, and Mandy supplied with the papers of a young slave who had died, they would take no chances. Bounty hunters and other agents roamed through all the states, including Pennsylvania and New York and beyond, and it was likely Mandy was still being pursued. Douglas would deliver them to a safe station, a house in Trenton that was on his route, and from there they would be driven by someone else to New York and then, in stages, on through the northern part of the state until they crossed the Canadian border.

The Graham house seemed so empty when they left. Jessica kept telling Aletha and Billy what a good life Mandy and Joseph would have together, knowing they were free and loving one another. But for a while Aletha cried for them and Billy made faces trying to keep his mouth from trembling. It helped when they talked of the flight from Virginia to Pennsylvania and the things they had shared together, the good times of the picnics and the frightening times when the patrol and the paddy rollers had come upon them. Whether or not they saw Mandy and Joseph again, they knew they all were eternally bonded to each other, weren't they?

"We'll see them again," Jessica said, not feeling as positive as she sounded.

"Will—will they come to us?" Aletha asked.

Jessica hugged the child. Poor little thing, she thought, so many separations—from her mother, from Julia and Cicero, from everyone she knew back home—and now this.

"No," she said slowly. "But *we* shall go, one day, to them."

"To Canada?" Aletha said. "It's so far away."

"We made one trip, remember?" She waited for Aletha to nod her head. "We can take another."

"I should go away, too," Billy said, "maybe to the West."

"Oh no, Billy!" Aletha shrieked, "the Indians!"

"I—we—would like you to stay," Jessica said, "that is, if you are happy here, Billy. You would be part of the family."

His eyes lit up.

"And I will really learn to read and write well?"

"Yes. And you could train for anything you want to become."

"But maybe I should go back one more time, to see my mother, to make it up to Cap'n Northrup that I ran away."

"Could you really do that, Billy?"

"And return sail with Cap'n Northrup, to stay for good?" he said anxiously.

"Of course. That could be arranged."

"Would First Mate—I mean Mr. Douglas—do it?"

"I think so—I really know he would."

Billy would not just be left behind, then, by Joseph. He would take action. He would go away, too. But he would return.

It was more difficult waiting than she had thought. Jessica knew now that whenever Douglas went out on one of the missions, she would live in great tension until he returned. Beyond the worry for his safety, which was foremost in her mind, seared into it by the knowledge of what had happened to Jason, she missed Douglas' presence. The first evening he was gone she imagined him sitting across the table from her, then holding her longingly in his arms, kissing her as he said goodnight and left. She found herself talking to him silently about the events of the day, about the children—Aletha and Billy—about her mother, how she would like her mother to know him.

In the morning she walked about the land, admiring its orderliness, the care that Douglas had given it. The coming winter would be a less busy time for him, she thought happily. A good time to be together.

Chapter Nine

The second evening of Douglas' absence was more difficult to bear. Time, especially after Aletha was asleep, seemed to pass very slowly. She went about the drawing room—which Douglas called the common room for anyone who wished to enter—tidying up where it did not require tidying. Picking up objects—a bowl, one of Douglas' pipes, a sexton he had set upon a table—she examined them and then returned them to their places. The house seemed so silent; she missed the pleasant sound of voices. Billy had gone to spell the Baileys' tending a sick beast; Jessica had thought it would be a diversion from his unhappiness about parting from Joseph and Mandy, as well as assistance to the farming couple. Now she wished she had the comfort of his company.

She was cold. She had forgotten to light the fire. She busied herself with the kindling wood and split logs stored in the box before the fireplace. Soon the room was alight and cheerful. Orange and blue flames leaped upon the hearth. The room resounded with the popping retorts of exploding knots. Drawing a chair close to the fender, she opened a book left upon a nearby table and thought she would read.

But after a few pages she set the book down again and just stared into the fire. A great sadness overcame her as her thoughts turned to Jason. She had had so little time alone since his death that she had not been able to mourn sufficiently. She took out her memories, as if from a hiding place, and let them reenact themselves before her eyes. She and Jason had had good years together. And Charles . . . she mourned him, too. A private cry . . . and she would store these memories away again, perhaps even more deeply, to surface unbeckoned in special times of need. No experience is ever lost, she thought. They pile one atop the other. They meld into the inner core to make us what we are . . . or shall be.

Stronger, she hoped. To be able to wait in calmness and conviction when Douglas left upon his missions. To accompany him, she would rather have it that way, but he had cautioned her no, her place was home with Aletha, the child had first priority. And she, Jessica, was needed to keep the safe house, in his absences, he said, for the increasing runaways who would come. Could she accept that role? She could, she would, she said.

And now she felt she was with him, driving that cart in tandem, sharing the risks. It would be cold in the darkness, in the open air. Joseph and Mandy, excited on the road to freedom, probably frightened, too. Had they already reached Trenton? Perhaps Joseph and Mandy were now at another drop-off place, hidden in a secret room, warm and fed, and waiting for the next part of their journey. Then Douglas would be on his way home, to her, and waiting to respond to the next call.

She rose to poke the fire. She would let it burn itself out and then lay another fire in the bedchamber to take away the chill before she slept. When she was about to go from one room to the other, there was a loud knocking on the outer door.

She did not keep it bolted. Douglas had said that out in the country, as it were, they did not need to lock up. Farmers were good folk, by and large, and the cutpurses and scalawags of the city seldom drifted out this way to prey upon them.

The knocking of her heart responded to the pounding on the door, and for a moment she stood rooted to the spot. It could not be Douglas, it could not be Billy—they would enter each with his own identifying step and greeting. Could it be—and her hand flew to her throat in terror—someone to bring dire news of Douglas' mission—failed, aborted, ending in death like Jason's? Douglas—the thought unfroze her, and she flew to open the door. "C-coming!" she called.

A man in gray Quaker garb, with a broad-brimmed hat he did not remove upon his head and a look of urgency upon his face, was waiting impatiently. She could see shadowy figures behind him.

"Graham?" he said tightly. "Where's Graham?"

Oh, she thought with great relief, he does not know where Douglas is, therefore he could not have bad tidings concerning him.

"May I help you?"

"He is away?" he asked, aghast.

"Yes."

"And thee is—"

"Mrs. Coopersmith, sir, widow, pledged to Mr. Graham in marriage."

"Ah, yes, yes, so I've heard. . . ." He looked at her keenly over his Franklin spectacles. "Thee thinks as Mr. Graham does?"

"I do." She trusted this man.

He seemed satisfied. He obviously trusted her, too.

"Where is the good man? Is he on a mission I have not yet heard of?"

"A sort of family mission—an escaped slave and her man—"

"Ah, yes, yes . . . but we must not stand here in the open, and there is no time to lose. Please, may we enter?"

She heard the faint sound of a woman crying behind his back.

"Of course," she said immediately. "Come!"

She stood aside for the three people to pass. For she had soon seen that a black man and woman huddled behind the Quaker. As the pair stood shaking in the drawing room, she observed that they were not the dirty, travel-soiled refugees that Joseph had described. They were neatly dressed in black clothing, the woman with a white apron half-covering her long skirt and a white starched fichu crossing her shoulders and enveloping her chest. The woman was small. The man was trying to comfort her, patting her reassuringly, though Jessica noted how fearful he seemed, too.

"Jessica Coopersmith," their conductor said, "we must act quickly. I am Elias Pancoast."

She interrupted, "Friend . . ."

"And these people need harboring and transfer as soon as possible."

"I understand."

"I thank thee."

"Are they hungry?" And then she felt the insult of not speaking directly to them. "Are you hungry?" she asked the couple.

"No, mistress," the man said, with perfect diction. "I thank you, but we are not."

"I'll tell thee quickly, and then we should proceed," Friend Pancoast said. "Dorcas and Thomas—man and wife—have asked repeatedly for manumission . . . my Society offered funds for this purpose . . . but their Philadelphia master and mistress would not comply—"

"Even here," Jessica said wonderingly.

"Indeed even here."

"Can they be returned to servitude against their will?"

"Yes. Legally they can. . . ."

Elias Pancoast explained that although Pennsylvania had become a free state in 1780, manumission was a private action. The intent was that it be gradual.

"But there are many ways to get around a law not popular with everyone," the Friend said scathingly.

He told Jessica the law provided that after 1780 a slave mother's child could be held in servitude until the age of twenty-eight. Then, if that child were a female and before the age of twenty-eight had produced offspring, her children automatically became slaves until they were twenty-eight years old, and so on and so on.

Perpetuating the cycle of their own mothers' slavery, Dorcas' and Thomas' mothers—before they were twenty-eight years old—had given birth to the children that were now this poor couple. If Dorcas and Thomas, prior to Dorcas' reaching twenty-eight years of age, should have a child, then that baby could be held in bondage until he or she reached the specified twenty-eight years.

"A woman can have a parcel of children before she is that old—and usually she does!" Elias snorted.

He went on to say that every twenty years a slave woman

could have children born into slavery, free state or not. There were masters who took advantage and many saw to it, despite censure from others, that the continuing lines went on as their property. Literally, the mother could be freed at twenty-eight if she left the child behind her. Usually she stayed on—even if she knew her rights, which most times she did not. A vicious, self-perpetuating legal tangle, Friend Pancoast said angrily.

Dorcas' crying heightened.

"Dorcas and Thomas are both twenty-five and feel they cannot bear the bondage another day," he said gently, and then he fumed again, "Vague provisos . . . meant to pacify the opposition, to provide an easy transition . . . at what cost in human despair—"

"We must hide them."

"Yes. With all haste. I wish Graham were here," he said worriedly.

"He may return tomorrow or the next day. We can handle it, Friend Pancoast."

"Elias, Friend Jessica."

"Friend Elias, we'll take them to the safe room."

"Yes."

"And then we shall notify the Baileys . . . they must know. . . ."

"Yes, of course. Good and dedicated people. Let's be on with it!"

Jessica reached for a lantern on the fireplace mantel, but Pancoast held up his hand in protest.

"No light."

"Of course. Then you must all follow close behind me. I know the path so well. . . ."

She snatched her long, much-used woolen cape from the peg upon the wall.

"Take this, Dorcas; you must be cold and the hood will shield your face."

The woman smiled tremulously at her, managed a small curtsey, and murmured, "I thank you, mistress."

Thomas, though his hands were shaking, gently helped her into it.

Jessica found a shawl for herself and led the group outside. They quietly went behind the house, single file, and down the dark path to the barn. It was a large building, brightly painted. Jessica reached up for the crossbar to unfasten the huge door. Elias took it from her hands, to spare her she knew, and she quickly ushered the party across the dirt floor inside. The horses neighed and the cows lowed and Jessica spoke quietly to settle them down again. She had half-expected to find Jeremiah Bailey and Billy still here, but it was evident they had completed their ministrations to the sick heifer. It would have simplified matters, making it unnecessary to go later to the Bailey house. Then past the stalls and past the shelves of pails and strainers and churns and wash basins and bars of homemade lye and ash soap they made a silent procession. Jessica led the way to the back of the long structure, where on one side carefully tied bales of hay were stored. Across the end wall under the uncovered wood beams was built a loft where loose hay was kept and, when needed, pushed down through a trapdoor to the floor below where it could be shoveled for daily feed. The loft was where the slave hunters were wont to look, Douglas had told her when he had first taken her to the place. They would come and clump up the stairs and kick the hay about the platform, certain that their leather boots would come in contact with the rump of some poor shivering runaway. "Hah!" he had cried, "we circumvent them."

"It's in here," Jessica said, motioning to the wall behind the ricks.

Thomas looked at her in puzzlement and dismay, as though she had tricked him and Dorcas.

It was a blank wall that looked like the other side of the outer planking.

"It's wonderful . . . really clever," Jessica said reassuringly. "See, you cannot tell. There is the second outer wall inside this, and you cannot see how the false one opens."

She pressed a wooden knot on one of the boards, and a narrow aperture, large enough for a good-sized person to enter sideways, unfolded slowly.

"Come," she said and slipped through it, showing the couple how. Elias was smiling. He knew the place well.

They entered a small room. The inner walls were draped with quilts to absorb any noise inside. Straw was spread upon the floor.

"No fires may be lit," Jessica made the obvious prohibition. "There are many blankets provided for warmth."

As their eyes adjusted to the even greater darkness of this compartment, they could see the blankets piled upon the pallets—and there were as many of these as the room could contain—laid atop the straw. To one side were jars of water, a box of hard tack (Jessica smiled even in her anxiety—that was Douglas's sea background showing itself), and slop pails.

"You can gather up the unused pallets and stack them, for more room," she said to Thomas.

"They will be comfortable here," Elias said.

"Rest well, and we will bring you an early breakfast."

"About two o'clock?" Elias said questioningly to Jessica.

"Whatever is best."

"Rest thyselves," he said to the couple. "Of course thee will not undress; be ready to move at the very moment of need."

"Yes sir," Thomas said steadily, "How can we thank—"

"No need," Elias and Jessica said in unison. They all smiled now.

"There are slight openings in the roof above for air," Jessica reassured them. "You will be all right. And you can see the stars," she added kindly.

Thomas bowed and Dorcas curtsied unsteadily.

"Rest well," Jessica said again and preceded Elias through the opening. "I'm closing now," she said, to prepare them, and as she pressed the knot again the gap in the wall disappeared.

Jessica and Elias went back along the path to the house. She asked him inside but he would not enter this time. He told her he had to see the Baileys and would spare her the trip.

"Will Dorcas and Thomas wait for Douglas to return?" she asked fearfully, dreading that Douglas might be asked to start out again for Trenton without an interval of relaxation—and, she realized selfishly, without time to spend with her.

"No, it would not be wise for him to leave again so soon—it

would be unusual for him to go in the same direction twice in such a short space. It might draw attention."

"Jeremiah Bailey?"

"No, he's needed here while Graham is away. I'll hasten back home and another Friend whom I shall contact will come with a wagon at half after two. Thee and Sybil Bailey will have time to see to Thomas' and Dorcas' food."

"No need to trouble Sybil. Billy, our helper, will be back later and he and I will take the pair a hearty breakfast, and a hamper of food as well for the journey."

"Thee is most kind, Friend Jessica."

"I am with you, Friend Elias. It is my wish to join this movement."

"It seems thee has already joined," he said, smiling broadly. His eyes twinkled.

When he left, she went back to the fireplace and added another log. There would be no sleep for her this night. It steadied her to have work to do. She was still too trembly—in a delayed reaction to danger—to begin at once the more careful preparation of food, but poking now at the fire drained some of the energy of tension.

She sat down again to rest a while.

She pondered over Dorcas and Thomas, who though living in the North still needed to follow the North Star like Mandy and Joseph from the South. Jessica remembered the worried faces of the newcomers to the barn. It was too soon for the exhilaration of freedom to elevate their spirits. The main flight was yet before them. They had left too recently the relative security of what they had always known to face an unknown future. The conviction must have been strong in Dorcas and Thomas for them to make the risky escape. Brave souls.

And Mandy and Joseph—their courage was an inspiration to her.

The thought of them brought a mist of tears to her eyes. She was too weepy this night, she thought, spiritedly shaking her head to cast away the moisture. But she did miss them so, already. It had been a wrench to see them go. She had come to love Mandy as much as Joseph, though her relationship with Joseph went back even further and the pride she had felt in his learning and growth had added another dimension to her feeling for him. Jessica hoped they would get to Canada and live there freely under the protection of her own Queen Victoria, who did not believe in black slavery. Joseph and Mandy would be happy, she felt, once they were safe. Joseph would miss Julia and Cicero, and Aletha, and possibly herself and of course Billy. But he would have Mandy as his wife, and they would work together to provide for themselves and the family they would surely have and raise as free citizens.

She realized how far Mandy had come to forget the prohibitions of slavery when before she left she placed her arms about Jessica, a white woman, and hugged her tightly.

Oh, she prayed, a safe passage for them . . . please . . . please . . . and then she went on to include a safe passage for Dorcas and Thomas, newly run.

She was staring into the flames, hypnotized by their leaps and flickers, when suddenly the silence was broken by still another noise.

The clop, clopping of a horse's hooves. She listened to their approach—not a wagon, so it could not be Douglas as she had hoped with a first great surge of expectancy, nor could it be Friend Elias' Friend so soon. There was no creak of wooden wheels. She strained to hear the iron horseshoes turn back from the private lane to her door. But to her dismay they came right ahead and stopped before the house. She knew she was to have no respite; there were to be more surprises played out this night. She imagined the man or woman dismounting, could hear the hooves make a few scrambling steps, imagined the reins tied to the post. Then the footsteps—too heavy for a female's; they had the ring of sturdy shoes—upon the doorstep. Again, she sighed, again. . . . She waited for his knock.

It was loud and authoritative, a man accustomed to having his way.

"Yes," she called clearly toward the door, letting him wait a few minutes as she tried to assume an expression of composure.

He knocked again.

"Open, please! Urgent business here."

There was a man of handsome appearance waiting upon the stoop where not long before Elias Pancoast had stood. The newcomer was not in somber gray; he was elegant.

"Mistress . . . ?"

"Coopersmith."

"Ah? I do not have you on my list." He looked at a paper in his hand.

"This is the home of Douglas Graham."

"Ah, yes," he said, as if ticking off a name. "May I see him?"

"He is not here at present."

"Will he return soon?"

She shrugged noncommitally.

"Perhaps you can tell me then. . . . Have you seen two slaves, unknown to you, a male and a female, come by here today?"

She could scarcely breathe. She tried not to show her sudden fear—all could be lost; this man could blight their lives.

"And who, sir, are you?" She heard her level voice with surprise.

"Their owner, James Appleby." He bowed.

Her fear intensified. Confused, she wondered what to do. She did not want this man to go to the Bailey house, with Elias undoubtedly still there. To come upon so late a visitor at the simple farmhouse would arouse his suspicion. And especially a visitor in Quaker dress.

"Had you sent the man and woman upon an errand?"

"No, no," he said impatiently. "They have run off. Mistress, may I come inside and beg a drink of water . . . or tea . . . of you? It has been a long and dusty ride, and all those stops talking to different householders . . . if you please?"

It was not wise, her thoughts scurried about, to permit him to enter, with Aletha asleep in her room and no other adult there for the sake of propriety. But she must delay him.

"Come, sir," she said shortly.

He paused to look appreciatively about the room and then sat down in the chair she indicated before the fire. He loosed his cape from his shoulders, and she noted the fine tailoring of his garments, the blue coat, the stitching of his ruffled stock. She looked at him and saw a bluejay, strutting before he came to rest.

Unobtrusively, she covered with other innocuous newspapers a copy of William Lloyd Garrison's *The Liberator* that had been left upon the table. She took the copper kettle from its crane that swung outward from the fireplace, carried it to the kitchen, and filled it with water. As she assembled a tray with the tea things in the inner room—glad to have a respite from Appleby—she wondered why he had traveled this way. Douglas had told her his group was most careful—there could be no leaks of information—and keeping secret the locations of safe houses and the people involved in the transfer of slaves was of the utmost importance. And the fewer people, even those trusted in the group, who knew where all the hiding places were, the better. Jessica well knew the harm that could come to everyone involved if identities were known to the proslavers, the roving bounty hunters, and the federal agents empowered to take runaways back to the South.

She returned to the drawing room with the tray, set it on a table, and carefully hung the kettle on the crane again and swung it over the fire. She then sat on a chair facing the visitor. Appleby, who had politely risen at her entrance, sank down again.

"The tea should be ready soon."

"Very good of you, Mistress Coopersmith. You are kin to Mr. Graham?"

"We shall soon be wed."

"Oh," he said, looking at her with heightened interest. "What a lucky man he is."

"I am fortunate, too."

"I do not know him." He smiled. "But I have seen you."

She flushed.

"How did you compile your list, sir?"

"Oh, this?" he said, looking at his paper again. "I am an investor in land." He waited for Jessica to recognize the importance of his position.

"I am not long in these parts," she said slowly. "I have recently come from England. . . ."

"Oh? How utterly charming. I should have known by your speech."

"But your list?" she persisted.

"Well, the records of property deeds. Who lives in this area, who lives in that, don't you know. . . ."

"Oh."

"I've heard tell," he said, "that runaways head out this way on their trek."

"Why should they?"

"It's a northern route out of Philadelphia."

"And that is where you live—in Philadelphia?"

"Yes. And where we kept the pair, Thomas and Dorcas . . . good house slaves . . . an irreplaceable cook and butler . . . our dinner parties are known for miles around. My wife is at her wits' end with their going . . . ungrateful wretches! And it is a criminal act to run away!"

"So I've heard."

"But I shall find them, have no doubt of that. I have been going from house to house, asking for them, before I turn the matter over to the city officials."

"Would that not . . . perhaps . . . be the better choice?"

"No, I am a man of action, and the wheels turn very slowly here . . . probably antislavers hindering the progress," he said darkly. "You can't count on anyone, even the law! And my wife is at home having a fit of hysterics."

"Have you had any information given you by my neighbors? Has anyone seen the man and woman?"

She held her breath until he answered.

"No," he said, disgruntled. "No one has seen any unfamiliar blacks. And they are annoyed that I should ask them! They could not have just vanished—impossible! But no one has admitted seeing the damn ingrates! Running off, when they were in the best home possible."

"No doubt no one has seen them."

She rose to take a woolen mitt from the tea tray. She gingerly took the kettle from the crane. She could see the man's eyes on her as she steeped the tea leaves in the silver pot, a Revere work.

Douglas had told her he had purchased it from the previous owner of the house. Odd that she should think of things like that in this danger-fraught time. A protective device, she knew. Keep calm . . . act normally . . .

"Sugar?" she asked politely.

"Please . . . just one, no milk. You are very kind and hospitable."

"We cannot turn away a weary traveler."

But, she thought, he did not look so worn. His clothing was not disheveled; his hair, but for the forelock, was neatly in place. He no doubt sat his horse quite well.

"The trouble is there is too much loose talk of abolition. Fanatics stirring up a lot of trouble, poking their noses into other people's affairs—plain jealousy and spite, making a man's slaves run off!"

"Will you have a cake?"

"Truth of the matter is," he said, "it's the natural way of things, masters and slaves, those who order and those who serve. It's the way it has always been and always will be, no matter whether it is called slavery or not!"

She had poured tea for herself after he was served, but she left it upon the table, for her tentative reach toward the handle of the china cup revealed her trembling hand. She quickly drew it back, hoping he had not seen.

"Don't you agree?" he asked.

"Well, I have not been in this country long," she reminded him, "and—"

"You'll soon learn," he told her grimly. "You'll soon learn."

"Perhaps."

"And Mr. Graham, he has slaves?"

"No, there is no need. The land does not spread far. A tenant farmer and his wife and a young male helper. It is all the help required at present."

He looked at her more boldly.

"There are no others in the house?"

She flushed. She had walked right into this embarrassment.

And should she mention Aletha? She hoped the child would sleep through this visit, as she had Elias Pancoast's.

"My daughter," she said.

"Oh?"

"I am a widow." The word still pained her.

His interest became something else. Jessica could sense it.

"A beautiful young widow." Now he was looking at her sensuously, his eyelids half-closing.

If only Billy would return. Or if Elias could be well on his way back to the city. She listened intently, hoping she would hear Elias riding on the outer road where their private lane joined it. She should hear, if she kept alert and did not panic.

"If I were Mr. Graham I would not leave you of an evening. . . . What a nice arrangement he has here, with you in the house. . . ."

Her temper flared, but she kept it under control. She would not inform him that Douglas spent his nights at the Baileys', let the man think whatever he may.

"It must be urgent business that has taken him off–"

"Marketing."

"A farm market? Ah, then he will be gone all night . . ."

"Your slaves," she said quickly. "Can you describe them?"

"Oh." Now he was reluctant to come back to the matter that had brought him here. But, never taking his eyes from her, he answered her question. "They are full-grown hands, a buck and negress–though," he amended, "they are not outside workers; they have had the advantages we have given them, a fine house to serve and profit from."

It still astounded her, though she realized she should have known–she had certainly been told–that the same sentiments existed north and south. But James Appleby, though at times he spoke like Charles and Duane Bellows, was no true counterpart of these special Southerners. He was more like Donald Avery, an ordinary man in fine clothing.

"They may have gone off for the day."

"Hardly."

"Some urgent business of their own–"

"What business? Slaves have business? They wouldn't dare, without permission!"

"Without thinking, perhaps?"

"How would they dare to do that!"

"But–"

"They were so docile," he said in amazement. "It's hard to believe. . . ."

"Well, then. . . ."

"But beneath the surface one never knows."

"One doesn't."

She thought she heard faint hoofbeats upon the outer road. Appleby paid no attention. He was growing ever more intent upon her. Jessica listened again. Yes. Just a little while longer–and she could send Appleby on his way.

If Aletha should wake and come into the room, though she was generally a sound sleeper now, Jessica would say–would say what? That her father, Jessica's own husband, had come from the Mediterranean, a handsome man, she would sigh, with olive skin and the deep dark eyes of that region . . . Oh, don't wake up, Aletha! Jessica willed, don't wake up until morning, as you usually do.

James Appleby had set down his cup and was rising from his chair. If he left now, Jessica thought desperately, Elias and he would overtake one another on the road. That Quaker figure would take on special significance.

But looking at James Appleby, Jessica could see now that he was aroused by other emotions.

"I need not return home this night," he said, taking her hands from where they lay upon her lap and drawing her upward. "No one will make much of my absence."

Shocking her further, he tried to kiss her, but she turned away, and his lips brushed her ear.

"You are too much of a woman to be alone at night," he murmured. "Let me comfort you."

"I don't need comforting. And you are forgetting yourself!"

"No, on the contrary, I am very mindful of myself . . . and of you."

Then he spent a few more minutes sparring with her. He complimented her complexion, how fair, how English it was, how it contrasted with her dark hair, the mystery of it, dark as night and soft as . . . soft as . . . her bosom promised to be. She gasped, but he kept staring at her bodice.

He tried to take her hands again, but she pulled back.

"If you please—"

"I please very much—"

"You are outrageous."

"I rage for you."

"Impossible!"

"Don't play the innocent." He clucked his tongue disapprovingly. "Inviting me in—"

"But not on—"

"Oh . . . on . . . on. . . ."

She glared at him.

"You are insulting."

"No, it is complimentary, it is the way you accept it. Accept me, mistress, and you shall see. . . ."

Time enough, she thought decisively. Elias must be sufficiently ahead.

"I shall have to ask you to leave."

"So soon?" he mocked. "Oh lady, and I am so unspent."

"You will need to do your spending elsewhere."

"You are being coy."

"And you are being dense. I want you to go!"

"No, you don't really."

"I do!"

"Resistance is part of the game."

"But not *my* game."

"What is your game? I'll play it."

"Will you please leave! You tire me."

"That I would love to do."

"Go! Immediately!" She did not raise her voice, but it had a cutting edge.

He sighed and flicked at his clothing.

"Ah, mistress, you are cruel."

She was silent as he fastened his cape.

"I would suggest," she said finally, "that you not rout out the neighborhood this time of night. Tempers run high when unleashed from sleep. Do your looking tomorrow. . . ."

"Oh, mistress, you would protect me?"

"No," she said wearily, "just good people's rest."

"No reprieve?"

"No."

"You are sure?"

"Positive."

"Your tea is warmer than your heart," he told her and bowed with exaggeration as she held the door open for him. "I thank you for the one but I cannot forgive the other."

She was automatically buttering slices of bread when Billy returned and found her in the kitchen. The hamper was finished and she was stirring porridge for breakfast. She was feeling better now.

"I'm sorry I'm so late," Billy said. "We pulled the cow through, though at first it was not certain that we would. And then we went back to the Bailey house for refreshment."

"You know?"

"Yes. Elias Pancoast told us about the runaways. Jeremiah vouched for me." He looked at her carefully, puzzled. "Are you angry?"

"Of course not."

"I stayed longer, so if anyone watched there would not be two of us . . . bad enough one. . . ."

"Yes, yes, Billy, it isn't that at all; you did the right thing. In an hour or so I'll have to wake Dorcas and Thomas . . ."

"I'll carry the hamper."

"You want to involve yourself even more than you already have?"

"Yes, Miz Jessica."

"You are sure?"

"Yes. Joseph and Aletha . . . and Mandy . . . are like my own family. . . ."

"Yes."

"And," he said shyly, "and especially you."

She smiled at him.

"And Douglas and the Baileys?"

"Yes. I want to! I want to help."

Dorcas and Thomas ate sparingly. Their faces still looked pinched and tired. It was obvious they had not slept. They had tidied up the hidden room, leaving it as they had found it, and now sat with Jessica on chairs around the edges of the cubicle while Billy waited outside the barn as lookout.

Jessica tried to ease their anxiety by distracting them from the coming journey. She asked where they were born: in Philadelphia, Dorcas in the Appleby family, where her mother had been a slave before her. Jessica kept secret that their master had visited her some hours earlier. Thomas volunteered that he had grown up in a neighboring family's house, and when the Appleby butler had died he was purchased from his original family for this role. Had the couple known each other beforehand? Jessica asked. Yes, they both said. The Applebys had hoped Dorcas would have children, but she had not and, Dorcas said angrily, they wanted Thomas to take another woman.

"You were not mistreated physically?" Jessica asked them. No, not beaten, they both said, though worked without proper rest day and night, and Dorcas added that planning to take Thomas from her was mistreatment enough.

"Well, you will be set free and then there will not be that problem," Jessica assured her.

Thomas smiled. Indeed not, he said, clasping Dorcas' hand.

"All my life," he told Jessica, "I have thought about freedom like all my brothers and sisters in slave quarters, wondering what it is like to go to bed a free man and wake in the morning knowing that you can say what you think and feel and go where you want. All my life, long as I can remember—you can't do this, you can't do that because you're colored, everybody said. My mammy always said smile, never show anyone what you are really like, what you are thinking. You are not allowed to think when you are a slave."

"At least, tell nobody what you think," Dorcas added, "unless it's a dear one, colored folk you can trust and well out of the hearing of the master or," she said bitterly, "mistress."

"I would look at the free men, the manumitted colored, and say, why not me too? Why not? I would work in the middle of the night, if I could, to buy my freedom. Day and night. I could do it. Why not me too?"

"It is difficult," Jessica said, "very difficult to see others gain what you want and not be able to have it. And yet it is not easy for the manumitted. There are many restrictions and prohibitions for them as well."

She was anxious about his expectations. He must know that the life ahead could still be difficult.

"But it is better than slavery," he insisted. "I would work as hard as two men, even three, to buy my freedom and Dorcas' freedom. I didn't want to run—"

"They would never let us," Dorcas said.

"There was nothing to do but walk away."

"But Friend Pancoast? How did you know?"

"In the quarters sometimes we hear," Thomas finally answered, and then he was grimly silent.

"Yes," Jessica reassured him, "I understand."

"Wagon coming!" Billy whispered, though they knew it as soon as they saw him.

"I suggest," Jessica said slowly, "that all of you stay here while I go see the driver."

Just to make sure it was the right one, she thought. It was the specified time and the specified place, but it was best to be cautious.

The night air cooled her as she came to the entrance of the barn and opened the door that Billy had carefully closed behind him. He had evidently not waited for the wagon to roll to a stop and had come to tell them when he saw it down the lane. The driver was a woman! It excited Jessica to see her. Though she should have been prepared, she told herself; there had been Mrs. Danby who had nursed Jason, and she had heard enough about the women making forays into the South to whisk away what slaves they could.

The woman, tall on her seat and thin as a fence rail, was smiling wryly at Jessica's expression.

"My husband was on another mission, and so I took his place, as I often do, when Friend Elias told me what was needed. I am a farm woman. See my baskets of eggs and clutch of chickens there?"

Jessica nodded.

"Well," the woman said practically, "I shall sell them at our destination. But no time to lose—where are my passengers?"

"I'll fetch them," Jessica said and disappeared into the barn. "It's all right," she told the party inside, and they came silently, Billy bringing up the rear, hamper in hand.

They, too, looked at the woman in amazement.

"I have done it before," she told them matter-of-factly. "Many times. I am Luisa."

She showed them a hidden section in the wagon, under the unseen shelf that held her provisions. The passengers would be cramped but not visible to any rider who came beside them on the pike.

Dorcas and Thomas made their farewells and thanks and nervously clambered aboard, following Luisa's instructions on how to sit in the least possible space. Billy thought of his journey from Philadelphia to Virginia between the wheels of the stagecoach. And Jessica, of the trip from Virginia, much more comfortable than this, inside the well-built carriage, and sometimes walking beside it.

They will be all right, Luisa promised, rearranging her wares two and three deep so the wood of the shelf would not show. The contents of the open wagon seemed a complete jumble.

"Good luck, Luisa."

"Prescott," she smiled at Jessica. She waved a large, thin hand.

"Good luck, Luisa Prescott."

"Good luck," Billy said.

"I'll see thee again!"

Luisa clucked at the horses, and the wagon, with its special contents, was off.

Chapter Ten

Douglas returned home the next day. When Jessica saw him a warm rush of feeling overwhelmed her. She did not need to ask him—the journey had been a success; Joseph and Mandy were already on the second stretch of their reach for the North Star. All doubts fled, and Jessica unselfconsciously threw her arms around him and held him close, and tenderly. For a moment he stepped back from her to look steadfastly into her eyes. What he saw there pleased him—a long-awaited gift. She knew he recognized what it was.

She was deeply in love with him. Not an ordinary love, if any love was ordinary, but an extraordinary love.

He was now forever in her thoughts. She wanted to be with him, to share his life, come what may . . . that was deeply in love. Perhaps it had begun that very time on shipboard, when there had been the first spark.

And it had grown, through hardship and commitment.

He would be her husband, she thought, the pleasure of it lighting up her face.

"Douglas, Douglas, I am so happy you are safely back," was all that she could whisper, but it told him everything he had waited to hear.

They were married in the Friends' Meeting House, a quiet

avowal of intention. He, seated on one side, and she, on the other, breaking the silence of meditation, to pledge their lives together. Afterward, the happy congratulations, the modest reception at the Bailey house. Jessica drifted through the groups of guests, members of the Meeting—the Pancoasts and Prescotts among them—and other neighbors, her eyes always searching out Douglas. He came to join her.

"How beautiful you are," he whispered. "Your inner light is showing in your face."

"I am so happy," she said simply.

"I aim to keep you that way, Mrs. Graham."

"That has a nice sound to it, Mr. Graham."

It was a testing place for Aletha. Jessica watched carefully. The child was made known as a ward of the Grahams. Aletha's good looks were duly admired and she seemed to be accepted. She clung shyly to Billy. Mrs. Bailey had charged him with her care that day. She had also invited Aletha and Billy to spend a few days at the Bailey house so that, as she told them, smiling broadly, the Douglases could get to know one another.

"They awready know," Aletha said sourly.

"Well," Mrs. Bailey said, undaunted, "then, better."

"It's time," Douglas whispered to Jessica.

"May we just slip away?"

"Yes."

He fetched her wrap and they left with the sound of good wishes following them. They walked arm in arm down the lane leading to their home, and at the doorstep he swooped her up into his arms and carried her inside. He did not stop in the outer rooms but took her directly into the bedroom. Some good neighbor had quietly left the party and started a wood fire buring brightly in the fireplace and turned back the coverlet on the bed. Douglas gently set her down upon the sheets. Jessica knew he meant to undress her and, smiling, she helped him.

When she awoke again, sunshine was streaming in the window, but it was no brighter than the joy she felt inside herself. Her hair flowed over the counterpane that he had tucked about her bare shoulders when he left her. She heard him in the kitchen—a bar or two of his singing and the chink of cups and saucers. She ran her fingers hurriedly through the dark cascade, finger-combing instead of getting out of bed to find a brush. The room was fragrant with his scent—salty and a little heavy—she liked it. Her body was perfumed with his flavor, too—everywhere he had touched her, where their bodies had joined, where they had pressed together and lain side by side.

Later in the day she would bring in the large wooden tub, and they would fill it with buckets of hot water from the cauldron on the stove and she would soak. Perhaps he would soak with her, too.

She could scarcely believe her good fortune. This man, this steady man, who had waited for her, who had kept his feelings in check for so long, was so expressive in love and lovemaking. At first he had been so careful and shy, but then their passion had exploded and carried them away. He had had to realize she was sensuous, that she was an experienced woman. He was an experienced man—there was never any doubt of that—and they had quickly learned through the night to adjust to one another, what pleased the other, when to hold back, when not to hold back. And there was a spontaneity, too. And a great lovingness that came with the physical pleasure.

She was smiling to herself when he came with a tea tray.

"You are always smiling," he said approvingly.

"Am I?"

"Yes—and it's lovely."

He set the tea tray down as he helped her up and piled the pillows behind her. The coverlet fell away and her breasts were exposed. He leaned over to kiss them. She rested her cheek on the top of his head for a minute, and reluctantly, faces flushed, they parted. She reached for the robe on the floor, but he shook his head.

"I'll build a fresh fire," he said.

He handed her a shawl. Then as she straightened herself, he took logs from the huge copper pot on the hearth and set them ablaze. He poured tea from the teapot into the cups he had brought and uncovered a plate of sweet rolls.

"Hungry?"

"Ravenous."

"You are . . . and I am. . . ."

They laughed at the *double entendre.* They sipped tea between their praises of each other and fed each other pieces of bread. When they were finished, he set the tray on a chest and they both watched the fire silently. Then he slipped out of his nightshirt and came to join her again in the large double-poster bed.

"We have much work to do in the outside world," he said gravely, and then he grinned crookedly, "and much work to do here in our room."

"Work?" she said, putting her arms around him.

"Anything you work at becomes worthwhile. Even play."

"And love?"

"Most of all, love."

"I shall work to make you happy."

"And I, you."

She wanted to ask him "Forever?" but for one fleeting sober moment she thought of the finiteness of life. The underside of joy always had a tinge of sadness, the fear of its loss. But she had been given another chance at happiness and she was going to hold on to it. She held him tightly.

"Always," she whispered.